Also by Tim Sebastian

THE SPY IN QUESTION

SPY SHADOW

SAVIOUR'S GATE

TIM SEBASTIAN

A Dell Book

Published by
Dell Publishing
a division of
Bantam Doubleday Dell Publishing Group, Inc.
666 Fifth Avenue
New York, New York 10103

ISBN: 0-440-21193-X

Reprinted by arrangement with Delacorte Press

Printed in the United States of America

Published simultaneously in Canada

May 1992

10 9 8 7 6 5 4 3 2 1

RAD

For Anthony, Alex, Anna and Charles

12/6

1

He could hear the plane when it was still way out over the northern cape; and in his mind's eye he could even see it, streaking low over the icepack, sucking the snow from the surface, blasting the thin atmosphere, two hours from darkness.

The morning had been bright and glorious and the sun just a block of gold, kneeling on the horizon. But by afternoon the weather had changed and the plane had been warned of the storm clouds that had hurtled in over the tundra.

The whine of the jets changed tone and he knew the pilot had flown past, initiating the 180-degree turn southward on final approach.

At about three hundred feet the aircraft cut through the darkening sky. It was dropping fast—a tiny silver pencil that shattered the polar silence as it fell. Ahead of it just a gray smear of a runway, half eaten, rutted by the cold. Not much of a welcome, he thought. Not when you've come this far.

Gennady waited until the wheels slammed down before turning toward the command center. A long line of white domes with their sheaves of antennas—the loneliest of Moscow's ears, tracking whispers and shimmers and shadows across the top of the world. And now a plane.

The noise of the twin jets faded as he pushed through the

double doors and into the front lobby. Still Russia with the bundles of dirty laundry waiting for pickup. Still Russia with the broken and irreplaceable light bulbs, the prefab walls with the missing bolts.

Take Russians to the Arctic, they had joked, and there'd be a shortage of snow within a year. That's what they'd said when he had accepted the assignment all those months ago in Leningrad, in the bloom of an early spring, when the world had seemed so good, and the friend of a friend had said you could make it even better. We need you, Major. They need you. And it had been such a time since anyone had.

He turned into the corridor and caught the smell of perfume, almost before he saw her. She was reading the notice board, she the captain, duty officer. She the rarest of all species in the Arctic bases. She nodded—not exactly all things to all men, but one or two to a few. On cold, comfortless nights when a fellow was depressed, they said, she could transport you into most of your fantasies. He took in the high boots, the tight uniform, the plume of black hair.

Not now, though, not with the plane arriving. Not when you needed the few wits you had left.

From his window Gennady saw the jet trainer had parked out on the southern tip of the runway. A fuel truck was skating toward it, snorting the snow in its path. Same plane as last time, same flight plan, or was it?

He turned away and punched the computer into life. Think carefully, walk carefully for later they'll know where you've been. But there, without hesitations, were the words in the bank. Order out of chaos. So little room for doubt or deception. The computer, it seemed, was everything Russia was not.

Gennady summoned the flight schedule for the northern air command: the catalog of routine patrols against which all flights were checked. The trainer had been logged in. He checked the authorization. The computer demanded his key.

He tried his own password: *moroz*—frost. "Play with me," he muttered. "Let's play." But it wouldn't.

So many times they blocked you. He rubbed his hands together and found them wet. Worse, the information was often incomplete, served up in niggardly droplets as if it were holy water.

He rubbed away the condensation from the window. Outside the fuel truck had withdrawn and from the blur behind the jet turbines he could tell the aircraft was ready to leave. Gennady saw the single helmet in the cockpit. Just like the last time, and the time before that. And once again no contact with the pilot, no overnight stay, no glass of tea in the canteen to meet all the other comrade pilots, no air force gossip about the shits back in Moscow.

It was, as they would say about the duty officer, just a quick in and out, and no one the wiser.

For days afterward, Gennady had no idea what made him go out again. Gloves, parka, boots, because if you don't do it properly, you don't come back. And he was in time to see the trainer screaming north even as the storm winds gathered and the first shard of lightning cracked around it. The nose wheel lifted, and in a second the others would follow. Two seconds, three. And you couldn't see where the runway ended, but you have to land or fly, you can't do both for long. Standing out there with a thousand miles of sky closing in, Gennady could have sworn he heard the pilot scream. It wasn't till much later that he realized he had been too far away to hear anything of the kind. Besides the wind had come up sharply, and the din of the fire engines and emergency trucks, and the twin explosions from the wreckage seemed to pierce right into his head. So he concluded, like all the others, that the scream he had heard had been his own.

Gennady had taken two days off work. That was orders. Like not talking about what he'd seen, like not speculating, like nothing had ever happened. Put it out of your mind for good. And he had looked through the window past the lecturing security man, with all the gold braid on his shoulders, and seen the last of the salvage trucks returning. Then they had switched off the floodlights and left the remains to the northern snows.

Two days and they had let him hitch a ride in a transport plane to Murmansk, two days sitting in the kitchen, listening to his mother, staring at his father. Two days of vegetables and fish soup. "What kind of fish is this?" he had asked her over dinner. "Fish," she had replied. "It's fish." What did he think it was?

On the second day he put his arm in his father's and led the old man gently down the staircase and out over the frozen pavement, past the lampposts that leaned crazily in the wind. Father seemed not to notice the horrendous cold, and why should he? Gennady knew he had suffered worse, shunted from one labor camp to another, dying a little in each of them. They bought cream and yogurt at the store. No fish that day. "What else is there?" Gennady had asked. The shopkeeper had shrugged—"only me." Back in the flat father had gone to bed early. His mother had turned on the radio and they had listened to the tinny voice from Moscow—and that had been new. In the old days, of course, they had never bothered, never even lifted a newspaper. Suddenly, it seemed, there was so much going on in the land of Russia, where the age of silence had melted and moved on.

The old lady shifted stiffly on the kitchen chair.

"Such a world," she whispered, pointing a finger at the radio. "One day change, one day stop. Forward then backward, who knows where it will end?"

Gennady seemed not to hear.

"Dad's tired." He looked up at her. It sounded like an accusation.

"He's been tired for years. Most days he says nothing then suddenly there's a smile, and I think to myself . . . finally it's going to be all right. But then come the tears, and he stands by the window, sometimes for a whole week, and I pull his arm and talk to him, but it's as if he's not there." She dragged a hand across her eyes. "In his own way he's survived. Now it's me who's dying."

They looked at each other in silence. The distant lecture from Moscow had paused and there was only the low static from the radio.

Gennady's mother stood up and leaned over the kitchen table, reaching for the cupboard. In her hand he saw an official sheet of paper. She put it in front of him.

"Came three weeks ago . . . for your father. I haven't showed it to him."

As he picked it up Gennady could feel his hand start to shake. His breathing quickened. He had never seen a letter like it. Such an admission, such a change. And then suddenly he saw it for what it was and the panic and excitement turned to anger.

Report of a commission . . . former political prisoners like you . . . miscarriage of justice . . . no legal basis. Full recognition of your loyal service to country. Party deeply regrets. In the name of so and so and such and such Union of Soviet Socialist Republics. And then the kick in the teeth—sixty-four rubles a month—and a fucking insult it was even to a dog.

They both heard the old man cry out but Gennady reached him first. He had thrown off his blanket and was sitting up in the narrow bed, clawing the air, his eyes shut tight, like a blind man questing for the world that had darkened and disappeared around him.

Gennady put out a hand to the moist forehead and eased his father back onto the pillow. But it was some time before his mind quieted. In the dark, overheated little bedroom, a former prisoner shook himself free of his memories.

Gennady stood up, knowing exactly why he'd done it: gone to the American Consulate in Leningrad, targeted the diplomat with the curly black hair, followed the man to the

Kirov, fallen in beside him, and made the first of a dozen contacts that could lose him his freedom and even his life.

And yet it could be no worse than what his father had suffered. Gennady looked at the crumpled figure in the loud striped pajamas, asleep in the Russia that could hurt him no longer.

They reached the command center at dusk the next day. Even before the plane had stopped the runway lights were extinguished and Gennady felt a door closing behind him. For once the wind had dropped and he stepped down from the aircraft humbled by the beauty around him. To the west a jagged red line cut into the sky, above and below it lay the deep dark blue of the Arctic. You could visit here, he thought, you could pitch your tent and play your games, but you couldn't win. And in the end the vast expanse of ice would drive you out, eating away at your soul—with loneliness, depression, and fear.

There was no sign of the wreckage. How quickly and efficiently it had been cleared away. He joined the little gaggle of returning officers as they made their way to the domes, long shadows across the snow and the last of the sun on their faces.

And he wouldn't worry, would he? Not about the accident. Maybe he'd plan an assault on the duty officer. Not that she was difficult. Maybe he'd overestimated the plane's importance. Maybe.

Almost twenty-four hours passed before he heard the scream of the jets. He was sitting at his computer and knew he didn't have to turn to look out of the window, knew the jet trainer was slicing a path across the runway, knew it had come from Moscow and carried no markings. Why now? Why again? Why at all? Questions that had echoed across Russia for centuries.

The trainer carried a single pilot. But that was strange too. Trainers trained. Designed for two at a time, like weddings. If it was a practice flight, for whom was it practicing? And why come here: the most distant of all the outposts?

You couldn't ask. He knew that. The time for asking hadn't lasted long. Too many asked for too much. They'd tolerated a few years of it and then the caravan had pulled up sharply. They'd all terrified themselves, leaned too far over the cliff. And now the pullback.

Gennady made his way to the canteen. Fish soup again. The way his mother made it. Maybe there wasn't any other way. Just one fish soup in the whole of Russia, he thought, and you're looking at it. All around him they drank from identical bowls—the officers, the monitors, the security guards, under the neon lights, in white plastic splendor.

On the notice board was a rare picture of the General Secretary in open-necked shirt, sitting on the ground with his family, picnicking by a lake. Remember that man, thought Gennady. Soon he might have a lot more free time on his hands. Or so they said. Anyway, in times of uncertainty you didn't rock the boat, you didn't even stand up in it. You didn't question and if you could stop yourself thinking as well, then so much the better.

But Gennady couldn't. Whatever the weather, day after day the plane would return. A grotesque homing pigeon that carried no message and seemed to fulfill no function. The next week, the week after, streaking down onto its concrete slab, departing again into the Arctic night.

Once he consulted Volodya who worked the opposite shift.

"Who cares?"

"I do."

"You're a fool." Volodya's voice carried conviction.

"But what about the accident?"

"What accident?" Volodya stared into his briefcase. "I've lost my sandwiches. My God, and you talk of stupid accidents. Something of great personal value is missing."

Only here, thought Gennady, can truth seem irrelevant.

Russians always knew the truth. Volodya would have known full well about the accident. But it simply would not impinge on his life, wouldn't alter it, color it, or materially affect it in any way at all. So he had dismissed the crash from his mind, just the way his entire generation and so many before it had dismissed all the crashes and casualties and disasters of Soviet power, never discussed, because they simply weren't relevant. You lived your own life, got buried in your own box, and left the grand designs to the state.

And that's why father, and all the other fathers, lay groaning at night like the tortured souls they were, with sixty-four rubles a month to compensate mind and body. And that's why Gennady waited another week, returned to Murmansk, and placed a two-line advertisement in the local edition of *Polyarnaya Pravda.*

It was as the American diplomat had told him—easy. You find something out, you tell someone. Simple communication. Been that way since man was a monkey.

2

It was spring in Murmansk. And yet the ice still clung to the city as tightly as a ferret's claw.

Marcus entered the hotel lobby and shook himself. Tiny frost flakes cascaded from his shoulders, where the wind had left them. He could hear his colleagues in the downstairs bar —Western journalists, hunting in a pack far from home, their raucous voices fighting a single accordion. They never went quietly into a foreign land.

For a moment he stood still, letting the warmth wash over him. A dark, almost skeletal figure, like a tree that's lost branches in a storm. You're tired, Marcus, you want to sleep, Marcus—and he knew he had to rest—just for a while, just till it was straight in his mind.

Tomorrow the press party would travel to the submarine base on the Kola peninsula: first visit ever by a foreign group. Russia dropping its trousers in public—and weren't they all anxious to get a look!

But that was still to come. Take it in order, he thought, climbing the stairs. Take it slow. First, get through the night.

He had, of course, made sure of the rendezvous, crossed the main square, climbed the two hundred stone steps to the war memorial and the blocks of flats. And the wind had seemed to tear the skin from his face.

A hundred yards to the right and Marcus had cleared the first of the apartment buildings. In the valley below he could see the football stadium. Hurry, he'd told himself. The light is failing. Another few minutes and you won't see it.

He tore off a glove, reached into his anorak, and brought out the tiny binoculars. And there so far away he could see the goalpost, with the snow gray and trampled around it, and tied to the netting was the little red scarf, flapping wildly as the Arctic sun sank away out of sight.

Marcus could have cheered. Down the steps and he could have hugged the old woman at the bottom, standing there with her baskets, coated and covered, snorting like an animal.

But even here, he had thought, you can rise above it, score, make a difference.

Now back in the narrow bedroom he turned off the light and lay still. Outside he could see the cold blue streetlamps, pools of light and dark etched on the snow beneath them. Somewhere a neon sign flickered incessantly. And from the shacks and the flats, along the rutted ice paths, past the gray, long-suffering city-dwellers would come a contact. Not a friend, not even an acquaintance, but a soul driven along a similar path, preordained in another country, at another time.

Do us a favor, Marcus. He could hear the voice so well. Do us a favor, when you're in Murmansk. Just a little job. Nothing risky. And you haven't done much for a long time. So they're not watching you, not taking any notice. There's a good fellow.

He swallowed hard and stared up at the ceiling. He'd told them how hard it was now that Helen had gone, now he was alone with the baby, now he had responsibilities. But they hadn't listened. Give it a little while, he thought, and I'll get it over with. There's a side door, so warped and misshapen they can't even lock it. Like the rest of the place. Not as clever or efficient, not as dangerous as we think. Maybe.

Marcus turned onto his side but the voice still droned on. You see the Russians know we never use reporters. Stopped all that years ago. Besides most of them were piss-artists, talked their heads off as soon as they got hold of a gin and tonic. But you're not like that, Marcus. You're the exception. That's why we're going to break all the rules and put you in.

So many years back: the little speech. And yet it sounded so clear.

He picked up his watch from the nightstand, and wound it noisily. It was nine-thirty. He'd go at ten.

Two miles west of Murmansk, the hills dip down almost to the sea. It's so hostile and desolate that if it hadn't been for the weapons of war and the insecurity of a super power no one would ever have gone there. The czars had declared the region unfit even for birds.

Gennady wedged himself between two giant rocks. He was out of the wind but his body was shaking badly. There'd been nothing for it. He couldn't have left the city in full arctic gear. People would have stopped him—a young man in arctic gear—asked questions. He'd had to go off wearing only his office clothes, an old overcoat, thin black shoes, with the soles falling apart—and now, God only knew, he'd probably die of frostbite.

Suddenly from far away came the sound of a barking dog. For a moment he crouched stock-still on the frozen ground. One minute, two. But there was no other sound, only the chattering of his teeth and the constant moaning of the wind.

From under his overcoat he pulled out the tiny transmitter and extended the antenna. This is for the one day when you'll need it. That's what the American had said. Insurance. You can leave signs and service all the drops in northern Russia, but if there's an emergency you'll need this little baby —the best we have. Won't let you down.

Christ! The Russian had sworn silently. You don't make promises like that. And he had crossed himself and tried to forget it had ever been said.

For a moment the wind dropped and he could hear the sea crashing along the coastline. And you wouldn't know you were in Russia, he thought. Not out here, where it doesn't matter at all what side you're on. You have only to survive.

Gennady turned on the transmitter, and his hand shook again, but it wasn't from the cold. He'd been wrong to answer the phone, wrong not to hang up once he'd heard the voice, the poor Russian accent, the nervous quaver.

"Is that Intourist? No? I'm sorry. Mistake." And he'd known that was the signal. They wanted final confirmation before the contact. They had to know it was clear.

It took him only twenty seconds to send the message. Just his code and call-sign and somewhere out beyond the waves they'd hear it, wouldn't they? Someone at sea or in a plane locking on to the little message from Russia, the little bird in the cage, singing his song to the wind.

Wearily he climbed back up to the road, his feet numbed and his heart pounding away. It had to be big, this one. Had to be important. This dark night in the city of Murmansk.

Marcus thought—you go now. And I promise you won't feel the cold. The excitement will carry you through. You used to call it fear, but now it's under control. You've got it together. You can do it.

Out the side entrance. Rubber boots on ice. Instantly the wind lifted and shook him. You fight all the odds, and when you've finished fighting, there's still the weather.

At the other end of the street he heard voices. A night club had thrown out its patrons. Teenagers mostly. They stumbled into the square, drunk, underdressed, calling out, their voices shrill in the silence.

For a moment Marcus held back beside the door, hidden from their view by an outcrop of the building. But as he

peered toward them he blessed the little crowd. Out of nowhere it seemed a militia patrol car had pulled up beside
them. Two officers had gotten out and he could see the silhouette of authority, the peaked caps and sheepskin coats;
and the little group had gone quiet, their bravado ebbing
away under the yellow headlights.

He didn't wait, took the back road, not running, but fast,
skirting the square and this time you head for the football
field. So few people on the streets and that's the best time to
go. You're not alone and you're not surrounded. You have
room to move.

Beside the tall iron gates he took a quick look behind
him. A wide concrete boulevard bent its way down toward
the port. No lights burned in the shop windows. A hundred
yards away he could make out the pillars of a local government office, dark, frozen, iced-in. How did they ever get the
city to move?

He pushed at the gate. For a moment it resisted, probably stuck by the cold, then it opened soundlessly and Marcus
swung through. He hadn't done too many of these, but you
always hope there'll be a premonition. A warning pulse if
only you hear it. But all he could think of was the cold, the
biting, deadening cold, under the clear, dark sky with the
stars out on parade. And how he'd watched those same stars
as a child in a safer land.

As Gennady walked, the moon dived in and out of the
clouds and the shadows flickered across the snow-covered
streets. Block after block, tall and rigid, windows illuminated or darkened at random, like squares on a puzzle.

Gennady only wanted to hurry. Figures drifted past him
in black coats and hats. For a second he wondered if they
were all on their way to a funeral. There were the same vacant expressions numbed by the cold, the stooping backs, the
air of miserable resignation. Maybe the Russian winter was a
kind of funeral after all.

But if you keep your head down, no one has to recognize you. You're all wearing the uniform. You're all the same. Just hurry home, wait an hour, then make the contact.

And he'd almost made it, almost at the steps for the long climb to his parents' flat when he felt the pressure on his arm. He tried to ignore it. But if a Russian grandmother gets her claws into you, there's little chance of escape. Gennady looked down and saw the tiny gloved hand locked on to his sleeve.

He knew the eyes above the scarf, the black eyes, and the old Georgian woman who owned them. Sharp eyes they were, that had watched his parents for years from across the corridor, eyes that had followed all the comings and goings, that had bored indifferently into their lives.

"Sorry to hear about your folks." The ancient voice croaked at him from behind the scarf.

Gennady turned and looked down at her. "What d'you mean?"

"The ambulance came for them about an hour ago." The old eyes looked away. "The concierge told me, just as I was leaving."

Liar, he thought. You've been lying so long, and yet you still can't do it properly. He brushed past her and headed up the steps and he wasn't at all sure what made him stop. He must have stood there for a full minute, his eyes tracking along the landscape, seeing nothing.

Something was wrong though. The ambulance was wrong. They don't send them out at night for old people. If you were lucky, very lucky, a doctor might visit. But an ambulance . . . for his father? And what had the old bag said? "The ambulance came for them." Both of them—together?

It was then that he felt the cold inside him—the kind that grows from within, sharper, more intrusive than an Arctic gale. In that instant he knew the walls were tumbling around him. Soon, as his mother used to say, sooner than he had ever imagined, the dogs would be looking for a meal.

* * *

Marcus reached the stands and stopped. Around him the rows of empty seats stretched away into shadow. He descended quietly, keeping his head low. Of all the games they've played here, he thought, this is the strangest.

In the moonlight he could see the goalposts. The southern goalpost. Which was it? And then he saw the distant cranes of the port and forced himself to work it out.

Last steps now. We'll meet behind it. Four minutes to go. Wait five and then get out. The psalm, the liturgy, the whole Order of Service.

So many details, and you've quite forgotten that the fellow will have something momentous to tell you, that he's summoned you all this way for a reason.

From the edge of the stands, there was a four-foot drop to the field, half cleared, half scraped. They must have had a game that night. Or half a game.

Wait here. Don't go down. Timing just right. Maybe he's here already, watching.

Marcus crouched on the steps. What was that on the ground beside the goalpost? Forget it. One minute, two. And then you're counting the final seconds and you start to know that he isn't coming, that somewhere over time or distance a thread has snapped, or a nerve.

And he had to get down onto the field to see what it was. It was light and fluttering, carried along by gusts of wind. As he bent down he recognized the thin red scarf that had flown almost defiantly from the goalpost and had meant so much to both of them. Now it was cold and discarded, like the property of a corpse.

You can't run away from them—so you run toward them. Gennady knew the theory, standing out there on the dismal, frozen street.

And then he saw it—the ancient truck with the monster hood, grunting along, only one headlight to show the way.

Easy to step out in front of it, arms raised, easy to tell the driver it was "national security," cajole him, threaten him, kick just another submissive Soviet into compliance. Easy when you have to.

For twenty minutes they drove in silence, slithering, grating along the sanded ice tracks. Gennady leaned against the passenger door and shut his eyes.

If they're in a hurry, if they're confident, if they want to keep the credit for themselves, they won't have put out a general alert and you can slip through their fingers like jelly.

Theory again. That's all it was. He looked at his watch. Two transport planes, he knew, would be preparing to leave for Moscow. It was one of the busiest routes in the Union. He'd verified it often enough on the computer.

In the distance the lights of the airfield were coming into view. The driver hesitated.

"What now?"

"Drive. We go straight in."

As they approached, a guard emerged from the gate house, semiautomatic rifle across his chest.

Gennady wound down the window and pushed his identity card into the freezing night air.

The guard shone his flashlight, then saluted. "Your travel warrant, comrade Major."

"My travel warrant awaits me at the departure gate."

"You know that I'm required to examine it here."

Gennady smiled. Every door has a lock, they say, every lock has a key. Like all Russians he knew the code.

"I would be exceptionally grateful, comrade corporal." And he could see the young man's eyes had started to move from his face, following the arc of his right hand, with the fifty-ruble bill clenched between thumb and forefinger. The right hand stopped a few inches from the corporal's face.

"The gate, comrade, the gate."

As they passed through, Gennady let the note fall into

the soldier's hand. He looked at the driver and read his thoughts.

"There's one for you too, my friend."

They stopped in front of the main building. Gennady leaned forward as if to open his door, then swiveled back and slammed his fist into the driver's face, the full weight of his body behind it. He left the money on the dashboard—just an inch from the unconscious head.

It wasn't that it came easily. Gennady knew such things either worked or failed in a spectacular manner. But they didn't check his travel warrant, because everyone knows that the guard at the gate does that. They'd become lax about security, because there seemed no need for it. And the great dark-green Ilyushin shuddered down the runway, rose slowly and noisily as if in pain, and left behind it no record of those on board.

Gennady huddled in a military parka, but the cold seeped in regardless.

Only then did he remember his mother and father, forcing himself to picture the scene in the cramped apartment, the clatter as the pigs would have forced their way in, yelling and smashing whatever they could find; Mama would have been in tears, Dad bewildered and confused, the two of them, half-clothed, stammering out their prayers, herded like cattle into the cold.

How could he have done that to them? Hadn't they earned their miserable square of peace? He turned his head away from the other passengers, clenching his fist, weeping tears of helplessness. All his ideals, all his hopes had been squandered and betrayed. The only people he'd loved would die in fear and misery, just like the old days, not even knowing what they'd done.

3

Cold, bad tempered, sleepy eyed, the press party gathered at dawn to wait for Yuri. Yuri from the Foreign Ministry. Yuri who'd arranged the trip, Yuri who carried the burden of it like a reluctant donkey.

He didn't look well, stepping over a pile of bags, cameras, and outstretched bodies in the lobby, much on his mind.

"C'mon fella—get the show on the road."

The shout from a cameraman seemed to galvanize the Russian into action.

He reached the front of the group. "Please to be silent. Listen to me."

The low murmuring continued. Marcus counted twenty or more in the press party. They would give Yuri a hard time just on principle. If there wasn't an adversary, there wasn't any journalism. Yuri was that day's main course.

"Shut up, I say."

The high-pitched screech made them stop and look up, mild amusement on a few of the faces. Yuri had lost it. Yuri would make a fool of himself. This was going to be more fun than they'd thought.

Marcus could see the exhaustion in Yuri's face. Had to have been up half the night. Probably at the local KGB station. They'd have had him crawling and stammering and apologizing for being alive, while they worked out what to do.

What to do about what? How much would they know? Had they detained his contact? Or had the man got away? What was a party of foreigners doing in the city in the middle of it all?

From his window a half hour earlier Marcus had seen the police activity. Unmarked cars and militia trucks racing across the city center, chasing their tails. In the main square disgruntled foot patrols stood around doing nothing, knowing nothing, a show of official impotence.

And they wouldn't have told Yuri either. They'd have hauled him in at the first sign of trouble. Routine. Back to basics. A Russian with foreigners in tow. Had to be suspect.

Marcus knew what was coming.

Yuri held up his hand. "I have bad news. Understand please. This is difficult, also for me. But trip to the dockyards is cancelled. We must all return to Moscow."

"Hey, what the fuck's going on?" The cry seemed to go up from a dozen people at the same time.

"I have not been informed . . ."

Marcus smiled thinly.

"It has been decided at the highest level. There is consideration of safety."

"Are you saying there's been an accident?" An American reporter nudged his cameraman. Suddenly a battery light flooded Yuri's face.

"I am saying nothing. No interview—nothing." He turned to go. "There is a bus to the airport in fifteen minutes. You may have breakfast first if you wish."

"You saying we've come all this way to Murmansk for nothing?"

The questions followed Yuri as he fled upstairs and out of range.

Marcus almost felt sorry for him. The trip would have taken months of preparation. He could almost see the acres of paperwork and clearances involved, the passes, the traveling to and fro because you could never get anyone on the phone. Yuri's world would be in pieces and he'd never know why.

Not the way Marcus knew, sick at heart, as he was, staring at failure.

It was still dark when they climbed into the buses. Only as they took off from the airport could Marcus see the late Arctic dawn, pallid and fragile toward the east.

He put his hand in his coat pocket and felt the red woollen scarf, still wet from the melted snow that was rushing beneath them.

4

Twenty-four hours went by before they summoned Marcus via London—to Washington.

To his surprise they booked him Air India to New York on an extra-cheap ticket. And he could only assume that a cost-conscious and dutiful bureaucrat had gone out in his lunch hour to buy it.

For much of the flight he slept, unaware of the children who played in the aisles, the women in their saris, the bustle of Asia around him. He had left Moscow in a rainstorm and even as the droplets battered at the aircraft's windows, he had felt cleansed, freed of the tugging, gnawing emotions that the city always provoked.

What was it about Moscow that forced you to examine your conscience? What made you search for guilt deep in your own soul? Not a calm place, he decided. Not a place to enjoy God's peace. Not these days.

A stewardess brought him a meal of Chicken Tikka. It was better food than he'd eaten for weeks. Moscow's supplies had worsened dramatically in recent weeks, and even the Westerners had caught the low, whispered predictions of food riots. Reforms were one thing, went the cry, hunger was something else. And hunger was on its way in the shape of the full and total dislocation of the economy. No more talk about the waking Soviet giant. The giant, they all agreed, had died long ago.

Marcus looked at his watch and decided to leave it on British time. That way he would know what the baby was doing—when she'd be sleeping and eating and playing—each stage in the soft, undemanding routine of childhood.

For now, he'd decided, she and the au pair would stay at his mother's house near Hatfield, with a garden of apples and pears, and cream tea by the hour. It would help the little girl forget her own mother, forget that she wouldn't be seeing her again.

No one met him in New York, where he stood an hour in line going through immigration. But they watched his progress.

No one offered him transportation as he waited twenty minutes for a taxi to change airports. And he was sleeping again as the Pan Am shuttle hugged the eastern seaboard, then dived abruptly toward the nation's capital—where they would ask him what had happened to their agent two days and a continent away.

You're not a reporter anymore, Marcus. At least you won't be once you're over there.

That voice again. Face had been a little older, more lined, more tired than Marcus had remembered.

Years earlier the man had introduced himself as Foreign Office Liaison as if that were his given name.

And this time he had shown Marcus to a chair in the dull gray office at Heathrow Airport and smiled without warmth.

"Just tell them what you told our people in Moscow. Stick to the facts. You turned up at the rendezvous. Their man didn't. You don't know what went wrong—so don't guess, okay?" It wasn't a question.

"They simply want to hear it from you. No hassle. That's if you can put up with the climate in Washington."

And now it was on him. As he left the terminal the heat

wrapped itself around his body like a cheap woman, cling-
ing, sticky, making it hard to breathe. Brits abroad, he
thought wryly. We always wear too many clothes. He removed his heavy worsted jacket and prayed silently for a
storm.

The cab took him to a hotel just off M Street. "Get along
to see them as soon as you like," Foreign Office had said.
"They're on K Street. That's two streets away from M."

"Really?" Marcus had raised an eyebrow.

"Mmm. Tell you what. On the floor below them there's
this place called the Intelligence Bookstore. Mainly for
weirdos and Soviet diplomats. Books on cryptology and mar-
tial arts. Assassinations we have known and loved. That sort
of thing. Bloody funny place, America."

The apartment was numbered but carried no name. Nor
did the silver blonde with the sixties wave, who sat him
down in reception. Would he have coffee or a soda? He chose
coffee, uncertain what a soda was.

It was, reflected Marcus, like waiting in a hospital for the
results of your test. Would they smile at you, would they look
at the floor? If the news was really bad, would they even tell
you?

In any event, the man who advanced on him seemed
cheerful enough.

"David Russert," he said quietly. "Good flight?" And he
smiled as if sharing a secret.

They sat on low, dark-green armchairs, a coffee table
between them.

"By the way. Really appreciate you coming." The smile
faded. Russert began to look genuinely upset. He hung his
head like a bulldog, the skin drooping in folds from his chin.

"We just wanted to hear your side of things back there.
You know, the pulse, the drumbeat, the colors. Smoke?" He
pointed to a leather box on the desk. "I've asked a colleague
to drop in once we've had a talk. Sound okay?"

"Sounds fine." And to Marcus it really did. He had expected more formality, preparing himself for a bronzed, hand-pumping, freshly showered twenty-year-old from the Agency. Instead Russert seemed more like a small-town college professor—understated, unambitious, unhurried. Late fifties, Marcus guessed. Probably too late to get where he'd wanted to go.

They studied each other as Marcus began to talk. He felt no pressure. Far below, the early evening traffic jammed solid. Russert loosened his tie and sat back. Only much later did Marcus realize that the American had not even asked a question. And yet when he told of the dawn return to Moscow, the red scarf in his pocket, the sense of disappointment, Russert sat up and opened his eyes wide.

"You tell the facts well, my friend. But what about impressions? Why did it all go down the drain? What did our comrade have to tell us that was so important? What made him press the panic button?" The gray eyebrows raised.

Marcus shook his head. "You know more than me. You received the initial contact. What did that tell you?"

"You don't need to know . . ."

"I can't help if you don't tell me . . ."

"You can't help at all. That's the way we see it." Russert stood up as if to regain control of the conversation. "We ask you people for a favor. We have an agent requesting contact in Murmansk. We don't have an officer who can get there. You had the perfect cover. The press trip. First of its kind. So we give it to you. What happens? The agent never shows. A fuck-up of truly cosmic dimensions. Excuse me." He turned away and picked up the phone. Marcus hadn't even heard it ring.

"Show him in."

The man who entered slid rather than walked through the doorway. Marcus was aware of a gray double-breasted suit, balding black hair, the olive coloring from weekend beaches and private money and seniority.

"Fox," he said simply and offered a cold left hand. "Kind of fits the job, doesn't it?" He leaned against Russert's desk. "So how far have we got?"

"Our friend was about to share some of his impressions. . . ."

"Oh yes, impressions. Such a difficult area, don't you think, Marcus. You don't mind if I call you Marcus, do you?" The voice was soft New England like Russert's. Same school, thought Marcus, only this one had got better grades.

"I haven't been to Russia, Marcus, so excuse my ignorance. Interesting times there just at the moment." Fox lifted a magazine from Russert's desk, examined the front page and put it back.

"Do you have any sense where all these events are leading? The power struggle, reforms, that kind of thing?"

The atmosphere had eased perceptibly, the air conditioning whirred. Russert shut his eyes. Marcus talked of what he knew. "It's not much, but the General Secretary may be unable to hold on. That's becoming clearer by the day."

"And what about you?" The question thrown, it seemed, from another room.

"I'm sorry . . ."

Fox raised both eyebrows. "What about you, I asked? Your position in Moscow, status, hopes, dreams. How much do you earn, Marcus?"

"That's my business. . . ."

"I know how much you earn. . . ."

"Then why ask . . . ?" In the back of his mind something told him to stay cool—the line from an ad—never let them see you sweat.

Fox wandered over to the window. "I wanted to see what you thought of it . . . your pay. Is it an issue?"

"Of course it is."

"Are you unhappy about it?"

"Are you?"

"We could play another kind of game if you don't like this one." Fox looked at his shoes.

"Is that a threat?"

"Marcus, Marcus, Marcus . . . you're among friends. Okay?" He clapped his hands together as if signaling the end of a chapter. "Okay. Look, we have to find a way to figure this thing out. That means the whole picture, you with me? An operation goes wrong. On the fifth floor they want the full, uncensored version—everything: the food you ate, the shoes you wore, the color of your underpants, the change in your pocket. You're a small part of the scene. You're here to help me write it."

The voice was steady and clear, no hesitation, no room for doubt. In the corner Russert stood up stiffly and yawned.

"You guys want coffee?"

No one answered. Russert had somehow become irrelevant. Marcus heard the door close behind him.

Fox took his place on the sofa. "Your family situation, Marcus. That must make things hard in Moscow."

"It doesn't help."

"Care to talk about it?"

"Not much to say." He looked the American straight in the eye. "And you know it anyway. My wife, Helen, was killed in a car accident last year. We were in West Berlin. We'd driven out of Moscow to get the car serviced and have a few days off. A decent cup of coffee, some shopping, that kind of thing. I was waiting in the hotel for a phone call, so she took the baby out for a drive. The car was hit by a truck. It just pulled in front of her without looking. The baby was thrown clear. No one knows how."

Marcus looked up. Fox hadn't moved. Odd, he thought. In Britain they'd be squirming with embarrassment by now, mumbling condolences and straightening their cuffs. But maybe death was part of this man's life.

"What made you go back to Moscow?"

"What else could I do?"

"Fall apart, disappear. Others have."

"The baby was a big help. She wasn't even two when it happened. And you know, or maybe you don't, that for a child there's just a daily routine that keeps on going. Feeding, washing, playing. Even without a mother it had to go on."

"How did the Russians treat you, when you got back?"

"The foreign press department was polite, sent a note. In the compound the staff were great, especially with the baby. She's called Cressida, by the way. . . ."

"I know."

"Of course you do. Anyway they made a great fuss over her. She was always in and out of the office. . . ."

"How about women?" An impatient tone had crept in.

"I beg your pardon . . . ?" Marcus felt the jolt and knew he'd been lulled.

"Did they put any women your way? I do have the authority to ask these questions."

For a moment Marcus didn't answer. The question was how *much* authority the man possessed. Had he caught his fish, or was he still trawling?

"One or two I suppose," he replied. "You never really know. There was a girl in the Ministry of Foreign Trade who got quite friendly. . . ."

"How friendly?"

"She would have gone to bed with me if I'd asked."

"Why didn't you?"

"Not my type. . . ."

"Which is?"

"Not your concern."

Fox smiled. "You've been a great help, Marcus. Thanks for coming."

"That's it?"

"For now. Have a good trip back."

He walked to the door and held it open. There was no sign of Russert, and the blonde had also disappeared from the outer office. Marcus had the sense that they had run out of time. Maybe the office was rented by the hour. Maybe the actors had lost interest and gone home.

He took the elevator to the ground floor. The traffic was still crawling. And it had to be a serious indictment of Western civilization when it was quicker to walk.

Russert had brought the car around to the front. The silver blonde sat in the back, the magazines and the coffee machine from the office were on the seat beside her. Facilities had been overstretched that day. She'd had to do it all herself.

Fox got in on the passenger side and they pulled out onto K Street.

"Don't you have a siren?"

Russert shook his head. "They took them away from us. Some people were abusing them to beat the rush hour."

"What did you make of our friend?"

What do you care? thought Russert. You've made up your mind.

"He seemed harmless enough."

The senior man shifted in his seat, examining his colleague. "When will you learn, Russert? Brits are never harmless. Look at history, look at the trouble they caused all around the world. Oh they may say 'please and thank you' more than we do. But they don't mean it. All that old world charm covers up all that old world deceit."

They pulled onto the Whitehurst Freeway. Along the Potomac the sun left an orange sparkle, the trees like a dark border, marking the edge of Virginia.

The younger man was warming to his subject. "You see, Russert—I know Brits. Half the time they treat the world like elementary school. All nicknames and initials. 'See you in the bugger house, chaps, biccies for supper. Anyone for a G and T?' " He mimicked the accent. "But underneath it they're tough, fucking tough. And you know why? Boarding schools —that's all it is. Shove the kids out the door when they're eight, pack 'em off to join the rest of the stuck-up junior rat-pack. Little kids, I'm talking about, in jams."

Russert braked hard to avoid a sports car that had pulled in front of them. The blonde drew in her breath audibly but the two men ignored her.

"Anyway, for the first year these little creatures cry themselves to sleep in dormitories. Then, pretty soon they stop crying and don't feel a damn thing. Next stage is they don't recognize a feeling if it bites them in the arse. So they're hard and they don't give a shit."

They were up on Key Bridge, turning right onto the GW Parkway and the traffic had picked up speed. A smooth fast road to Langley and Russert hadn't been expecting the question.

"You handled this one yourself, didn't you?"

"You know I did." He shifted his hands on the wheel. "Anything that goes this high. Comes to me. The embassy station knows that. It's policy."

"Nothing came back from Murmansk, did it?"

"Nothing will." Russert had lowered his voice. "Watch for the small print in the local papers. A year from now they'll announce a fatal accident. We'll never know what really happened."

"Why so certain?" His colleague turned in the seat. "We normally hear something."

"Just a feeling on this one." Russert turned off the parkway, down the winding avenue of fir trees and neat grass shoulders out of sight of the rush-hour traffic. "All that Arctic ice," he murmured. "Seems to bury most things."

5

They were in the garden at Hatfield, where the cedar tree sat over them like a giant umbrella—a summer garden of flowers and rugs and sprinkled toys—forever teatime.

Marcus had watched his mother playing with the little girl, running after her as the tiny brown legs pedaled the tricycle toward the shed. Only the lucky ones ride a path like that, he thought. Such a straight and peaceful path.

And yet now the peace had gone. He knew that. Helen had taken it with her, and after that both the Department and the Russians had contrived to siphon off his emotions like so much dishwater. There were no longer any quiet and comfortable thoughts to take with you and lie with under the cedar tree.

Only you, Cressida, he told himself, you blot out so many of life's sharp edges. Your face, alive with humor and agility.

The child was running toward him, the brown curls shaking, eyes bright, and as he put out his arms, she ran around them, laughing. You won't be tamed, he told her silently. Helen's child there. You're a free spirit just like I was before it all began.

As Marcus looked around the garden he could see his mother, red in the face, panting. "Sit down, Ma, for God's sake. You're pottering about like a thing demented."

"Is that any way to talk to your mother?"

She smiled and settled down heavily on the blanket beside him.

He examined her eyes. If you could read my thoughts, he wondered, what would you feel about them? As you're walking in the supermarket, going to church, visiting patients in the hospital, what would you think if you knew that I had crossed into East Berlin once on a forged passport, that I had picked up two microdots in Kiev and delivered them to the embassy in Moscow, that I gambled with lives and secrets, that I had won extensions for the ones, and sometimes lost the others?

"More cake, dear?"

He took her hand and squeezed it, the hand that was firm, cool, unchanging.

"There's a chap from work, come to see you, Marcus."

He had fallen asleep under the cedar tree. She was shaking him gently. It was dusk and cool. "Cressida . . . ?" he murmured.

"She's fast asleep. I've put this fellow in the drawing room and given him a drink. He said it was important."

"Thanks, Ma. I think I know who it is."

Foreign Office was sitting on the sofa. A long curl of black hair hung down over his spectacles. Even on a Sunday he wore his brown suit and paisley tie, but he just missed being elegant. The shirt collar had frayed, the front was creased, the trousers carried a small stain on the knee.

"Hallo, Marcus." He got up awkwardly.

"Couldn't this have waited? I don't get much time to myself."

"Sorry. There's been a meeting this weekend. Country house. You know the kind of thing. Cold pie and a beer. Round the world in a day."

Marcus sat down. Why did Foreign Office always talk like a telex?

"Anyway, wanted to fill you in. Lot of talk about Russia. Appears the General Secretary may be in trouble. More trouble. They want you back in. It's that woman of yours, really. The one in the ministry. Best contact we've got. Best contact anyone's got. The Americans would kill for her. . . ."

"What trouble are you talking about?" Marcus could barely contain his annoyance.

"The conservative group in the party has formally broken links with the rest." Foreign Office gulped with excitement. "Says it's too reformist, says the economy's in chaos and discipline has gone to hell." He looked around the room, examining the pictures. "All true of course, but it means things could move rather quickly from now on. It would be good if you could get stuck in again. . . ."

"I am stuck in."

"You know what I mean." Foreign Office stood up. He was a whole head shorter than Marcus and didn't like it. "By the way, how did you get on in Washington?"

"I'm not sure why I was there."

"Funny that." Foreign Office picked up his raincoat from the floor. "We're not sure why you were there either. The Americans are being very odd about this one. They lost an important man in Murmansk. As you know that tracking station is of more than passing interest to us. And yet they haven't followed it up, haven't sniffed the air or dispatched the dogs, haven't done a thing. They've closed the book without even looking inside. Almost as if they don't want to know what happened."

"Any idea why?"

Foreign Office put his hand on the front doorknob.

"Probably nothing to it." He looked down at his feet. "Fact is there was a little trouble at the embassy in Moscow while you were in the States. . . ."

"Whose embassy?"

"Ours. Russian chap rushed the entrance, got into the compound. Unfortunately wasn't there for long. The guards came in, grabbed him, beat him senseless. Head of Chancery came out, ordered them off the grounds, but they took not a blind bit of notice. Kept smashing this young creature over the head. Our man even struggled with them, got pushed to the ground. Quite a battle really."

"Christ." Marcus drew in his breath. "I didn't hear anything on the news about it."

"Course you didn't. We didn't exactly shout about it."

"Why not?"

"Little chap managed to leave a note in a box on the ground. Guards didn't see it. Told some story about a fellow in Murmansk. Apparently he'd been plane spotting. Seems to have been something odd with a training flight. Couldn't work it out myself. Anyway this Russian was supposed to hand over the information to the Americans, only he got betrayed before he could. Seemed to think the Americans were to blame." Foreign Office looked at his watch. "Lord, I must be off. Have a care, Marcus. Stay in touch."

Quickly Marcus reached for the man's arm. He could feel himself shaking.

"For God's sake, what happened to this Russian? Didn't you protest or something?"

"Course we did. So did they. Told us he was a crank. Said it was none of our business." He shrugged. "That's it. I shouldn't really have said anything." He patted Marcus on the shoulder. "Anyway, old chap, don't let it worry you. Mmm? Just one of those things."

6

The envoy was a man in his early fifties. Well traveled for a Russian, but his name meant nothing to anyone.

He had grown up in a miserable mud-heap of a village in the Transcaucasus, where the inhabitants had once contemplated a food riot, but called it off because no one could agree when it should start.

As a boy, therefore, he had witnessed both poverty and indolence, and might have spent his life enjoying both, had it not been for an unexpected occurrence, shortly before his twelfth birthday.

The ancient village teacher, who had forgotten most of the things he had ever known, finally forgot his way home. He was returning blind drunk from a wedding party at the collective farm, wheezing and singing his way along a narrow path beside the river. Instead of turning left where there was a bridge he turned right where there wasn't, landing forty feet below on a disused railway track, from where, it's assumed, he began that final journey, slightly ahead of his appointed time.

In the absence of another teacher the children of the village were bused each day to the neighboring town of Shelepin, where they were obliged to attend the already overcrowded classes. The envoy found himself next to a boy who was clearly more intelligent and dynamic than himself, but with whom he was to form an unusual bond.

Mikhail, as he was called, took pity on his less fortunate colleague and went on to fashion a relationship of mutual benefit. In return for help with schoolwork, the envoy would offer Mikhail his muscle—protection, the kind of thing a bright, go-ahead twelve-year-old needs when he walks home late among envious fellow students.

The envoy was strong beyond his years, with legs and arms like small tree trunks. More importantly to Mikhail he was totally trustworthy. Soon he was carrying out errands for Mikhail's family. That earned him both food and affection. He began to feel part of a new family. He belonged. So when Mikhail left school and joined a collective farm, the envoy went with him, smoothing his path, running his errands, persuading, where persuasion was needed. From there to the party institute where the envoy's own skills were insufficient to get him accepted as a student, but where he could be "found" a job in the office once his loyalty and reliability became known.

The big leap came in 1958 when Mikhail won a place at the Law Faculty of Moscow University. The envoy remembered his feelings when he heard the news—joy and pride at his friend's achievement, but also acute sadness at the thought that the two of them would finally have to part.

To avoid embarrassing Mikhail, he made the most difficult decision of his life and simply disappeared from the scene. Without hesitating he took a bus back to Shelepin and rented a room. He recalled the blustery day in October, his own sinking spirits, and the little sprawl of a town that he had hoped never to see again.

The envoy signed on at the local timber yard, worked three days, collected his pay and then walked into town to wait for the *chas volka* —the hour of the wolf—opening time —and a few hours of oblivion.

At some time during that night he remembered a hand

that seemed to pull him out of the crowd, a strong hand, but not an unfriendly one. Past the grinning red faces, it pulled him, past the senseless figures lying in swill on the floor, out into the darkness where the first snowflakes of the year fell softly into the dirt. Barely visible in the streetlamps had been a shiny black car: the ultimate symbol of officialdom, and his heart had sunk again, thinking that he was being arrested, that he had shamed the party, that he was to be sent into exile.

The car belonged to the local party secretary, but the hand was Mikhail's stretching out to support the one friend he had ever felt able to trust. Mikhail took him to the local government guest house where a room had been prepared, along with coffee and a gallon of water. And by morning the envoy was sitting up pale and sober as Mikhail informed him of his plans. In a month they would travel to Moscow together. There, through his party connections, the envoy would be found work and given a room. Mikhail would pursue a career in politics, they could work together in between his studies. Who could tell, one day they might set foot in the Kremlin itself.

The envoy couldn't help smiling when he looked back. "History," he muttered to himself. The strangest tale of all. What a long way they had traveled from Shelepin. What an odyssey it had been. Now he was on his way to the airport. He barely noticed the road. So often had he traveled it, in so many weathers. On this day the city seemed hot and lifeless, the policemen in their caps and blue shirts, lounging at the intersections, taking only a passing interest in the traffic. Dust and the laziness of many centuries hung in the air.

Of course he hadn't been at the Kremlin meeting that morning, but the reports of it were common gossip in the corridors of the building. Mikhail voted down, Mikhail up a blind alley, the old wolf unable to kill the calf, the pack at his heels. And they all knew what that meant.

So the envoy felt sick at heart to be leaving. In the old days, he reasoned, there had, of course, been battles. To rise in that system you had to claw others out of the way. You prodded, you cajoled, you extorted. That was the political currency in the land of the proletariat. But these battles were different. There was envy, there was greed, there was confusion at every level.

Before leaving he had called the only secure number that the Kremlin had ever operated. A single communications link unconnected to either the city or government network. An army team, working under his own supervision, had installed it during a May Day parade, when everyone had piled into Red Square and the Kremlin guard had its hands full with the crowd. To make quite sure the envoy had even arranged a brawl beside the Saviour's Gate. By the time it had been broken up the link was established.

That morning he had listened to his friend's voice, and noted the instructions. But the tone had shocked him. For a moment he had thought it was someone else, so deep and halting and care-laden were the sounds that reached him.

The envoy didn't need to be told that there was little time left, that his mission was risky, that the two of them might never meet again. Such things were understood. You know when a dream is over, he told himself, you know because you wake in your own room, cold and disoriented, sitting bolt upright, with your mind in pieces on the floor beside you, just as Mikhail would be sitting at this moment, inside the Kremlin that he had come to rule.

"Documents."

The KGB guard at the diplomatic departure gate seemed bored and inattentive.

Even when he looked at the envoy's letter, he barely reacted. Only the rapid scanning of the eyes gave him away.

His right hand reached out languidly for the gray telephone beside him.

"Wait," he told the envoy, then whispered into the receiver.

"My plane leaves in thirty minutes," the envoy replied coolly. "I am not accustomed to being kept waiting."

"This is not the Kremlin, my friend, this is the airport. I said wait."

As he looked toward the customs area the envoy could see two men approaching. Both were in plain clothes, wearing the red armbands of the airport security service. Their trousers were baggy, in the modern style of the West, their hair slicked back. They were confident, sure of their own domain.

"You will follow us, please." The taller of the two led the way to an anteroom beside the immigration booths. Just a desk and two metal chairs. The envoy took one of them.

"What is the meaning of this?" he asked.

The security man held his letter up to the neon light.

"We are simply checking the validity of this authorization."

"It is not for you to check." The envoy stood up. "I take it you can read the signature."

The security man smiled. "I can read it but there is a problem with it. Please wait here."

The two men left the room and for the first time the envoy felt nervous. This had not happened before. On the contrary the airport staff had always been courteous to the point of obsequiousness, falling over themselves to smooth his path.

Suddenly the door reopened and the younger security man came in, his face flushed. He seemed in a great hurry.

"Quickly, come with me."

"What the . . ." but the envoy could see from his face that it was not the time to argue. Out of the room, the man led him, down the shiny lino corridor, toward the immigration booths. He didn't stop, waving a plastic pass, guiding the envoy through, toward the departure gate.

"You're leaving on a different flight," he whispered. "British Airways to London. It's the first one out of here. I suggest you do not wait for your own plane."

"What's going on?"

The security man was striding ahead through the departure lounge.

"Let me just say this. The signature on your letter no longer carries the authority it did. Someone here wanted to make an example of you, but there's a row about it. The General Secretary still has a few friends left."

They had reached the ramp. A single guard in uniform was checking the boarding passes. The security man brushed him aside.

"Have a good flight, ambassador . . ."

"But . . ." the envoy hesitated.

"Go while you still can, comrade. There's nothing more you can do here."

He saw London through the dirt-spattered windows of the plane, London drenched by summer drizzle, the red brick houses and roofs, blurred in a damp pathway, stretching to the coast. A credit card, drawn on a numbered account at Moscow's bank of foreign trade, bought him the ticket to Washington, and he waited anxiously in Terminal Four as the people grazed past the food counters and duty-free shops. He had never felt secure in the West, never at ease. And he deplored the arrogant condescension that many Soviets adopted when they left their country.

Seven hours later the aircraft lowered itself over the Virginia countryside to the west of the U.S. capital. Right to the heart of the beast, he told himself, and he couldn't suppress the thrill at arriving unknown.

"Enjoy your stay, Mr. Konstanz," said the immigration officer. "How's the weather in Switzerland this time of year?"

"Better than here," he replied and shook his head. Talk of the weather, smiles, nice days. What a contrast America provided with the country of his birth. There you didn't just smile for the sake of it. You smiled when there was something to smile about. And God only knew that hadn't been often.

He settled himself in the back of a cab and looked out at the houses. Everything seemed new, a small estate with the buildings dotted along a hill, trees and green and the wide highways that could take you out across the time zones.

Each time he came to America it was the same impression. Roads and movement, a country in transit, while on the other side of the world, Russia sat like a broken-down car at the side of the highway, its hood up, its driver asleep on the grass shoulder.

We tried to change it, he told himself. Tried to wake it up. But maybe it died long ago. You don't take an express train into a cemetery and expect people to clamber aboard.

In the city he rented a car and headed back the way he'd come, taking the Chain Bridge across the Potomac, turning up the air conditioning. In the driving mirror he caught sight of himself, nervous, poorly shaved, a wide bulky face, with pouches under the eyes. "You should have stayed in Shelepin," he murmured, "stayed there and died there."

As he neared Great Falls Park, the country began to remind him of Moscow, the outskirts, where the leadership kept their country retreats, where the roads were smooth and the forests impenetrable. He recalled the unmarked turnings, with the houses well out of sight, and you didn't go near them unless you were meant to.

The envoy pulled up at the gate house and paid his fee.

"We close in about two hours," the ranger told him. "Dusk."

He nodded and drove slowly into the parking area. Only a dozen cars remained. A family was clearing away their picnic, all plastic and cellophane, clusters of wasps, and children yelling at them. He got out and walked toward the overlook. A light wind had taken the edge off the heat. Far below he could hear water coursing on rock, could sense the urgency, the dynamic.

The envoy knew him from his walk, even before he saw his face. The walk tells you the kind of life that a man has lived, the kind of troubles he's faced, the speed of his progress, the ambitions still unfulfilled. And this man meandered along the pathway, unhurried, as if his life were behind him.

They had never met and yet there was a familiarity between them. The man from Russia wearing the tired creased clothing of a traveler, the American, relaxed and confident as only Americans can be, in pink shirt and slacks, also creased, but in his case to perfection.

The envoy looked him over and recalled with scepticism what he'd been told. This is an unusual man. Don't lean on him, pressure him. Neither an agent, nor an ally. We owe each other no favors or debts. But even people like us, right at the top of the political tree, we need someone like this. A friend, a simple friend. Nothing more. That's what Mikhail had said.

They sat at one of the wooden picnic tables as the last of the picnickers prepared to leave. "I can tell you," said the envoy stiffly, "that he misses the talks you used to have." He looked awkwardly around the park. He wasn't good at feelings.

"You didn't come all this way to tell me that."

"He asked me to come."

"Mikhail asked you?"

"Yes."

The American put his head in his hands. "You are taking quite a risk."

"I don't think so. Not here."

For a moment they listened to the crickets. All at once the noise seemed deafening.

"We were good friends many years ago. You know that, don't you?" The American leaned forward, his voice a whisper.

"Yes."

"Sometimes he wrote me letters. Oh not frequently. Twice maybe three times a year. Even when he got to Moscow and became so well known."

"I know."

"Yes, well . . . It was so strange of course. You know, this public figure, and me getting letters from him, not just a former friend, but from the leader of the Soviet Union." He shrugged. "I mean it wasn't something I could shout about, was it?"

"Shout?" The envoy looked puzzled for a moment. "Of course. No."

He stood up. Enough of the pleasantries. Surely. Now they could move to business. He leaned against the table, turning toward the American.

"I have come to ask a favor." He was watching the man so carefully.

"Ask it."

"You know of some of Mikhail's problems . . ."

"Ask it." Louder this time but the American wasn't moving. Not his hands, not his eyes. Stock-still. Controlled. The envoy realized they had not underestimated the man.

"I have to tell you that we know your business."

"What does that mean?"

"It means your business in the intelligence community. Not your business at the State Department where you are listed as working." The envoy took out a handkerchief and dabbed his forehead. A wasp buzzed angrily around him and he waved it away. The crickets rattled on ceaselessly. Nature, he realized, was unconcerned by his revelations.

"Go on."

"We have never used this information. Mikhail has never used it, and never would. To him you are a friend. In Russia that is no simple statement. It has much meaning. More perhaps than anything else. It's because of that, that he now asks your help."

"Shall we walk for a moment." The American rose stiffly and gestured toward the overlook. They fell into step along the uneven gravel.

"I remember very clearly that time in Moscow." He had his eyes fixed on the ground. "Remember that winter of '59, and that group of us all crowded together in the student hostel. Miserable conditions. Miserable time, when you think about it. And yet we were all so . . ." he looked up for a moment, "so intense about everything. Loves, hatreds. Everything meant so much. The end of Stalin. For the first time it seemed as though there might be a future instead of just the terrible past."

They reached the overlook and gazed out for a moment in silence.

"Of course they still didn't know what to make of me. An American student. I was one of the first. Meant to symbolize the thaw. Only everyone thought I was spying. So that didn't help much."

"Were you spying?"

The American grinned. "Of course I was. Did you think all those clever fellows in Washington would let me go to Russia just to read poems?" He stood up to his full height. "I was there to do my patriotic duty, same as everyone else." He smiled. "Had to keep my eyes open. Make contacts, pass them on, addresses, telephone numbers. We were all new to the game in those days, weren't we, my friend? Only you guys weren't as new as we were. You'd been practicing on your own people for thirty years. So you knew a few more tricks. . . ."

"And Mikhail . . . ?" Steer him, thought the envoy. Bring him around. He's wandering, giving himself time, working out what he'll say.

"Mikhail?" The American looked away from the waterfall. "Mikhail was my roommate, a friend. A great friend."

"We want you to come into Russia. Such a man as you could find out things that we can't. Who are our friends and enemies, who is working against us. Often such people approach the foreigners. They talk more freely to them than to Russians. Such a man could help us talk to Washington." He paused for a second. "Such a man could wait for the time when his friend might need him." He turned away and looked back out over the falls. "Will you help?"

The American smiled again. "I already did."

By the time the envoy turned back, the sky seemed to have darkened and the man had gone. All around him the paths and the picnic areas were empty. From the undergrowth came the sounds of clawing and rustling as the animals reclaimed their domain.

He recalled seeing a telephone beside the visitors' office. You could wait, he told himself. You could make the contact later. Take five minutes to breathe the fresh air. Take your thoughts back to Russia. But he knew he couldn't.

The envoy called a voice bank in Britain and left a recorded message in the Telecom computer. It was short and precise, and required specific action. Within a few minutes he knew the message would be retrieved and sent on to Moscow.

That at least was a relief. He replaced the receiver and took the path to the parking lot, noticing that he wasn't alone after all. A red truck had parked close to his car and it wasn't till he'd gone a few steps farther that he realized how odd that was. Out of all the empty spaces, in an all but deserted parking lot, the truck driver had stopped right next to him.

And yet it could have been a warning. It was late. The park was closing. Perhaps the rangers had come to remind him.

He took a step back from the path into the bushes and then he saw them—two figures, carrying plastic bags. They must have been emptying the garbage cans. Unhurriedly they flung the sacks into the back of the truck and drove toward the exit. The envoy emerged into the open. The sun was way down behind the trees.

You should have stayed in Shelepin, he told himself, and died in Shelepin; and for just a brief moment, he could see the broken-down wooden houses along the main street, the muddy uneven cobbles, and the troubled gray sky. Behind him, he felt sure, was that same wind that never quieted for long.

7

The three men were a team. Anyone could see that. Three chunky faces, three expressions of awkward nonchalance, three jackets almost aggressively ill fitting. Together they stood in the midday glare, waiting for the Moscow steamer. Rechnoi Vokzal—the river station was their destination—just as the envoy had instructed. For they were his men.

If he was aware of their attentions the figure in front of them showed no sign of it. Besides he had other distractions. Locked around him was a girl, no more than nineteen years old, painfully thin. She had about her an air of defiant possession, as if her parents had told her "Don't go out with this man, he's no good for you" and she'd taken pleasure in ignoring them. Now she clung to his waist, her pale skin clashing with his tan.

As they boarded the vessel, they stood out from the crowd. A few of the passengers stared, a few of the blowsy Moscow blondes, loud, cheeky, good-time girls who giggled a lot and shoveled ice cream into their mouth. They could see it: the couple were *inostrany*—foreign—untouchable, and out of reach. Not that they hadn't seen foreigners before, but these were different. Distracted, disinterested, not bothering to blend in or mingle. "Americans," whispered one of the blondes. "Bet you."

The team looked at each other. Half right, thought the

leader. Half right. He motioned the junior officer to go below
and get them a drink. They were all hot and anxious. They
couldn't afford to bungle this one.

Fun for the passengers was gliding past the tugs and
barges, past the fishermen and the sun bathers. By the
churches with the golden cupolas, they fell silent in wonder-
ment, and it was only when they reached the eyesore of Moscow University, standing like a rocket launcher on the Lenin
Hills, that they again found their shrill voices, all agreeing
they lived in a beautiful city.

The team nodded their approval. It was good, disci-
plined behavior. The people were law abiding and content,
unlike the scum they had to deal with.

At Serebryany Bor the couple made their move, dressed
in white, easy to follow. The beach lay close to many of the
foreign dachas, so the sandy strip was peopled by diplomats
and their families. There were swings and a merry-go-round
or two, snack bars, a Ping-Pong table in the open air, but the
couple paid no attention to the attractions. They walked not
for pleasure, but to get somewhere. Behind them the team
split up. One of the officers went for the phone.

Abruptly the young couple headed inland into the forest.
They took the lovers' path. Maybe they sought quiet and se-
clusion, but now they seemed hurried.

In a clearing they stopped and looked about them. Satisfied they were alone, the man set down his camera bag and
extracted a leather pouch. The girl seemed to be shaking her
head from side to side, singing softly. For the first time her
lips broadened into a smile. Then a tiny vial appeared in the
man's hand and she was feigning surprise, putting her hands
to her mouth in mock horror, before bending low over the
white powder, huddling close to him, blocking the team's
vision.

To them it was the final episode in a surveillance pro-
gram, authorized long before the summer began. Each time
the man had been the same, each time the woman different,

each one Russian. Just a job, log and watch, watch and log. But the team hadn't liked what they'd seen, and when the order had come to reel him in, they weren't slow to comply. The account, they reckoned, was overdue.

Fifty yards from the couple, they received word that the cars were in position, away from the beach, at the edge of the forest, engines running, destination cleared. Then they moved.

As they reached the clearing, the couple lay dozing, the vial almost empty beside them. And even when the two of them were dragged to their feet, they seemed unable to comprehend what had happened. They took the woman first, stunned, almost lifeless. It would be a long time before she came around.

As for the man, it seemed he struggled a lot, and had to be restrained for his own safety. That's what they said later in their report. That's how they explained the fractured rib, the bruising and lacerations to the face. He'd hit himself against a tree, scraped the bark. Lucky he was, that it hadn't been worse.

Six hours later they called the American embassy to come and get him, and get him out of the country. Lousy way for a diplomat to behave, they said. He and others like him could count on being persona non grata in the Union of Soviet Socialist Republics. Maybe okay on the streets of New York, but we don't like that here.

"You going to go public on this one?" The U.S. chargé d'affaires looked over at the deputy foreign minister. The summons to the ministry had ruined his Saturday.

"Depends if you retaliate," the Russian replied genially.

"Then I think we can terminate our business right now."

"Quite." The minister watched him leave. He'd had to come all the way into Moscow, just to authorize the arrest. What had the Kremlin said . . . "We need a U.S. diplomat with problems, preferably a sensitive one. Whatever he's doing, catch him doing it and chuck him out." The minister had been glad to oblige.

The chargé was just as glad to return to the embassy, glad that he hadn't been asked about the diplomat's other activities, glad that he wouldn't have to do Langley's business for them, appalled that they couldn't find a station officer for Moscow without a heroin addiction.

He drafted a coded message to Washington informing them curtly that the embassy was now one officer below strength—and better for it.

The envoy didn't know his request had been fulfilled so quickly and with such precision. He was halfway out over the Atlantic on the direct New York–Moscow flight, with no idea at all of the kind of reception he, himself, would be facing.

8

Look at you, Marcus.

Moscow was sleeping. One in the afternoon with the summer heat baking the cracked, uneven streets of the suburbs. Far below in the little park white-hot shafts of sunlight glared through the plane trees. And as ever, in the land of the powerful, no place to hide.

He ran a hand through his hair and moved closer to the window, but there was no breeze. In Moscow the seasons didn't just come and go, they smacked you across the face—heat and cold, like cudgels, beating you, wearing you down.

Look at you, Marcus.

Look at her.

She lay half-clothed on the rough, dumpy mattress—long red hair all over the place, laughing up at him, because it had been so good and they had waited so long, summoning their courage, choosing the moment. No flurry of spontaneity but, instead, the deep warmth that had built and built as the summer gathered around them.

It should never have happened. We both know that. But it did. And while you can run from almost anyone, you can't run from yourself. Not once she's gripped you, squeezed you, taken you over.

Look at her, Marcus.

And maybe she was thinking the same. For the smile had

hardened and there were new lines indented among the freckles on her forehead. She knows the consequences, he thought. Has to. Knows how they can make her pay.

She pulled herself up, leaning on the wall, back arched against the cheap striped wallpaper.

Look at you, Marcus.

He pulled his shirt toward him.

"You feel bad, don't you?" She put out a hand to him.

Like you're reading my face, he thought. "No."

"You sure?"

"No."

For a moment, above the rooftops, he could see the sun pass behind a cloud.

"Maybe it would have been better . . ."

"Listen, Marcus. You and I—we don't think about 'maybes' . . . we see a door, we open it, go inside, take a look . . ."

"Then how d'you close it?"

"Don't ever close doors, Marcus. Some days you go forward, others in reverse. Leave the doors open. They always taught us that."

As he sat there in the lazy stillness the panic hit him. Get out now, Marcus. You've gone way past the line on the map, dropped off the edge of the world even, torn up the only order in the book that really mattered. Hold an agent, comfort an agent, cry and laugh with an agent, but never, ever, till the sun does a dance in the sky, never fall for one.

They both put on their clothes. She, pulling and wriggling into white blouse and black skirt, office best, uniform of the new professionals—a million miles from the Revolution.

"You go first. Try for a taxi. Sometimes they wait by the metro station."

And he wondered again who was running whom.

"What about you?"

She grinned, bending down to stare at herself in the mirror, reclipping the red mane that hung so long and thick. "You forget, Marcus. I am so important these days. They will send a car for me." She slid into her shoes. "Oh nothing very grand, but if I'm lucky there'll be four wheels and I won't have to push it. Go!"

Out then into the courtyard, where the grandmothers, like ancient soothsayers, shook their heads at shadows, lazing in their speckled summer dresses. This day of sunshine in Russia.

Suddenly he felt like walking. It was the southern edge of Moscow, flat, ragged, the grass brown and dying along the sidewalks. Not the scenic route, but . . .

Got away with it, Marcus.

He looked at his reflection in a grimy shop window. Who was it who'd told him that the Russians employed fourteen surveillance officers for every foreigner in Moscow? Sounded improbable. Seven would be bad enough. But if you're caught with your pants down, one's too many.

Who was she really? Anastasiya—what a name. She'd called herself Nastya. Was she back at work, and if she was, what did she do?

Two months had passed since they'd met. He, the guest at a Kremlin banquet no less—an event revived to mark the appointment of the first General Secretary in twenty years, capable of staying awake through it. She, apparently, a hostess, with both a hairstyle and a brain.

She. Thirty-six years old. Once married to someone. He recalled her effortless American English. "I'm a dissident, Marcus," and then she'd smiled and laughed out loud. He had looked around to see if anyone had heard, but he needn't have worried. Under the vast crystal chandeliers of St. George's Hall, the Kremlin guests were being smothered in hospitality. Where had they all come from, he'd wondered. The beautiful people from the world's first socialist state— silked and jeweled, brushed and groomed—a coming-out party, like none he had ever imagined.

Anastasiya. She had led him through the crowd and gone on leading, he realized. They had said good-bye at the giant ornate gateway, and then he had stopped.

Who were you in that moment, Marcus, when you asked for her number—reporter, agent, or just a fool taking more of a risk than you could handle?

She had handed him her card, smiling again with eyes that said: read me, there's everything to read, and some of it's true and some of it's not, but read it if you can.

Anastasiya, new diplomat. Dissident. We want to go further and faster, she had told him. We want the reforms to be permanent and they're not. We want more than changes of atmosphere, we want a new climate. And we'll fight for it if we have to.

Marcus, turning away from the shop window, realizing that others had come to stare beside him, curious as to what he might have seen.

He took a taxi into the city, settling back on the clammy plastic seat, hearing the urgency in her voice, the passion. Did you really imagine you could stay indifferent . . . did you think you could walk away?

You, who've broken all the rules in all the countries: what made you believe you'd keep this one? You, the hider and seeker, the doer of things impermissible.

Look at you, Marcus.

If they find out, they won't forgive you.

Back in the center of Moscow, back in the foreigners' compound he found a telex message from the paper. Suggest trip to Armenia, it said. Lot happening. Time you left Moscow. Got out and about. Marcus shook his head. Maybe they'd heard of ethnic unrest there, maybe someone had read a book or seen a film. Who knew what went on in their minds? He screwed up the message and flung it in the wastebasket. He didn't want to go to Armenia. Not now. Not any time in the near future.

Marcus was walking out of the office, intent on going to the flat, bathing Cressida, reading a bedtime story, when he caught sight of Helen's picture on top of the filing cabinet. Who had put it there? Why now? Had someone been in and moved his things? It wouldn't be the first time.

He lifted the picture and held it to the light. Helen's eyes bored into him from a cloudy day and a beach in England. A year had gone by since she had died. And he hadn't told anyone about the circumstances. Oh yes, the truck, the accident. They all knew about that. But not the terrible row the night before. The tears, the accusations.

Helen had never believed that he cared for her, and somehow he had never managed to tell her. You only stayed for the baby, she would say. And was that true? Could he have loved her more, done more? Was it enough?

He thought back to the afternoon, and the red-haired Anastasiya who came from a different planet than Helen.

You can't go back, Marcus . . . and he knew then that he didn't want to. He'd follow this, wherever it led.

There must have been eight security men in the detail. The envoy took them all in as he came down the steps of the aircraft. Three black Zils, and a Mercedes from the militia protection unit, and they had ordered the Finnair plane parked at the western end of the Moscow runway close to the perimeter gate. They'd done him proud.

Over their shoulders he could see two officers from the KGB border troops watching with binoculars. It wouldn't have been a pleasant scene—Kremlin security, pushing its way through into the international concourse, elbowing guards and troops out of their way, and just daring someone to object. He knew they all carried Colt 9mm pistols. There would be semiautomatic rifles in the trunks of the cars. And would the Kantemir division have stood by? The General Secretary's own troops. Not yet. It hadn't come to that. Not yet.

They ushered the envoy onto the backseat and piled in after him. Very slick. He'd watched them perform a thousand times with the General Secretary. They sat facing outward, quiet and assured. They would have been given orders to get him through the airport, come what may, and whatever opposition there was would know it. The Kremlin's own security apparatus had been separate from the KGB since the new leadership was sworn in. They were quite capable of starting a full-scale battle on a public street. Their reputation was unblemished—they always delivered.

As the cars sped along the wide boulevards the envoy studied their faces.

All right, he thought, today they're ours. Loyal, committed, and very confident. But they were products of the system, just like all the others. And the system had taught them to make rapid accommodations within it.

Once they became sure the General Secretary was on his way out, they'd be the first to turn on him, to stab him in the chest.

It was simply the Soviet way. None of them would give it a second thought.

9

"Two visits in a week from you people. We're flattered." Fox took off his jacket and laid it on the back of the chair. He would maintain the fiction that this was his real office, even though the visitor knew it wasn't. The man didn't fit the room, didn't connect with it, didn't have the familiarity or sense of ease that comes from being where you live.

All this Foreign Office took in as he sat down on the dark-green sofa, high above K Street, luxuriating in the coolness of his welcome.

"Frankly, you could have picked a better day." The American perched against the desk.

"We thought it was important."

"We being . . . ?"

"I thought it was important." Foreign Office took off his glasses.

"I see, the royal *we* . . ."

"I didn't have to come. . . ."

Fox smiled for the first time. "Oh yes you did, my friend. If you had anything that even looks like a hole in our armor, and you didn't come to us . . ." He left the sentence unfinished.

"Shall we start again perhaps?" Foreign Office drained his coffee cup and put on his most schoolmasterly tone. It was going to be one of *those* meetings. "You've read the report," he said, "so you know what this Russian left in his note. Pretty unusual that, and I'm afraid my view is that the whole thing stinks. This was your courier," he raised a single eyebrow, "there can be no doubt about that—he loses his rag, barges into our embassy and announces, just before they beat him stupid, that you've shopped him. Worth a plane ticket, don't you think?"

"On any other day it would be."

"Explain."

"I . . . I . . . No," Fox seemed to pull his words from an air pocket close to the ceiling. "What the hell—I'm going to tell you anyway. You come over here, complaining about a low-grade Russian major who's blown. Today, of all days, that barely even rates a sentence in the Intelligence digest. Why? Because I've just lost my deputy station chief in Moscow. Why?" The voice rose an octave. "Because out of all the wonderful things this guy could have been, he turns out to be a heroin addict." He opened his hands in disbelief. "D'you realize how many briefings he attended, how many interrogations, how many of his friends and relatives we questioned? We knew him so well, we could have torn him apart and put him back together again. Christ almighty! Now it turns out he could have compromised the entire station."

"As you say, I picked the wrong day." Foreign Office shifted in his seat.

"They're all wrong days in this business."

"I have a theory about that."

"Spare me."

"All right." Foreign Office rose and inelegantly pulled up his trousers.

"Okay, okay. Tell me on your way out."

They rode down in the elevator to the ground floor, marble underfoot, neon above, and most of the world seemingly going home.

As they stepped out into the street, Foreign Office was struck by the contrast between the city and its climate. Washington lay stifling, yet civilized, in the heat of the tropics. Perhaps there was hope for some of the other swamps and snakepits around the world.

"Your theory." The American surveyed the passersby without interest.

"It's not mine." Foreign Office blinked in the glare, wishing they'd stayed inside. "Your Russian had a theory. He believed he'd uncovered a mystery flight. A decoy flight, if you like. A plane that was flying decoy, waiting for the time when it would fly for real. Only when that happened, it wouldn't attract attention." He looked around at his host. "Trouble was this one crashed."

"You didn't put that in the report."

"It's why I came."

Fox bit angrily into his lower lip. "You Brits amaze me. D'you ever come out straight and say what you mean? You always seem to dance around the subject, takes you forever to get there."

Foreign Office looked pleased. It was good to upset the Americans from time to time. So easy too. Their pride seemed to walk the streets just waiting to be wounded.

"Well, let's see if this is straight enough for you. What your man may have discovered is a training flight that could one day carry no less a person than the General Secretary out into exile, if things continue to deteriorate, as we think they will. That flight may be his final insurance policy—an escape route."

The American laughed, without humor. "That has to be crazy. The General Secretary? My God, you really are crazy."

"Problem is that someone else didn't think so." Foreign Office continued unfazed. "Which is why your Russian is sitting in the Lubyanka as we speak, or worse still, under it. And that's something for which he blames you."

But by this time Fox had caught sight of a face in the crowd, and his attention had wandered.

He turned to his visitor. "Would you like to meet the new guy going to Moscow?"

"Not really."

"Well he's here."

There was no time for Foreign Office to get away. Before he could step back the hand of the amiable David Russert was extended to him across the pavement. He had the impression of a man both relaxed and confident, and he wondered, under the circumstances, how that could possibly be.

10 _____

It was good to work again. Marcus with notebook on the front seat beside him, nosed his Volvo through the mid-morning traffic. Past Tass, once known as the Lie Factory, now simply the Grand Excuser, past the new pizza restaurant, past the new boutiques. And how soon would it be before Moscow was no longer Moscow, no longer different from anywhere else in the world, no longer abroad? When would the con men and the entrepreneurs bring neon lights into Red Square and sell hot dogs beside St. Basil's Cathedral?

I will miss it when it's gone, he thought, miss all the dark streets and crumbling byways, the sleepy, seedy suburbs where every summer day felt like a weekend, every hour a siesta. If Russia ever woke up, he reflected, it wouldn't know itself, wouldn't be happy.

Anastasiya.

Don't think of her now. You're going to a news conference and it's important. The new conservatives in the party, splitting from the reformists. See how they tell it. See how they run.

"Good morning ladies and gentlemen, welcome to the Foreign Ministry of the U.S.S.R.," and hadn't they learned since the old days. Marcus took his seat among other British journalists, realizing suddenly that it was Yuri holding court.

Yuri, fresh from the debacle in Murmansk, more tired, more subdued. Had he lost his place in the promotion line—or didn't they do that anymore?

Marcus looked around. At the side of the theater were the same craggy, gray faces that had always been there. The old men of the system, the apparatus, the rigid, inflexible core. No longer were they acceptable as spokesmen. But in one form or another they'd always be there, exploiting limitless power and cruelty, spread out across the continents, awaiting their time.

Yuri had made opening remarks. Further signs of the new democracy, he said. Opposition and government side by side. Not a split in the party, but differences, right and proper. People free to go their own way, make their own choices. Questions? No it wasn't dangerous. Like so much else it was the best thing that had ever happened.

The effort appeared to have exhausted Yuri still further. Marcus waylaid him later in the corridor and suggested tea. They made their way to the cafe and found a table.

"I also would like cake." Yuri got up and returned with a sad-looking cream object.

"You keep up your strength," Marcus told him.

"It's not easy." Yuri licked his fork. "Maybe it is just me. But I have nothing to report except failures."

"Welcome to politics."

"No, but it is not so simple. Look, we have two bosses. One has three private telephones, the other two. Which is more powerful?" He could see Marcus smiling. "Of course it is the one with more telephones. So I go to see him. He tells me: 'Report facts, Yuri Sergeyevich, tell the truth. Naturally you must make bad things look good and good things look even better, but try not to tell lies.' 'Okay, I tell him, fine.' " Yuri sighed and pushed away his empty plate. "Two minutes later I walk out and see the other boss. He says: 'Come to see me at four o'clock, Yuri Sergeyevich,' and he doesn't smile. At four I'm in his office. He doesn't tell me to sit down.

'What's the matter with you, Yuri?' he asks. 'You don't want to work here anymore? What's all this bad news? What's all this sudden fascination with the truth? You're supposed to serve the government, not embarrass it. You're talking to foreigners. The eyes of the world are on us, Yuri Sergeyevich, and my eyes are on you, and I don't like what I see.' "

A cleaning lady cleared away the tea glasses. At the counter Marcus could see the cook, dressed in surgeon green, ladling soup.

"What can I say, Yuri?" Marcus smiled thinly.

"Of course the events in Murmansk have not been helpful. Even now I do not know what was happening. And then the questions . . ." He sighed again. "Really it is too painful to think about . . . so much work, so much time totally wasted." The little brown eyes closed for a moment in despair. Marcus had forgotten Yuri's theatrical talents. But then they all had them, didn't they? Slavs were chameleons—sinners one moment, confessors the next. Different facets of the same person acted and counteracted with equal strength.

Marcus got up to leave.

"Nice to see you, Yuri."

But Yuri wasn't about to go.

"Please sit down one more moment," he whispered. "I have been thinking where my duty should lie and wondering what is best to be done." He flicked some bread crumbs onto the floor. "But finally you ask me for tea—thank you for that —and I think I must say something."

Marcus put his elbows on the table and leaned almost imperceptibly forward.

"When I got back from Murmansk, I told you this, there were many questions. All right. Always there are questions. But some of them were about you. Who you met on the trip, who you talked to, what was it that you were interested in." He shrugged. "You know, just like the old days."

Marcus nodded. Give him a smile, Marcus. Relax your face, relax your hands. Not a hint of concern. Lead him, oh so gently and he'll open the box. Good boy, Yuri, come to dad, spit it all out.

"Of course I tell them nothing. I know nothing. Mr. Marcus is journalist, nice man, always polite, not like some of the others. 'We have different impression,' they say. 'We think Mr. Marcus is troublemaker, hooligan. We do not wish him invited on any further trips out of Moscow. Maybe that will teach him lesson.'"

Yuri's eyes darted across Marcus's face.

"Look, I know nothing more than you. I tell them this is all nonsense and they have no right to give me orders. Those days are over. 'You think so?' they say. 'You think so? Just wait around a little and you will see who is giving the orders. Uhh?'" Yuri lifted his palm and slammed it dismissively on the table. The color seemed suddenly to drain from his face.

"I have said too much—right? Maybe you think I've been drinking. Maybe I should drink. Maybe everyone got it wrong here. Instead of drinking too much, it is very possible that Russians don't drink enough. Then instead of forgetting just a few things, we could forget everything and"—Yuri rubbed his eyes—"who knows? Tomorrow there may be a boss with four telephones and different orders. I cannot keep the track."

They stood up. You don't say anything, Marcus. You don't say "Thanks for the warning" or "Look after yourself" or "Come and have a chat anytime you're worried." You don't give any encouragement at all. Yuri could have been testing, could have been setting you up. Was it an approach or an apology? Was he wandering blind or following orders?

They shook hands by the staircase. Yuri climbed, Marcus descended.

Whichever way you look at it, Marcus, you leave this building under threat. And you can never pin down what it is. That's the beauty of Soviet intimidation. No need to arrest, or harangue, or interrogate. Just float a warning on the wind, watch it envelop its victim. Abstract fear, the worst

kind, because you can't grip it, can't focus it. There's no enemy to confront, just the knowledge that he's out there.

Marcus could have looked the other way. Traffic was
heavy enough along the Garden Ring. Tiny cars, bashed and
battered, were coughing their way beside the oversized
trucks—fortresses on wheels, their great rubber tires en-
crusted in mud. Stretching out before him was an unending
line of stinking metal hulks, some without windshield wipers, some with their paint peeling, others sporting great
gashes of rust. He could have looked the other way, but he
didn't.

She was standing beneath the clock at the entrance to
the Puppet Theater. Anastasiya, mingling with the crowds
who come to watch the chiming every hour, when the
brightly colored animals and figurines open their doors and
look down on Moscow. Even across the six-lane highway he
had caught a glimpse of her red hair, the supple, elegant
figure—such a rare species on the streets of the Soviet capital.

Hurriedly Marcus parked the car, turned the key in the
door, noticed his hand was shaking. Up fifty yards to the left
and he took the underpass, sprinting. Anastasiya stood at the
top of the steps.

He called out to her: "How did you know I'd see you?"

She was in his arms before she could reply and he could
feel the laughter through her dress.

"You always look this way. I've watched you." She pulled
away, grinning. "Must be all those dissidents you used to
meet here in the old days."

"You're very well informed." He took her arm.

She swung it high in the air. "That's the thing about us
Russians. We're always well informed. We just never talk
about it."

They made their way toward the subway. Perceptibly, he
could feel her mood darken. He knew the signs, he'd seen

them with Cressida, the fidgeting, the nervous eyes, the sudden listlessness. How quickly clouds can cover the sun.

In a cafe on Gorky Street, they pushed their way to a table. There was no coffee. They ordered juice.

Without thinking Marcus took her hand. "I didn't expect to see you today."

She withdrew her hand and looked at him icily. "It is not always a question of what you expect."

"Figure of speech, I'm sorry. Just something to say. Didn't mean anything."

"Doesn't matter if it did."

He looked at her carefully. A thin trickle of sweat had broken through the makeup on her forehead. Her blouse was creased, hair untamed by the two clasps that held it.

All at once a woman with a large wicker basket bumped Marcus from behind. He turned around angrily, but she was busy assaulting each of the patrons in turn, ruthless in her quest to clear a path to the door. He smiled.

Anastasiya balanced her head on her hands. "How much do you know about me, Marcus?"

Mentally he took a step back. Right from the mountaintop—that one. A low, curving ball in a clear sky. Careful.

"You're thirty-six, clever, highly desirable."

"The details, Marcus. Not the decoration."

"You work at the Foreign Ministry—but you liaise with the Kremlin. That means you could even get to see the General Secretary. Only you're very discreet, so you don't tell me that." Her eyes hadn't even flickered. "Your work involves policy toward Western Europe, Britain in particular. In the early eighties you were married, now you're not."

When someone says something quite simple but invests it with enormous meaning, you think about it for days afterward. You remember the way they formed the words, what their eyes looked like, the weather, the time of day, the smells. And Marcus could register them all as she spoke, raising her head high, shaking the hair, daring him to be surprised.

"I am one of only two liaison officers, assigned from the General Secretary's personal staff to the Ministry of Foreign Affairs."

He was suddenly aware of the color of the room, and everything in it. All his senses seemed heightened.

"It is my responsibility to brief the General Secretary on an informal basis." She looked down at the table. "I brief him on Western reactions to our policy. I brief him on rumors and impressions and he tells me his."

He should have taken her out then and there, spirited her away to a safe location, asked her a thousand questions, squeezed her dry, and pushed her back out again for more. She could name her terms, the world, he told himself, and all that therein is. She was water in the thirstiest of lands. She was the answer to prayers that hadn't even been uttered. And she was offering her treasures to him.

But at that moment in the crowded cafe, with the cadences of the chattering patrons and the clink of a hundred glasses, he could only reflect on how lovely she looked—and now, suddenly, how very vulnerable.

He couldn't have known the reason for the tears. Not then. Not until much later. For she had never said much. Generalities about the office, the comics, the thieves, the informers. The way they all wasted time, went shopping during the hours of work, played truant, laughed and cried.

Nowhere in this daily catalog had Anastasiya ever spoken of her own feelings, her most valuable thoughts, the tiny quiet corner of the mind where all souls seek refuge. Hers was down deep somewhere, out of sight, only a tear to hint that it even existed.

For a long time Marcus held her in his arms as the traffic outside dwindled into the suburbs and the daylight seeped away. Hours later she got up and made soup and they sat in semi-darkness in the kitchen, not daring to talk.

As he left he could see relief in her eyes. He had asked no questions, applied no pressure. Later they would talk, and gradually and oh so gently he would begin to extract the jewels, as he had to. She would expect it, she would be prepared. Wasn't she, after all, a willing partner?

Marcus rode the subway back into the city center. The car was empty except for a handful of old people. Maybe they simply traveled for company or diversion. The men with their rows of medals and memories lolled, yawning, on the hard wooden seats. One or two women sat alone, expressionless, like houses boarded up for the winter.

By the time he emerged onto the street Marcus knew he didn't have long. If Yuri's story was only half true, they might well be watching him already. Almost certainly they'd be watching her. So do you get her out or leave her where she is?

He nodded to the guard at the compound gate and took the elevator to the sixth floor. The nanny had gone to sleep, Cressida had gone to sleep. No mental effort required until morning.

And then? Then, you could drive to the airport, buy tickets and get out of Moscow and never come back. You could. You really could. This time tomorrow you could be in Hatfield, with supper on a tray under the cedar tree and mother clearing away the dishes and fussing over the little girl.

And you'd never know why Anastasiya was crying.

11

The envoy hunted alone. For as long as he could remember the job had required him to shun the company of officials at every level. Not that there were many to seek him out. He was the exception in a land of rules. The personal property of the General Secretary, tolerated by all, courted by none.

He had instant access to the personal apartments in the Kremlin. His key fitted every lock. He was unaccountable and untouchable, until the day when his master's foot faltered.

Often when he drank alone, he would imagine such a day, when they would come for him, how they would do it, whether he'd cry out in the throes of agony. Lately the fantasy had seemed closer to home.

That evening he left the cabinet office in a summer shower, joining the headlong crowds outside the Kremlin's Trinity Gate, then through into the Alexander Gardens, where a few stragglers sheltered beneath the trees.

Each day the envoy parked his gray Fiat in a different side street. Each day he changed his route. It wasn't much in the way of security but it was better than nothing.

He headed north for a mile, then turned and doubled back. The car was outside a bakery. Two boys were lounging against it. Instantly they read the disapproval in his eyes and moved away. He took the windshield wipers from the glove compartment and attached them to the metal holders. He knew if he'd left them out, they'd have disappeared.

East of the city, the traffic was lighter and he picked up speed. Two cars seemed to keep pace, but that could have been nothing. In any case if they cared that much, they would always know where to find him. He just didn't want to make it easy.

Abruptly the envoy turned the car across a bank of twisting steel streetcar lines, making it jolt wildly. From the suspension came sounds of serious protest.

He found himself on a narrow track that led away from the main highway to a single modern apartment block. Evidently it was to have been the first of several. But the plan had become separated from its timetable.

Mountains of steel piping and concrete blocks rose up from the surrounding mudlands. A mechanical digger sat like a giant insect, its claw half buried in the ground. But there was no sign of activity and the envoy knew the site had not been worked for more than a year.

He stopped the car and got out. Rainwater had collected in a lake beside the entrance but he took no notice, striding through it, heading for the steps. He was faced with a long, poorly lit corridor that seemed to slope downward. He tried the light but the power was off. Satisfied, he went farther, his hand scraping along the rough, unfinished walls—until he came to a doorway.

The envoy called out a name that echoed far away on empty landings and staircases but there was no reply. For a few moments he stood motionless, then ran his hand across the doorframe, searching for a button. Without hesitation the door swung inward on silent hinges and he moved quickly inside.

The flat was light, the walls gray, but freshly painted. In the living room lay a pile of newspapers, yellowed and faded from the sunlight. All of Russia had rooms like this, he reflected. Spartan, functional, soulless—just the thing for socialist man, born to work in a factory and sleep in a box. A big one for the time when you're alive, someone had said, and a smaller one for when you're dead. Nothing like a good box.

The envoy removed his shoes, hurrying from room to room, checking the windows for signs of entry. In the bathroom stood a generator with cans of fuel stacked alongside. The kitchen cupboards had been filled with canned and dried food, cartons of juice and milk. Iron rations. Lousy and tasteless until the day you need them.

A final glance around and he stopped. What was it that had unnerved him, forced him to come out here, check on the last resort?

Perhaps the business at the airport—the certain and final knowledge that their power had limits and they were fast approaching them. Of course they'd seen it coming. Why else had he set the flat up in the first place, brought the food last winter from an army depot, when the roads had been covered in snow and the militia too cold and lazy to patrol?

But when you see things in the distance, there's no definition. You provide a shelter, but you believe the storm will pass. You take out insurance because it makes you feel better, not because you think you'll need it.

He peered through the window but the courtyard below remained deserted. God, what a bleak, deadly place! And that wasn't all. The whole project was one of Moscow's worst-ever building scandals. A low-profile, high-budget enterprise that should have been finished the year before.

The party had commissioned it through its own channels, intending to create a private city with pools and schools and shops, not open to the general public. Stuck out to the east of the city, it lay in an area closed to foreigners—so there wouldn't be any television crews wandering around.

The idea, he reflected, had not been a bad one. All right, the building was for the party hierarchy, but not for those with a future. This was a final act of largesse to a disappear-

ing species, the deadwood that they'd had to hack away from
all the dying trees.

"Here, comrades, is a token of our esteem for your years
of patriotic service"—that's the way it was to have been. A
pleasant little estate, best facilities, not far from the city center. "Oh yes, and this is where you are to stay. No further
duties are required of you. Your offices and your staffs have
been allocated to other people. Just take the apartment, live
prosperously, multiply if you still can, but above all else—
go."

The envoy shut the door behind him. A good idea, he
repeated to himself. But then, as so often, the incurable Russian disease—the botch-up, fruit of years of willful, criminal
incompetence—had struck. They had built the thing on the
cheap, so that one side of it had partially collapsed during a
winter storm. Oh they'd propped it up, slammed in a few
more girders, made a lot of fuss and filled files with dockets,
excuses, and caveats. But who would live in it now? In any
case the architect had been relieved of his duties—nice eu-
phemism for a residence permit in a town he'd never heard
of, the contractor had been imprisoned, and the work force
seemed to have disappeared. Yet another socialist triumph,
he reflected. As if the scorecard wasn't full up already.

He drove slowly back into the city. There was a bar on
Pushkinskaya Street where he could drink in crowded ano-
nymity. Not a pretty place, not a congenial place. You stood
in three inches of swill, your elbows resting on a wooden
shelf. Like many Soviet pastimes, the pleasure was watered
down by discomfort. That meant Russians could seldom
have just a simple good time—half of it would be good, the
other half terrible.

That night the clientele seemed sparser than usual. In a
corner a small group of loafers jeered and poked their fingers at each other. Beside him an old woman spooned salt
into her beer glass in an effort to strengthen the brew.

He finished one beer, then fetched a second. The barman gave him a scowl of recognition.

"Come to piss away your daily bread, have you?"

"Why don't you fuck off?"

The scowl became a smile. "Been doing that for years." He laid a wet cloth on the bar. "Only it doesn't matter now, does it? All you fat bastards in suits—you've had years of telling us to fuck off. Now you're going to sing a different tune with our boots up your arses."

The envoy didn't need any of that, he decided. But it always happened. If you drank more than two or three times in the same place they started to hassle you, pick fights, push you around, anything to relieve the miserable frustrations of daily life.

He turned away. That was it. Finish the beer. Get out. Mistakenly he bumped into one of the loafers who had separated from the group. Or had the fellow moved?

"Excuse me." The envoy reached for his beer. All at once the place seemed strangely quiet. But you don't get quiet bars in Russia. Russians don't meditate over alcohol, they shriek or cry, they drink to separate the mind from the body . . .

"You knocked me." A rude voice, three words slurred into one. A foot behind him.

The envoy swung around. The man was taller, filthy jacket, unshaven face. But the long arms hung comfortably at his side. Ready.

He could see two others shambling toward him. They weren't hurrying because this was to be their night. Despicable scum! He could feel his anger rising. They weren't fit to be Russians. Mean, idle bullies, oozing greed and envy, raised in the gutter and only fit for it.

They stood in a line before him, stupid grins across toothless faces.

I don't believe this, he thought suddenly. It must be twenty years since the last time. Shelepin. A group of thugs outside the factory. Whiners, strikers . . .

He took a step back.

You have to know how far you can maneuver.

Beyond them, he could see the entrance had been closed. The barman . . .

And then it broke over him—blinding, burning pain in his eyes, in the back of his head, so sudden and extreme that he thought it had come from another world that had nothing to do with him, forcing out his light and his life, laying darkness, like a shroud, across him.

"Thought you were dead, did you?" The voice carried detached amusement.

Years before, the envoy had woken midway during an operation to remove his appendix. He'd been lucky to get an anesthetic at all, but he remembered being laid out then as now, unable to move, to open his eyes, to cry out.

The beer. What had they done to the beer . . . ? He tried to move. In the distance a muscle stirred. You didn't die after all, and that isn't such good news, is it? Because they can make you wish you had if they know what they're doing. A beating is one thing. You've taken plenty of those, but if they do it with science, if they've read books about it and done their homework, you could be finished in half an hour. They can take all your weak points, all the major nerves, and break them into minor pieces.

And now he realized why he could no longer see. There was darkness around him, a breeze washed over his face. One by one the sensations hit him. Just one shadow in front of him, a light far away, the noise of cars. The city. Still in Moscow. Still there.

"In a few moments, you'll be able to move. . . ."

It was a different voice from the thugs who'd confronted him. Cultured. Sensitive. But there was something else.

"You've had a shock. Nothing more. But you won't forget it. And that's the reason . . ."

Something about that voice.

". . . we arranged this. Everything's slowing up: the re-forms, the freedoms, the rights we thought we'd gained. The tide isn't coming in anymore, it's rushing out."

The place seemed to fill with a sense of despair.

"All through our history we've seen openings, only to have them closed, opportunities that we lost, riches and prizes that were taken from us or simply squandered. We can't see that happen again. Not this time, not with the end of the century in sight. You understand that, don't you?"

The envoy tried to speak but the words wouldn't come.

"Thing is that when the door opened, there were mil-lions of us who ran for it, determined to get through. We didn't just support the new leadership, we worked for it night and day, broke our backs, believed in it. A choice. You see that? And we made it, knowing that sometime in the future, in a year, two years, ten—we'd have to pay for it. Because that's the way here, isn't it? Nothing for nothing. In the end no one lives without someone having to die. No one gets rich without someone going hungry. That's Russia—land of ex-tremes. Always has been."

There was a pause. The envoy could feel the wind gust-ing. From somewhere in the distance, a noise was growing louder.

"This time—whatever the cost—we're going to pay. We won't slide back to what it was. We won't let the leadership be diverted or stagnate. If no one wakes it, and keeps it awake, Russia will sleep for centuries." The voice coughed. It was getting harder to hear. "Tonight was just a little sample. Take it away. Share it. The day after tomorrow, there'll be a big demonstration along Gorky Street. Maybe you've heard about it. March for freedom. The militia have orders to break it up. Make sure that doesn't happen. For the sake . . ."

But the voice was lost in the pounding, clattering din that bore down on him. The envoy could feel the ground shaking. For the first time he registered the imminent, shocking progress of a train. The urgent pulse of steel on steel. He had to be on the line itself. The noise was indescribable. And is this the way you go?

Lying there, alone now, he threw up a hand to protect himself as the lights of the locomotive came startlingly into view. The speed, so close . . . he rolled onto his side as the sudden, buffeting wave tore past him, hostile and unstoppable, just a few feet away. And then, almost at once, there was silence, and the envoy lay gasping in the dirt. He was clutching handfuls of grass, his body numb, his mind bruised and violated, as once again the darkness settled over him.

12

To Muscovites a black car has always been the symbol of unattainable status. But a black American car is something even beyond the land of dreams. And yet the Lincoln Continental that ferried David Russert from the Moscow airport to the city center made little impact in the early rush-hour traffic.

Standing on the wide pavement, a group of schoolchildren barely turned their heads, an old woman screwed up her eyes, staring into the sunlight, and it was left to the militiamen, among whom old habits die hardest, to salute at the intersections. Irony of ironies, thought Russert. On my way to discover your secrets, and you wave me through.

The embassy apartment was in a building you'd have called modern, if it hadn't been for the building they put up behind it. Or tried to put up. From his window over the city center Russert could see the new American compound rising into the afternoon, useless and uninhabited.

More than two years had passed since the State Department had declared it to have been so fully wired for sound by the Russians that it could no longer be made secure. "Bugged to buggery" went the saying. But no one could decide whether to pull it down or forget about the whole thing. Maybe Soviet indecision was catching.

Russert looked around. Everything seemed new: and so

it would be. They'd have torn up the carpets, dismantled the kitchen, slit open the drapes and chair covers. Nothing would have been left intact. Not after the business with the heroin.

His predecessor, he realized, hadn't just upset his wine glass, he'd knocked over the whole banquet table.

"You'll like it here, sir." The marine had left his bags in the living room and was on his way through the door.

"Why will I like it?" Russert inquired, half amused by the assertion.

"Good crowd of people, sir."

Russert shook his head at the departing uniform. He was already going to meet the crowd. Drinks at six-thirty in the ambassador's office. Summons delivered. Hands to shake. Welcome, welcome and what the hell are you really here for? The standard and unspoken question. Informal. Means wear a tie. Dipspeak—language of the diplomatic service. It was coming back to him. All of it.

He opened the window, letting the smell of cheap low-octane fuel flood in from the Ring Road. A long line of cars was crawling into the underpass.

Abruptly he turned away and zipped open the bags. For twenty minutes he worked hard, hanging clothes, stowing belongings in drawers. It was the single man's discipline. You do it yourself because there won't be anyone coming along after you.

Fifteen years earlier his wife had told him exactly that, as she packed her own bag and flounced out of his life into a waiting car. She had been the last person to come along after him, always resenting his ways and his habits, and now he just had himself to please.

"Aren't you lonely?" someone had once asked him.

"Yes, I am," he had replied. "But at least I'm at peace with myself. I don't have to put on an act, don't have to smile if I don't want to. I'm not required to declare feelings I haven't got."

He made his way outside, conspicuous in dark gray suit, beside the brightly-colored inelegance on the streets. Just a few steps to the embassy entrance and even as he approached, the Soviet guards were converging on him, demanding his documents.

You're on a leash, he thought, remember that. It can be long or short, you can feel it or forget about it, but it'll always be there.

The ambassador's secretary showed him into the office. He took a quick look at the half-dozen faces, the shirtsleeves, the colored suspenders, the slicked-back hair, and his spirits plummeted. These were the new professionals—more like Wall Street, than C Street, home base for the State Department. Not the comfortable, thorough diplomats of old, who would sow their seeds and wait for the seasons to ripen them. These men would be in a hurry, wanting graphs and balance sheets and results that carried their names.

He waded through a mist of aftershave, seeing them rise from the sofas, seeing the hands outstretched toward him.

"Welcome to Moscow, Russert. . . . What's it like in Washington these days . . . ? Hear Charlie Peterson's not so well. . . . Get anything to eat on the plane . . . ?"

They retook their seats, edging up on the sofa to let the new man in. But not that much. The smiles seemed fixed. They were telling him this was a club and membership had to be earned. And you know instantly when you're not going to fit, when your clothes aren't right, when you're too young or too old, or you're facing the wrong way on the train—just the way David Russert knew it then.

The ambassador took charge, his the most expensive of the white shirts, the sleekest of the silk ties.

"Let me take you around the table, David. . . ."

And so it went: counselor, secretary, first secretary, attaché, assistant . . . Russert nodded at the jumble. There was only one figure he needed to register, and he'd stay behind at the end. That's the way it would be done. Inner circle first. The gesture to discussion and argument. Then the deciders.

"Drinks, anyone?"

It was the signal for socializing. The ambassador waved his hand toward a tray of drinks. Russert caught the movement of a gold identity bracelet. You're from California, he recalled, knowing there'd be a gold chain beneath the shirt, and plenty of gold left in a bank back home. Morton Cohen, longtime friend of the President, courtroom lawyer to the famous and badly behaved, was well known for taking on cases no one else wanted and making them pay. . . . Moscow was the exception.

"Fascinating times, David." He leaned expansively toward the table, as if, somehow, those times belonged to him. An unsolicited martini had been placed in front of him. "Open season, could go back, could go forward. Each day there seems to be a different faction opening up. It's like a pot with all the ingredients swirling around inside getting hotter and hotter." He looked around at the faces for appreciation. "Might explode of course if no one turns off the gas."

They chuckled politely.

"This kind of summer heat, doesn't help the situation. If we're going to get a meltdown, it could come soon." The commercial counselor spoke fast, as if he were reading from a text. Cohen leaned back, hands behind his head.

"Meltdown, huh? I like it. But let's define this thing. . . ."

For Christ's sake, thought Russert. Intellectual masturbation at its worst. The Soviets were outside, pulling their country to pieces, and the embassy was defining terms. His eyes drifted toward the windows, heavily shuttered, with double glass screens. When they returned to the group, he knew that one man had watched his inattention, one man reading him from across the coffee table.

"As I see it," the ambassador was saying, and it was clearly of no importance how anyone else saw it, "the General Secretary is boxed in. Go forward with the reforms and the conservatives will block him, go back and the new radicals could literally pull millions onto the streets to protest. . . ."

"If I were him," the counselor seemed emboldened after his interjection, "I'd take a Yak 40 jet and get the hell out over the Baltic to Sweden."

Cohen looked around his subordinates as if serious discussion had just ended. "On that note then, gentlemen, thank you and good night. We'll see each other in the morning. David," he gestured to Russert, "would you wait behind a moment, please?"

The counselor also stayed where he was, a thin smile twitching at the corners of his mouth. As the door shut, he broke into laughter. "I didn't know how else to get those bums out of the door. David, good to see you. Jim Tuckerman. We've never met, but we both know each other, I think."

Tuckerman was both fat and amiable, late thirties, Russert guessed, and highly deceptive. There were depths to Jim Tuckerman, to the unblinking eyes, to the dry and immensely powerful handshake, and somewhere in Russert's mind he caught a warning.

Cohen's smile seemed to envelop them both. "You people probably want to talk somewhere more private. But I just wanted to make a point of my own." The smile died. He went around the desk and sat in the large, expansive chair. "You should know, David, you're riding in on a kind of a black cloud. Your predecessor, Stevens, didn't win popularity points, even before he began mainlining—but he's left behind him one hell of a nasty smell. And some of it attaches to your outfit—" he poked a finger toward Tuckerman. "You know that, Jim, so don't shake your head like that. Christ, even the sweepers knew Stevens was Agency."

Tuckerman shook his head again.

"Oh, give me a break, this place is clean as a baby's butt,"

Cohen told him. "Your people checked it out yesterday." He grimaced. "What the hell, you guys go and talk about what you have to talk about. I've had all I can take for today."

He got up and held open the door for them.

"Let's have a chat when you have a moment, David. I'd like to hear some of your reminiscences about this place. After all it's not the first time you've seen Moscow."

Russert stopped in mid-step and turned back toward the ambassador, puzzled somehow by the man's tone. Was he asking a question? Or did he think he'd found an answer?

Twenty-four hours of unanswered calls and Marcus was worried. All day the telephone had been busy or had rung unanswered. Finally at lunchtime, when he'd least expected a response, the receiver was picked up.

"Anastasiya?"

"Not here." A man's voice.

"When will she be in?"

"Try after two."

He had put the phone down, feeling sick. It was just like the old days. Standard fob-off, the kind of sullen Soviet indifference that's impossible to penetrate. It's the ultimate brick wall. No recourse. No inquiries. You're out in the wilderness, blindfolded.

At two-thirty he called from the apartment and got a final response.

"Call tomorrow," said the voice and cut the connection.

Marcus looked around the apartment: a tiny Western island in the sea of Moscow. In that moment he could imagine the crippling frustration of millions of Soviets, spread out as they were over the six time zones. What if you needed an answer from Moscow? What if you needed to talk to a friend or relative a thousand miles away. What if . . . ?

And then he recalled the words of a Russian friend.

"Marcus, in this country, we make journeys where you would use the telephone. It is the only way to reach a person.

It is the only way to avoid ulcers and heart attacks. We travel. We love it. Sometimes for days and nights, weeks and weeks, because, you know something, there is no other way."

How many times had he heard that in Russia—land of such stark choices. No alternative, no other way. One truth for all of you—and you're lucky to have it.

Down the corridor he could hear the front door opening and then the cry of his daughter. Cressida. Had I almost forgotten you? And he pulled himself up from the sofa, running toward her, feeling the tiny arms wrap tight around his neck. Little fingers played with his hair, the way they always did—child of charm.

They sat in the little kitchen having tea. Doreen the nanny, standing by the stove, just as Helen had done, all those lives ago. "We went swimming," she announced. "Down by the river. You know that place you took us once." She flipped a boiled egg from the saucepan. "Getting quite good, she is, Li'l Cress." He smiled. Wonderful thing about Doreen. She'd taken to Moscow as if it were Southend. There were sunny days and rainy days, there were meals and shops and boyfriends. So what else did any of it matter? Of course she was right, decked out in her daily uniform of jeans and pink sneakers, slightly thin, slightly pale—with her very own file sitting back in London in the archives of counterintelligence. Not that she'd ever known about it, not that she'd ever seen the retired police inspectors in their tweed jackets, wandering from house to house, among her friends and family and acquaintances, asking questions. He could just hear them—and what sort of friends did she have? Has she, you know, had any serious boyfriends? Poor Doreen, never knowing.

She took the child from his arms. "I'll get her to bed then."

"Would you?"

He gave her up. Helen's child. Helps to say that. Removes some of the responsibility. Makes it easier to be father one minute, or reporter, or informer for the government of Her Majesty the Queen—and then, there's Anastasiya. Who am I to you, wherever you are out there in the city of Moscow?

Marcus hurried downstairs to the car, past the old kitchen basins with the flowers growing in them, past the other nannies and babies and wives, the human effects that always sat around in the Western compounds. Out into the city traffic, now easing, as the dust of the day began to settle.

Her apartment was empty. It wasn't just the lack of an answer. He had listened for several minutes before ringing the bell. He had heard the creaks from the woodwork, the water that coughed and hiccupped in the pipes. Far away a woman was shouting incomprehensibly. Take it from me, she seemed to be saying, Anastasiya isn't here.

He waited a little while by the entrance. Not too long because your Western clothes, and your haircut, and your healthy color set you apart from the locals. Hanging around is their natural pastime, not yours. And it's hard to adopt that belligerent slouch that comes from carrying so many chips on so many shoulders, for so long.

He had parked the car a half mile away, obscured by the trees along a side road, leading to other apartment buildings, and he doesn't remember why he didn't see her, or hear her, or even sense her presence, there in the backseat of the Volvo, until she reached forward and told him to drive.

While the tears had gone, Marcus could see that the cause of them had not. Eyeing her sideways, hugging the right-hand lane, feeling her arm loop itself around his. Not your natural state, Anastasiya. You're the talkative one, the gregarious one, the one who giggles in the bedroom. But now she looked more Russian than ever. The brow more furrowed, more thoughtful. There was a hardness and single-mindedness about the eyes that he hadn't noticed before. I could see you in the factories, he thought, with a checked rag

on your head and a rifle in your hand, shouting out the slogans, marching through the ruins, loving and hating, passion
in every pore.

They had traveled at least a mile before she spoke.

"Stop the car, Marcus."

"Where?"

"It's not important."

He pulled onto a back road off the main highway, Moscow, never short of sleepy roads, places to dream.

She turned to face him, tightening her grip on his arm.

"I cannot see you anymore, Marcus. It's getting too difficult. I am sorry, my dear. I did not know how to tell you."

Anastasiya. What *was* she telling him?

"We should not have been seeing each other. It's too dangerous for me, too dangerous for the things I have to do."
She was looking at the road, eyes fixed and heavy, as if there
were no tears left to cry.

"What things, what are you talking about?" The nausea
seemed to be rising in his throat.

"Look around you, Marcus. Every day more tension.
More chaos. The political leadership pulled this way and
that." She held out her hands. "I am involved in this. How
could I not be?"

"How involved?"

"Last night—" she stopped herself, then shrugged her
shoulders. "Last night a senior official. We took him. Held
him, warned him that the reforms have to go on. They have
to stand up to the old men that have ruined this country.
Now we must go further. There may have to be violence."
She touched him again. "I cannot say how sorry I am. If
things were different . . . well, they'd be different. We could
be together, lead a normal life. But there are no normal lives
in Russia. Not now, not yet . . . who knows"—she tossed
her head—"maybe never."

Swallow, Marcus. Get air. Somehow.

"But this isn't something that can be torn up as if it never happened." Was that his voice?

"It was wrong. Should not have happened. . . ."

Wait, wait, wait. She's digging in her heels now, he thought. She's upset, desperate. Don't push her or she'll never come out. But . . .

Her hand was moving toward the door handle.

"It is best I go now, Marcus. I leave from here. In a little while you'll forget me . . ."

"I can't let you do that . . ." again a voice from inside him that he hadn't heard before. "Whatever it is, Anastasiya, we'll work it out, we have to. There's too much . . ."

"Then we have to make a sacrifice. I do." She raised her eyebrows. "I will manage."

The anger hit him then. "Go on, do it. Do what you have to. Make your sacrifice, like the rest of the bloody country . . ."

She was moving so fast through the door, and yet he could still have stopped her, held her, turned back time. And it was only when she was out of sight that he pulled himself from the car, his heart heaving in his chest, and ran full tilt to the corner, ready to promise and deliver the world, if only she would come back and be held.

There were clouds moving fast across the city, the streets were full of people leaving a cinema, Moscow was halfway through another dreary evening. But Anastasiya had gone.

13 _____

Stripped of power, stripped of influence, friendless, without money or papers, the envoy viewed his homeland from an altogether new standpoint, clambering up the railway escarpment to stand looking across to the suburbs, with the giant electricity pylons low against the skyline. The urban wilderness was in darkness. And not only because it was night. Darkness that we produced, he thought. Darkness for all the years of silence and slogans, of lies and blindness. Soviet darkness, more complete, more deadening, than any in the world.

The envoy stumbled on a rock, picked himself up, and limped toward the road. His watch, like his other possessions had been removed and he had little sense of time, the sparse traffic his only clue.

For nearly an hour he waited, till it seemed no one would ever stop and he would be left to spend the night by the curb. Long after midnight a flimsy old Moskvich lumbered into view, the driver evidently cruising for any business he could find.

The envoy leaned down to the open window.

"I need Leninsky Prospekt. Been robbed. Can't pay you."

"That's what they all say. Oh get in, for God's sake." The driver must have been a pensioner. The envoy could make out small, wizened features. A sharp ratlike nose pointed upward.

"Fact is"—the driver shook his head and put the car into gear—"no one pays these days. If I ask for money they say they'll beat my head in. Others say they'll get it—then they disappear into a building, and never come out. Sometimes I think I'm working for the damned state, instead of trying to make some money."

He turned to size up the envoy. "Go on, tell me—just for the hell of it. You blew your money on some bitch, and she threw you out of her flat." He turned again. "You don't say much. I'll give you that. Dirty devil." He smiled. "That's the way it happened though, didn't it?"

The envoy hadn't the strength to argue. "You're right. I should have told you. After all you're a man of the world. I can see that all right."

The driver chuckled. "I knew it. Just knew it. Took one look at your miserable, bloody face and I could tell straightaway."

He dropped the envoy close to the Gagarin monument.

"Got another woman here, I shouldn't wonder. Wife at home with the kiddies as well? Oh shove off!" He slammed the door angrily and the car limped away north toward the river, only one of its taillights illuminated.

But the envoy had already turned down a side street, his feet numb and heavy. Here the houses were newer, the walls so thin that as he passed he could make out snatches of conversation and music. In the light of a streetlamp he caught a glimpse of a young man in pajamas, leaning against a car, shaking his head at the moon, and rocking slowly from side to side.

The envoy crossed to the other side, feeling his nausea return. In the old days they'd locked up the lunatics along with the political criminals. Now they'd let them all out because they couldn't distinguish between them. The results were all around—people who shouted at you on the street for no apparent reason, who ran out in front of cars, who jumped off bridges. What was the saying . . . ? "It's the idiots who're happy." Maybe that was the key to Russia. Be an idiot, shout all you want, then finish yourself off when you've had enough.

He hadn't come this way for some time. A year, maybe two. But it hadn't changed. Courtyards overgrown with weeds, cracked pavements, buildings tatty and rundown.

He was obliged to force the door to the apartment building. But it gave easily enough. Nothing was that secure anymore. People seemed to be forcing doors right across the country.

On the third floor he turned sharply to the left, knocked at a door and marveled that it opened almost at once. From the dim hallway with the smell of old books and the posters of London and the English queen, a voice he knew so well, whispered in faultless English . . . "Come in, come in, what are you waiting for?" It was like a trip back in time to a world of light and safety.

"I didn't have anywhere else to go." The envoy sat at the old mahogany tea table.

"I thought as much."

"But you couldn't have known I'd come here."

The teacher smiled. "I was looking out of the window. Besides, people tell me all sorts of things. Let's just say I'd expected visitors."

He patted the envoy on the shoulder, such an un-Russian gesture, even after so many years. "It's good to see you haven't forgotten your English. I expect you've been practicing."

He winked and got up to make coffee. A tall, lanky figure, haphazardly constructed, one arm seemingly longer than the other, his bald head shining in the harsh neon light. The envoy looked around the room. So little had changed: the old cigarette cards on the mantelpiece, a print of Westminster Abbey, a seaside view, a coronation mug. Same old things: the mementos, treasured and displayed.

"Still take it black?" the teacher was calling from the kitchen.

"Please." Yes, please, teacher. How odd it was to return to this room. A schoolroom really. The place where he had come to learn English way back in the sixties when they had wanted somewhere very private and confidential, because Mikhail had been sure he should learn a language. For the future. Just in case. And it had been better this way. The Englishman wasn't a defector or a spy or a misfit, but simply a harmless student who had stayed on, because there'd been nothing to return for. At home a broken love affair, parents dead. Living in Russia, he'd once said, was a kind of therapy. Helped him to forget. And yet he kept the mementos.

"There now." The teacher laid a metal pot on the table. He peered through thick glasses. "Are you all right?"

The envoy sipped his coffee. "I shouldn't have come."

"Why?"

"Dangerous for you."

The Englishman looked away. "When I lived in Britain, there was precious little in the way of danger. A mugging perhaps, a confrontation between human and motor car." He poured coffee for himself and looked up into the envoy's eyes. "There was absolutely no danger of becoming involved —in anything."

The envoy had always looked on his old teacher as remote, disengaged, but there was something new about the tightness around the face, the incline of the head, the rapid speech.

"Here it's different," the teacher went on. "Out there is real danger, for you and me, for Russia, maybe for everyone. Who knows how fragile the political balance really is? But d'you really think I want to sit and read books, and teach conversation to my fancy pupils while all this is going on?

I'm in Russia. That's why I stayed. If it goes to hell, I go with it."

The envoy got to his feet.

"Sit down, my dear fellow." The teacher stretched out his arm. "You need time to think, to plan. You don't have to tell me what's happened. I don't want to know. But if I can help, I'm ready to do so."

The envoy could see the suspicion of a tear in one of the teacher's eyes. And it struck him that for the first time in decades this man had found something to live for. In Russia the tragedy was always that the moment you identified a cause, you stood the greatest chance of having to die for it.

"Does the boy still come here?" The envoy broke the silence that both men had welcomed, sitting under the cheap neon lights with thoughts that had taken them over many miles and many years. They both knew who the boy was. No identification was needed.

"He was here yesterday."

"Good, good . . ."

"Not so good." The teacher pursed his lips. "He says his father's unwell. Oh not physical. But the pressure's getting to him. He's going to the meetings when he has to, but nothing else. He's shut away. The worst of it is, he doesn't seem to be fighting."

The envoy leaned back in the armchair, his pudgy face looking sallow and drawn. He put his hands to his mouth in the shape of a steeple.

"When is the boy here again?"

"In two days time. He has three lessons a week. Same as always."

They looked at each other without speaking. The envoy moved to the mantelpiece. He hadn't noticed it before, but there it was, right at the end, half-obscured by an envelope—a photo of a boy when he'd been much younger. Mikhail's boy, of course. A picture taken on a summer day next to a rose garden. Long before the thorns took hold.

14 _____

There are words in a news story that can get you a meeting in Helsinki. Put them in, Marcus, type the text, let it go. And by the evening of the next day the little man with the glasses and the wayward brown hair will meet you in Helsinki, just outside Stockmanns, the Harrods of the north, as if you're to go shopping together.

The instructions, he reflected, were always that easy. "Simple, simpler, simplest," Foreign Office had once told him, sounding, as he did so often, like an exercise in grammar. "That way we don't forget, do we?"

Marcus hadn't wanted to press the button. But when your mind's taken a walk without you, it's not good to stay in Moscow. Not clever. Not sound. That was the way London would put it.

And the walk? He had spent the night between the couch and the dining table, seeing the face of Anastasiya, computing, questioning. The woman who had untold stories to tell, the inner workings of the General Secretary's mind, his fears, concerns. A basket of golden nuggets, beyond value. Where had she taken them? Where do you look?

Every hour he had wandered into Cressida's room to gaze at the blond hair on the pillow. Same color as Helen's. Same olive skin. How much did I care for you? he wondered. What's changed? "You never needed me, did you?" He could hear her voice, recall the afternoon, a Sunday back in England, always the day for a row. And she'd been right. He hadn't needed her. Not this way. Not the way he needed the Russian with the red hair and the laughter that could fill your heart.

And when the dawn drifted in over the Ring Road, and the shoe repair shop across the way, when he could no longer decide if he wanted her for his country or himself, Marcus wrote the story.

He was good at that, he reflected. He wrote prose, some said, that could sit up and sing. In Poland, in Czechoslovakia, in South Africa—in so many of the changing political climates, Marcus had sung.

And there had always been two songs. Two different sets of lyrics. One for the newspaper, the other for a more select circulation.

Sometimes, Marcus recalled, he had all but forgotten about that other less public commitment. Months had gone by without contact. And then maybe there would be a package to collect or deliver, a man to drive or wait for, an unexpected guest in the spare room, some impressions or an interview, never destined for publication.

My part-time job, he called it—but only to himself. And yet it wasn't really a job at all. No contract had ever been offered, no terms of employment, no money. In fact it had never really been discussed at all. Marcus would "do little favors" in answer to "little suggestions"—the "why-don't-you's" and "what-about-its" that came from Foreign Office. Everything couched in vague, almost meaningless terms. Sometimes, in the quiet periods, he felt as if he'd imagined the whole thing. Perhaps that's why he had never really refused them: because they had never really asked.

Now it was different. Taking the stairs, five flights, into the courtyard and along to the office, the paper in his hand, turning on the telex, Marcus realized it was the first time since childhood that he'd asked for help.

* * *

The siren made Marcus look up. Through the passenger window he could see traffic at a standstill on the crossroads. And yet as always the central lane—that conduit for the mighty—remained open, and he sat in amazement as an unbroken line of yellow troop carriers droned into the city.

"Blimey!" Doreen was driving him. "Look at that lot. Anybody'd think World War Three was going to start!"

It reminded Marcus of the old newsreel films of Soviet mobilization. Your country needs you. Only this time half the country didn't. This wasn't a call to patriotic duty. These were the authorities' preparations for the so-called freedom march planned for the next evening. Was this the way they would greet it?

It took nearly ten minutes for the convoy to pass, with its outriders and escorts. In other countries, Marcus recalled, the military were always kept well out of sight, used only in the event of widespread social disorder. In Moscow they brought the soldiers in before anything happened, in case it happened. The act of a government that fears its own people more than its enemies.

Now he was leaving, even for a night, Marcus wanted to hurry. Hard to sit still in the car, stand still in the lines, to try not to mind when they rifle your suitcase.

And yet for the first time there was little thrill in seeing the lights of Helsinki airport in the distance, landing in the west, following the sun. The shops and cafes that had always lifted his spirits, seemed curiously dull.

An hour ahead of the rendezvous he booked in at the Intercontinental, noticing the thick, soft carpet, the hum of efficiency. Desk clerks were rushing to carry out orders. There was none of the instant bad grace that characterizes service in the Soviet Union.

He sat down on the bed, feeling the tiredness smothering him. Only fifty minutes flying time from Moscow. Another planet. And the burdens are supposed to drop away when you cross the border. You're supposed to feel light and free, leaving the monster city and its hordes behind. But not Anastasiya. With a start he realized her face and her presence had traveled with him. The expansive gestures, the sparkle that came from deep inside.

Marcus rubbed his eyes, went to the window and opened it. A light summer wind swirled in. He'd go early to the store, do some shopping, find a trinket for Doreen, a toy for Cressida, some food—that great missing pleasure of Moscow.

He located Foreign Office in the sock department. The man appeared to be holding several pairs of remarkably unpleasant footwear. Marcus could make out greens and blacks with yellow diamonds on them, there were spots and arrows.

He tapped him on the back.

"You're not seriously thinking of buying these, are you?"

Foreign Office seemed unsurprised by the sudden intrusion.

"Of course I am. Haven't seen anything as repulsive as this for years." He made for the checkout. "We're having a fancy dress party. Daughter of mine, Tiggy. Mandatory attendance. Prize for the one who makes the biggest cock of himself."

"Should be some stiff competition."

Foreign Office ignored the remark, paid the money and stuffed the bag into his jacket. "Right. That's that. Care for a walk?"

They joined the late-evening crowds, mingling in movie theaters and cafes. Again the contrast. Here was light-years away from the city of the drab, the land of the make-do.

"Well I've bought my socks. Now what do *you* want?" Foreign Office gestured to Marcus to cross the road and head for the lake.

"Where do I start . . . ?"

"Oh dear. Is it that bad? Thought it might be."

Marcus put his hands in his pockets. It was a warm

night. Most of the people seemed to be enjoying themselves. But then they hadn't come from Moscow.

"I seem to have lost the girl." He looked hard at Foreign Office, but the man had fixed his eyes on the ground.

"Go on, go on. What d'you want—congratulations?"

"She got into my car yesterday evening, said she couldn't see me anymore. Too dangerous . . ."

"So you offered your shoulder, played her along, gave the impression of agreeing. Standard procedure."

"I couldn't. It all happened too quickly." Marcus shook his head. "She was out of the car, down the street. I ran after her—but it was too late."

"What about her flat? Office?"

"Nothing. Disappeared. I'm telling you I don't know where to look."

They had reached the edge of the lake. Foreign Office seemed to be watching the birds, squawking, landing on the water, but his teeth were clenched and his lips had tightened. They sat on a bench.

"Right. Take me back. Motives. Hints. What the hell led up to all this?"

"Look, she let slip that she's in with the radicals, the people who want the reforms guaranteed, pushed further, cast in stone. . . ."

"Bunch of dreamers . . ."

"No!" Marcus was suddenly angry. "Not dreamers. They've thought it out. They're simply determined not to go back to what it was. At any price."

Foreign Office raised his eyebrows. "You seem quite in favor of this crowd. . . ."

"Not in favor. I understand them, see their point." He locked his hands together. "My job is to assess . . ."

"Your job," the official from London sniggered, "your job is to find the best fence going and sit on it. We don't take sides, we play all of them, back all the horses. Because whoever comes out on top, we'll be at their door with flowers and champagne, saying how nice to see you, and we were with you all the way. Get it? Politics." He stood up, thought better of it and sat down again. "There's more to this, though. It's the bloody woman, isn't it?" He paused for a second. "Christ, you and she have been . . . That's what it's all about." He looked at Marcus, not expecting a reply. "Oh for God's sake! That's really too much to take." He glanced around him. His face seemed to have reddened with embarrassment. A few feet away a man and a woman had locked themselves together, gazing toward the lake, seeing nothing.

"Time for walkies, Marcus."

They strolled unsmilingly. The northern night was falling. A dim, gray hue filtered in over the city, but it wouldn't get dark, not this time of year.

"Summing up then," Foreign Office said, sighing. "You've lost one of the best placed people we've ever had. Maybe you upset her. Maybe you had a tiff." He looked Marcus straight in the eye. "Maybe you're unreliable, dear boy. Should we be thinking that?"

"You seem to be forgetting something—I found the woman in the first place. . . ."

"Not your property, old son . . ."

"But . . ."

"She belongs to Her Majesty now, not to you. You're only the bloody messenger between her and us. She's on the eighth floor. Access to the Director. Don't knock—walk straight up. This goes all the way. Can't you see that? She's not just some little Joe you pick up, buy a Pepsi, and get a few facts about sausage production." His mouth turned down at the corners. "Or anything else."

Foreign Office paused. "I'm going back to my hotel." He pointed a finger at Marcus. "You're going back to Moscow. Find the woman and start bleeding her."

They parted, as they had met, without pleasantries, and Marcus recalled their first meeting in a room off King Charles Street in Whitehall. A high, ornate ceiling with a tasteless modern partition. Foreign Office had called him in on the pretext of a visa enquiry—were the Russians playing games, how long did the applications take? And then he had told him what he wanted, and left Marcus to get on with it. Just the way he'd done it this time.

15

He had known it would go badly—the safest of all assumptions in Russia, where the violence lies dormant so close to the surface.

The crowds began to appear in the early afternoon. All on foot. From everywhere and nowhere. Not the crowds of summer, not dressed for pleasure. The old men marched with their war medals in bunches on their chests. The women carried baskets of food, or babies, or both. Children waved hammer and sickle flags as if they alone had the right to them. Then there were the revolutionaries: earnest intellectuals, their hair waving in the wind, megaphones in their hands, leather jackets, jeans, and all the energy of passion. In the old days Marcus had met many of them in their dismal apartments out in suburbs where they would recite their plans and their dreams, and go to sleep knowing both were pointless. Individually they had been sad, sometimes pathetic. Together they began to seem dangerously like an army.

Rendezvous was the city council building, home of the mayor, less than half a mile from the Kremlin. It's a gray stone edifice in a courtyard off Gorky Street, a wide sloping avenue that feeds into Revolution Square. The courtyard was full and the overflow spilled out into the six-lane street, closed to traffic.

He had walked from the compound, taking the tiny side streets, around the Bolshoi. Don't look for the main picture, they said. The key is always the side streets, the backup. That's where you learn their intentions.

And they weren't disguising them. If the militia on the main streets were the normal traffic and patrol units, those waiting in buses were something else. He hadn't seen them before, because even in Russia they don't show them that often—KGB border troops in riot gear. Spanking new helmets, dark blue overalls, shields and truncheons—the full equipment, imported direct from France, where the state has never had much time for demonstrations.

But it was the numbers that shocked him, the communications trucks, the water cannon, and armored personnel carriers. All around was the static from radio transmissions as the soldiers waited for orders and the officers stood around tense and awkward. The sun was blinding in a cloudless sky. Conditions were perfect for anything except the events that were to follow.

Marcus could see television cameras at intervals along the route. The Western networks had moved to Moscow in force, bringing their satellite dishes, their phones and fixers and scribes, sensing a turning point.

This time, they all said, things will never be the same again. The oldest phrase in the book, the journalistic catchall, the portent of things momentous, with not a fact to back it up. He'd written it himself and hated the triteness of it. Things will never be the same. Things are never the same. A day can never be the same as the one that follows or precedes it. You live one day and die the next. You love one day and maybe never love again.

Some of the people had even climbed into tiny trees along the route and as Marcus looked up to the red and gray apartment blocks that line Gorky Street he saw balconies crammed with bodies, faces at all the windows. Above them on the rooftops, the silhouettes of riot police against the sky.

He caught the glint of the sun on metal and realized with horror that the men were armed.

David Russert abandoned his car a mile farther down Gorky Street. Three quarters of the embassy had gone out to monitor the demonstration and in the way of embassies, they had wanted him to sign up, and be organized, dividing the area with the rest of the political section.

But Tuckerman had got him out of that. You weren't head of station for nothing. And even those who didn't know his position bowed before the forceful personality.

"Up to you," he had told Russert, "but I should hang loose, get somewhere high. Last thing you want is to be trapped beside a million people."

Russert had said "thanks" and set off by himself. He hadn't, he told himself, come back to Russia after all these years to look out of a window. He headed for the city council, drinking in the fervor and commitment, so different from the people back home. No one in this crowd would be going home to TV dinners, or fried chicken, or fifty-two cable channels on television. If things went wrong, some of them wouldn't be going home at all.

It took him more than half an hour to cover just a hundred yards. Not quite Stalingrad, he thought, but close. The people had packed tightly together in the belief that that would make them harder to disperse. He had to push and cajole. Angry words flew over his head. A young boy tried to trip him.

Quite suddenly he found himself at the head of the demonstration. Around the entrance to the mayor's office, stewards of the march had cordoned off a section in the shape of a semicircle. Evidently there were to be speeches, demands, calls for action.

The designated leaders waited awkwardly in a group, about half a dozen of them, with beards and of indeterminate ages. You can't really believe you're there, thought Rus-

sert. After all these years, and you remember when they used
to throw you inside just for carrying a few lousy leaflets.

For a moment he stood listening to the conversations
around him, and was struck by the tone. Russians always
complain, but there was a sharp needle in the crowd that he
hadn't heard before. The talk was of power and what the
people could do with it. Pressure, violence, a swirl of public
opinion that the time had come—all their times had come—
to force through changes, to go for the gold, to widen the
doorway before anyone could close it.

"We did it once before"—a craggy, sticklike old woman
jabbed him in the ribs—"and now we'll do it again. String
em' all up." She opened her toothless mouth and cackled.
"Give 'em power for a few years, and they get fat, forget
about us, forget what it's like on the streets. Now we'll teach
'em."

"You tell it, grandma. . . ." a man in his thirties grabbed
her by both shoulders and hugged her. All around them the
crowd went wild.

And then the first of the leaders had picked up his mega-
phone and was calling for quiet. He was the tallest of them,
the palest, the worst fed. His diet would be ideas, emotions,
adrenaline. And yet somewhere in the political deserts of
Russia, this one had learned to press buttons. It was a well-
rehearsed tirade. Russert shifted uneasily as he listened. If
this was the start, what would happen when the crowd got
moving?

Patience, said the crackling, disembodied voice, patience
belonged to the old days. Now they would move. March to
the Kremlin, march to the leaders. Show them a tide and a
torrent that could never be turned back.

And then it happened quite suddenly. The sound of jeer-
ing from way back in the crowd on Gorky Street. Perhaps,
thought Russert, they couldn't hear, perhaps the police had
sent in thugs to disrupt the meeting. At any rate waves of
dismay and anger went through the people. In an instant a

murmur, like the gasp of a football crowd, turned into a roar.

Russert was thrown forward to the front, up against the door of the city council, flattened, winded as the crowd surged forward. He fell to the ground, aware of other voices piped through megaphones and loudspeakers. A boot caught him on the jaw and amid the sudden shouting, from way back, maybe half a mile away, he thought he could make out the sound of automatic gunfire.

Marcus had found high ground: the horseback statue of Yuri Dolgoruky—founder of Moscow—Yuri of the long arm. He had climbed onto the plinth to get a better look at the crowd.

With mounting horror he had seen the soldiers leave the buses, assembling in rapid formation at the edge of the side streets. Somehow it looked too slick, too un-Russian, and then he remembered—this is what they do well. Force, control—pacification. In this country, where they can't get the tractors to work or the light bulbs to light—this is what they can do. He watched the clenched, gloved hands on the truncheons with the sickening awareness that he was seeing true professionals in action.

It started as an attempt to push the crowd through into the courtyard, out the other side and divert them from the Kremlin. But the plan was ill conceived, based on hopeless underestimates of the numbers. Three quarters of a million people can't pass through a courtyard, and as they balked, pinning the outer edges against the walls, some of them began to turn back toward the troops, anger on their faces, their heels digging in.

In that moment Marcus saw the soldiers raise their rifles. The people nearest to them flinched but held their ground. Somewhere in the distance there was an order to fire. He saw the rifles aimed above the heads of the demonstrators, and heard the first crack echoing down the street.

Even at that late stage, even as the bewildered, mad-
dened crowd held its breath, they might have contained it, if
it hadn't been for one thing.

Around the trees the crowd had forced a space. Marcus
could see people on their knees. And then suddenly a woman
rose above them with a tiny bundle in her arms. Only it
couldn't have been a child, he thought, because it wasn't
moving and there were stains all over it—and in that second
he saw the blood and knew what had happened. The young
girl had been watching from the trees at the same time as the
troops had fired directly into them. Live ammunition. Live.
In God's name, what had possessed them?

Even as the thoughts hit him, he watched the woman
turn slowly around, offering the bundle to the crowd, like a
sacrifice. A strange, unnatural silence had fallen over the
people. And then she screamed: a cry of hatred, anger, and
despair, a curse that seemed to echo rooftop to rooftop
across the Soviet capital. To the demonstrators it was the
battle cry they needed.

This time they all turned and surged back the way they
had come, straight into the batons of the army. Marcus, sick
at heart, could only watch from what seemed a vantage point
in hell.

Fighting broke out spontaneously all along the police
cordon, and then he heard the troops firing again. Beside
him people had started to run, back down into the side
streets, kicking and overturning cars and military transport-
ers. And in that instant Marcus knew it was out of control.

Half-jumping, half-falling, he clambered down from the
statue. In the confusion another salvo of rifle fire smacked
out close to him. Someone a few feet away yelled out in
agony and he looked down and saw blood on his clothes. He
ran, not knowing where, dodging soldiers, people, anything
that moved. Hands clasped at him. He tripped against a man
lying facedown in the road. And then he saw a sight that
wrenched at his stomach: the distant blur of red hair, mov-

ing toward him. Like a drowning animal she seemed to come
up for air, and was then lost in the mass of bodies. Smoke
now, a heavy cloud, swirling down the street. He glimpsed
her again, and this time she didn't resurface, and he was
forcing himself through the people, marking the spot where
she'd fallen.

As he ran the tear gas hit him, burning his eyes and his
throat. He put his head down, almost groping his way along.
Somewhere in the confusion a truncheon landed on his
back, felling him to his knees. He got up, and saw her, half
sitting, head in her hands. Anastasiya. His eyes would barely
open and then the coughing came, and you will never know,
Marcus, how you did it, pulling her into your arms, dragging
her, hearing the grinding, jarring tracks of the motorized in-
fantry, the shouted incomprehensible orders. Around you
the battleground, with the hopes and the bodies of a generation strewn upon it.

He saw it through a daze. People were running, handker-
chiefs, shirts, rags over their faces, but the firing seemed to
have stopped. In the distance were the sirens of ambulances.
Moscow, Moscow—what have you done?

Suddenly he could hear his breath coming in shrieks and
he nearly dropped her as the coughing again racked his
body. He was into a side street now, blundering, stumbling,
his whole head ringing to a symphony of pain. Go, go, go, he
told himself. Get her out of here. But he knew he couldn't.
His strength was gone. Lay her down, gently—nothing for it
—fall into the gutter . . . He was slipping, bracing himself
for the impact, when a hand seemed to come from nowhere
and steady him. Anastasiya was lifted from his arms, and the
awful noise seemed suddenly to have been blotted out.

Marcus was aware that a door had closed behind him.

Somehow Russert had staggered to his feet, pushed on
by the crowd as it turned on the army and police. For him
though, it wasn't a long war, wasn't a good war, wasn't distin-

guished. As he hit Gorky Street the snatch squads pounced
on him and he was flung into a prison truck. Inside, his first
act was to throw up over the woman beside him.

A medical orderly leaned across, told him to face the
sky, and put drops into his eyes. Miraculously the blur and
the burning eased.

He looked back out of the window. The driver had
started the engine. And he watched in shocked fascination as
a young man, doubled up with pain, reached down and lifted
a red-haired girl from the rubble, from among the spent car-
tridges, from the ragged pieces of clothing that lay scattered
across the street.

The face of the man stuck in his mind, and it wasn't till
many hours later, when he had finally established his own
identity, and the embassy had sent a car for him, and he had
filed his account of the capital's worst carnage since the
Revolution, that he remembered who it was.

The teacher woke him. He was still sitting on the sofa,
where he had drunk his coffee, talked about fears and dangers, and worn out with worry, had fallen asleep.

Already the television set was on. But it was only the
station ID. Central Television, they called it. The much-ex-
amined, sanitized Voice of Moscow.

Again the teacher shook the envoy's shoulder. "Wake up,
for God's sake. They've just said there'll be an announcement. The General Secretary is to broadcast. Something awful . . ."

The envoy became aware of the Englishman's face leaning over him. For a moment he forgot where he was. Slowly
he sat up, letting the color fade back into the room, the sofa
draped with a blanket, the pictures, the neon light: all cheap
and shabby.

"How long have I . . . ?" He broke off, hearing the voice
on the television, seeing the features that were so familiar.

He hardly took in the words for he could read them in

the eyes. Key words of disappointment, of failure. Gone was the animated lilt from the provinces, the laughter around the mouth, the determination. Not the man I have known, he thought, not the man I accompanied to Moscow: someone else that I barely recognize.

When it was over the teacher turned off the set and looked at him. "I don't know what to say. . . ."

"Say nothing." The envoy closed his eyes.

"How can I say nothing? How can you? Eighteen people died on the streets of Moscow this evening. Three hundred injured, a curfew over the city for the first time since the war. And you tell me to say nothing?"

The envoy got up and looked out. There was a yard and a building site, and acres of wasteland and, beyond that, the impenetrable darkness.

He turned back to the teacher. "What would you have me do?"

The Englishman wrung his hands.

In the distance they could hear a siren, blaring out over the apartment buildings, the people locked inside them, and the empty streets of the capital.

16

In time Marcus could see a wide hall with stone staircases that led away from it. The light came only from a handful of kerosene lamps placed at random on the flagstones. Dark shapes hurried past him, paying no attention.

He rose painfully to his feet.

"Nu shto? Luchay tyebye?" "You better?" A short figure took his arm. Marcus could make out a T-shirt from the Moscow Olympics. They descended, and he looked around him, startled that he could recognize the place. The Russian was watching him.

"Know where you are then? Do you? You should. Probably eaten here a few times, uh?"

He could see it now. The Aragvi restaurant, one of Moscow's oldest and best known, just off Gorky Street. They were downstairs passing through the dining halls. More lanterns and shapes. From a corner a woman seemed to be moaning in pain. "We expected trouble," the Russian was whispering, nerves unlocking his tongue, forcing him to gabble, "the manager's one of us. He closed the place, let us use it just for today."

Marcus halted. Something was tearing at his mind. Anastasiya! "Wait. The woman who was with me."

He could see gold teeth as the man opened his mouth.

"She's all right . . ."

"I want to see her . . ."

"Already moved on . . ."

"But . . ."

"I said she's gone." The hand gripped his arm very tightly, passing a message of its own.

Through the kitchens now. Someone was boiling water. No faces, he thought, just impressions. Russia underground. God alone knew what was happening on the streets.

"Stalin's favorite restaurant." The man turned to him and smiled again. "He had them build his own way out. Always scared, always fearing a bullet in the back. Would have been too good for him."

They had stopped in front of a brick fireplace. "We have to hurry." Without warning the guide dipped his head under the mantelpiece and Marcus was instantly aware of an optical illusion. The grate was a stone slab that stuck out from the wall. To each side of it was a recess for storing wood or coal, but the man disappeared into it and Marcus followed, finding himself in a low tunnel.

The Russian reached for a flashlight, half turning in the narrow space. "This leads all the way to the Kremlin." He made a face. "But you're not going that far. Here—come here. Squeeze past me—that's it."

Marcus felt himself manhandled against the brickwork. When his hand came away from the wall it was damp.

"You go three hundred meters farther, keep your hand out, you'll feel a door. It's part of the wall of a block of flats, leads into the cellar. Listen before you open it, make sure there's no one there. It's just beside the Bolshoi." The man was moving back. Marcus could feel himself on a long path into darkness. And then he heard it. Anastasiya. For a moment he wondered where the word had come from.

The man must have been twenty feet away down the tunnel. "She said she'll contact you." Just a whisper.

"When, where?"

But the Russian had turned, and as he looked back Marcus could see the flashlight bobbing up and down like a beacon at sea in a storm.

In ten minutes he emerged into the street, shocked suddenly to find that darkness had fallen. The city was strangely quiet, streetlights on. Across the wide boulevards isolated militiamen stood guard at traffic lights where there were no cars. In the distance he could see the ancient water trucks, washing the streets. It was as if the violence and killing and the shouts of anger and terror had never been. A disaster had occurred, only now it was covered over, obscured—as only Russia could do it.

And how do you write it, Marcus?

He was sitting safe in the office, in the safe courtyard, where only the foreigners can go.

And outside, Russia had stood on tiptoe, and screamed loudly enough for the world to hear. A bloody and cruel event. And yet hadn't they expected it? Hadn't change always come violently to the people of the steppes?

As he looked back over a thirteen-year career Marcus recalled times of powerful and addictive exhilaration, but nothing like this. To light even a spark in Russia was to ignite powerful and dangerous forces that could only be imagined. A mother crying out to a crowd, holding up the body of her child, killed by the brutal stupidity of the Soviet armed forces. A symbol of primeval agony. Where would it lead them?

When he'd finished he sat back in the little office with the bare wood floors and reread the lead. Get that right, they'd always told him, and the rest would follow.

Of course it had written itself, the big events do. None bigger than this, he thought. The story of the giant rusting locomotive called Russia, idle for decades, now on the move.

In pin-striped splendor, wearing pained expressions, carrying letters that spoke of disgust and concern, the ambassadors of the Western nations queued in their black limousines to lodge protests at the Soviet Foreign Ministry.

It was a gray summer mid-morning, the humidity trapped by the clouds, not a breath of air. Moscow barely alive.

Marcus wound down the window as far as it would go, driving past the line, heading for the American embassy.

The U.S. ambassador was not to confine himself to diplomatic niceties. He'd been told to go public but go gently. The lightest touch you have, said the coded message. No threats, no rhetoric. Regrets only.

They held the news conference in the embassy canteen, the lunchtime hot dogs well out of sight, the kitchen staff ordered clear, Ambassador Cohen sailing in smooth and fast, the gaggle behind him.

"Ladies, gentlemen . . ." He knew he could do it, but did he want to? Shouldn't there be some needle? And then he recalled the briefing on his last trip home. Whispered conversation in the bar at the Willard Hotel, well away from State, just to let him know "one or two things."

Cohen had craned his head forward and listened intently. How Washington was too tied in with the current General Secretary to want to switch horses. How the leaders got on too well, how there'd been too many oral agreements that had never been transcribed or translated, too many winks and nods that the allies had never seen. Washington wanted this man and no one else. The parting advice had been painfully simple. "Don't fuck up."

At the back of the room Marcus read over his notes. It amounted to nothing. Washington soft-pedaling, running for cover. You could tell by the lack of adjectives. Cohen was using nouns: distress, regret, sympathy. Without adjectives they hadn't even begun.

"Mr. Ambassador . . ." A network reporter was on his feet. "This isn't exactly a strong reaction."

"On the contrary, Jim, it's very strong, and we've known

each other long enough, I think, to have some trust on this thing." He looked up from the table and saw incredulity in the reporter's eyes. "We are profoundly sorry that this situation came about."

"Just sorry?" The reporter's voice rose.

"Profoundly sorry, I said, Jim."

"What about who's to blame?"

Cohen looked on surer ground. "Not our area. Let the Soviets decide that. I've no doubt there'll be an investigation. Let's face it—this isn't the Brezhnev era."

"Yeah, well it didn't look so far from it on Gorky Street last night." The American sat down. There was a general buzz of conversation.

"If that's all, ladies and gentlemen . . ." Cohen got to his feet. It was a long time since he'd had to skate on ice as thin as that. "Look, the bottom line is this . . ." A few departing heads turned back in his direction. "We're worried, we're concerned, we're asking the Soviets for details, okay? Okay! That's it."

Marcus made his way to the door, nodding to colleagues, noting the wry smiles, watching the scepticism blossom. He was almost outside when a hand caught his shoulder. He turned around, hearing his name, recognizing the deep, southern cadences. A right, brown-suited arm was already extended in his direction. It belonged to David Russert.

"I thought we might talk for a moment." They stood in the courtyard. It was baking after the cool, air-conditioned canteen.

"Talk about what? Last time we met, we didn't have much in common."

"Last time we met there wasn't civil war on the streets of Moscow." Russert took off his jacket. To Marcus he seemed much older than he had in Washington, the facial skin more mottled, the hair thinner. "It was a bad time for all of us. One failure too many. Lots of heavy breathing from above."

"I didn't know you were coming to Moscow . . ."

"We try not to advertise these things."

"Good. Then it would be better if we didn't meet again." Marcus began walking toward the main embassy building. He looked around for someone to divert Russert, but the other reporters had hurried on ahead.

"I think we could help each other . . ." Russert had kept up with him.

"Help each other? I shouldn't even be talking to you." Marcus turned to face him, his index finger pointing at Russert's chest. "You know the rules. If there's a chance encounter like this: we back off, both of us. I've already forgotten we ever met—d'you understand?"

He walked through into the corridor, past the marines. The glass door opened with an electronic click. For a moment Marcus made the mistake of looking back.

"That was a brave thing you did on Gorky Street, my friend." Russert was smiling broadly, about fifteen feet away from him. "Looked like a pretty lady, too. That creature with the red hair. Not your average Muscovite."

Marcus turned away, but the words seemed to drill right through him. Moscow was like that. You could be content and at peace, and then something would stab you with a needle, and you'd be gasping for air. Just the way Russert had done it, with such finely tuned precision.

They had lifted the curfew an hour before dawn. And soon afterward the envoy had perched himself on the radiator inside the teacher's apartment and watched the shadows flickering on their way to work. Gradually the blue night sky gave way to daylight and the people kept coming. He doubted most would even mention the violence. Russians never talked about things they knew—just the rumors about things they didn't.

He couldn't go to the Kremlin. That was the rule. If there was ever serious trouble he was to be the man on the outside.

He was to go to ground, set up communications, make it work. He'd lost count of the times they'd discussed it.

For a moment his eyes lighted on a young woman far below on the street. She was walking, just like the others, bundled up in a gray coat like the others. But her expression was different. Her eyes were screwed up, and as he looked harder, he could see her dabbing at her cheeks with a handkerchief.

It hit him then: the remorse, the guilt, the full Slavic tour of doubt and introspection. Adults were going to work in tears, bodies to the mortuary, mothers to the graves. And all this in the name of change. All this . . .

"You won't help like that."

The teacher had come up soundlessly behind him.

"Like what?"

"Soul searching." The Englishman was biting his lip. He opened his mouth to say something but changed his mind.

"You were going to tell me that it's too late for that, weren't you?" The envoy smiled.

"Maybe. But it's not for me to say." He began putting food on the table, bread, jam, some yellow cheese. "What I should tell you is that the boy is due here this morning. Ten o'clock. That's if he comes."

The envoy had turned away and was staring once again out of the window.

The teacher looked up surprised. "Did you hear what I said?"

"My friend," replied the envoy, his face close up against the glass, "I have thought of nothing else."

In the old days the boy would have been better protected. There would have been a carload of official thugs to surround him, every time he set foot on the streets of Russia. Not anymore.

Now there was just a single trusty and a driver, both

armed with automatics dangling uncomfortably beneath heavy jackets.

But that day was more uncomfortable than most. So as they drove, they wound down the windows, removed their shoulder holsters and placed the guns under the front seats. The roads along the Arbat were empty. The most tangible threat, they reckoned, was the heatwave.

On the backseat the sixteen-year-old sat silent and nervous. He hadn't wanted to leave the Kutuzovsky apartment, but then he hadn't been given the choice. It was important everything should appear normal. Normal! Even the boy had sniggered at that, going off to a private English lesson while the rest of the city was licking its wounds, and the world was in an uproar about it.

He had listened that morning to the BBC World Service —a practice sanctioned originally for his English studies—so he had heard what no one else seemed able to tell him and he could sense the tension.

The boy was tall for his age and, somehow, old for his years. Long gone was the energy of youth, for he had no need of it. To him Russia gave, while from others it took. In tune with the times his hair was long and his clothes baggy. He carried no sign of rank or favor and yet both were with him. As the car bounced over potholes and ruts, he rocked gently from side to side, his thoughts at some distance from his body.

They should have changed the route each week. Those were the orders. But the men had been working the same shift for more than six months and were bored with it. They simply went the quickest way. Down Leninsky Prospekt, past the giant Gagarin monument, and right into the back-street sprawl.

The car drew up beside a line of people at the newspaper stand. A few pensioners, some housewives. They took no notice. The boy got out. Still no reaction. They would have known his name but the face meant nothing.

As he walked the bodyguard scanned the dirty windows. Habit. The instant, automatic search for a shard of light on metal, a face, the twitch of a curtain. All for this little devil, he thought, manhandling the boy through the main gate, up the stone steps to the first floor. And yet if things continued as they were, he wouldn't be doing it much longer.

The hallway was cool and dark. No proper lighting. Each apartment block halfway between a pigsty and a wreck. Now the hard part. Keep the boy around the corner, and knock at the door, and if there are any surprises, any dangers, any men of evil intent, it'll suddenly be the day you earn your money. He knocked twice and flattened himself against the wall.

Outside, the driver leaned against the car, enjoying the shade. While he shut his eyes a man in a yellow sport shirt took his picture, noting that he was unarmed. Along the street the scene was depressingly normal. The line by the newspaper stand had lengthened, a dog hunted through a pile of litter, two dirty children threw sand at each other. Another hot day going nowhere.

The teacher shook the boy's hand, and ushered him into the sitting room. The bodyguard stayed outside. Right from the first visit it had been understood that he would sit in the hall, watching the entrance. He knew his place.

Only when the door had been closed did the envoy emerge from the kitchen. The boy gasped, the twin corners of a smile spreading across his face. For a moment he looked at the unshaven face, the crumpled suit, the fleshy, peasant features of his father's oldest friend—and then they were clasping each other, laughing silently in pleasure, recalling the years of better times, the way, the envoy realized, they had all grown up together.

For nearly an hour he listened to the boy, often shaking his head in disbelief. Mostly the teacher left them in peace, busied himself in the kitchen. From time to time he filled the

teapot. Once he put a tin of biscuits on the table, but neither
of them noticed him.

At the end of it, the envoy felt bewildered. The boy bent
down to hug him.

"I should go now. They'll get worried."

But the envoy couldn't get to his feet, couldn't move. A
few moments later the teacher returned from the hall.
"They've gone."

"Did you hear it all?" The envoy was still slumped on the
sofa.

"I tried not to listen."

"Did you hear it, I asked?"

"Yes." The teacher's face reddened.

"I am too close to it. I see too much. What picture do you
have?"

The teacher sat down and shut his eyes. "It's the picture
of a man locked away on his own. Right inside the Kremlin.
He has all the trappings of power around him, but nothing
works. It's as if the phone lines go nowhere, no one comes
when he calls, no one heeds his commands."

"Why? Why?" The envoy's eyes flashed angrily.

"The police, the army, they're no longer under his control. The boy said it. 'No guard on the door.' They simply
isolated him, bypassed him. When the demonstrators took to
the streets, they ignored his orders and opened fire."

"Why don't they get rid of him, shove him out?"

"Something the boy said . . . he's too popular abroad,
carries too much weight. He's the one who brings in the
crowds, and the money. Without him, they know the economy's finished."

"And the man, what picture of the man?"

"Trapped. Tormented. You heard the boy. He no longer
goes to bed. He sits, catnapping for a few minutes at a time.
Day and night, it makes no difference to him. He knows
there's no way out. Even the reformists are beginning to feel
threatened, and sold short. It's they who will move against

him. And when they do the police and the army will make a great show of rescuing their leader from the very people he's encouraged. It's brilliant. He can do nothing."

"Then I have to do it for him."

"How? What can you do?" The teacher peered anxiously through his glasses, tired but exhilarated.

The car had almost reached the Kremlin. Carelessly, the driver had got stuck in traffic along Kropotkinskaya. The boy was nervous, drumming his fingers on the plastic upholstery. Maybe he had said too much. Maybe he shouldn't have gone.

But he felt better when they reached the Saviour's Gate. The guard saluted smartly. There was plenty of activity around the central committee. He was whisked quickly and respectfully toward the private apartments. There was no sign of hostility or condescension. Perhaps, then, he had got away with it, after all.

17

Foreign Office had always lived in the city. He rented an orange bedroom and a magnolia living room in Berkeley Court, just beside Baker Street, where the Arabs had arrived in force, provoking much talk of a bedouin diaspora.

But as it was England, nothing was said in public. The deep resentments were worn stoically on the faces of the other residents, with sighs and raised eyebrows and the clucking of tongues at the constant deliveries from Harrods and Fortnums that no one else could afford.

And yet, Foreign Office told himself, he enjoyed the ornate entrance, the uniformed and even sometimes polite porters, the feeling that his own flat was a haven of quiet among all the chaos.

On weekends, and sometimes with ill-disguised resignation, he would join the family in Wiltshire, where his wife had long ago decided to raise their progeny. Tiggy and Yol and Hoppy for the female contingent, Barry to shore up the male domain. It was boarding school, get-togethers, committees, and flowers: the lifeless tapestry of rural Britain, supported by money that he could never earn, and that his wife had never had to.

It was hard to admit to himself, but he always enjoyed returning to London, mind back in gear, work in place, all things personal consigned to the countryside.

That night he had decided not to eat. He wanted to listen to music. He had been tired and rushed all day, his stomach felt tight and knotted. He would relax the system, ignore the television news, drop out.

It was soon after eleven when the doorbell rang and he could feel his annoyance rising instantly. Visitors were supposed to check in with security downstairs, security was supposed to telephone ahead. Really it was too bad. If you complained they always said it was someone new and wouldn't happen again.

He could see the gray suit, even before he took in the American wearing it, and he groaned inwardly.

"Hallo."

"That must be English for 'come in.' " Harry Fox looked amused. He sidestepped Foreign Office and walked straight into the sitting room, his eyes on tour.

"You're supposed to say, 'Nice place you've got,' to which I reply, 'You're too kind, it's just a humble pied-à-terre.' "

Fox took off his coat. "As a matter of fact it does look humble. D'you like bare walls?"

Foreign Office gestured to the sofa. "I don't suppose I should ask why you're here."

"Why not?" The American yawned and rubbed his eyes. "We have a monthly intelligence meeting in London: all the heads of the European stations. We started it when the Eastern bloc began falling apart. Call it our preparations for the afterlife." He paused and looked around. "D'you have a drink?"

Foreign Office went over to the sideboard.

Fox sighed. "In the old days it was easier. No one mistrusted anyone. Mistrust suggests there was a basis for trust. There wasn't. Each side *knew* the other was cheating. Now that we've climbed into the same bed, there's raging paranoia. Like a jealous married couple we've begun to suspect all sorts of betrayal. What if our new partner is lying, covering up, making love with someone else? Goes back to what we always said. . . . It's easier to deal with an enemy than a friend. Anyway that's why I come over: to help check on the friend. I coordinate." He took a long time over the word, letting it fill the room.

"How quickly we all lose our innocence!" Foreign Office smiled sweetly and set a whiskey glass in front of his visitor. "What did you want to tell me?"

"Ask you, not tell you. Your fellow in Moscow . . . we'd like him to work with us."

"You amaze me."

"Why?"

"In Washington you didn't have a nice word to say about him. In fact you thought he was responsible for bungling the thing in Murmansk."

"Right."

"So what's changed?"

Fox shrugged. "Maybe nothing. Maybe we still think he's an idiot, but times are hard out there, the place is becoming a slaughterhouse, it's moving faster than we can follow. We need extra hands."

"Russert still there?"

"He was the last time we looked. He just arrived . . ."

"And you want Marcus to hold his hand."

They looked at each other. The American lifted his glass and emptied it.

Foreign Office broke the silence. "Want to know what I think?"

"It's why I came."

"You don't trust Russert . . ."

"You're out of line . . ."

"Oh I don't think you trust Marcus either. But you'd just love to lock them together and see which one floated to the surface. Think of it. If one of them's bent, the other stands a good chance of finding out about it. If they're both useless, they'll help each other. And if our man's a lot better than

yours, you can only benefit. Wouldn't you love to find out
who they really are?"

The American got up and walked over to the mantelpiece. He studied a row of printed invitations, lots of scrawly
print and coats of arms.

"Wouldn't you?"

Foreign Office stayed where he was. "You don't trust Russert because you still don't know how you lost the courier in
Murmansk—and Russert doesn't seem to know much about
it either. Funny, that. He was the case officer, wasn't he? He
could have leaked it. He could have been playing . . ."

"I want those two guys working together."

"Like hell."

"I can go to the top with this one." Fox picked up his
raincoat. "This Friday—Camp David—our two sainted leaders will be walking arm in arm, as they always do. And you
know how they hate to refuse each other anything—" He
grinned. "As you people say . . . I hope I've made myself
clear."

Left alone, Foreign Office turned up the record player,
removed his brown carpet slippers, and stretched out on the
sofa. You couldn't have heard it above the music, but he gave
a small sigh of pleasure. Fox had no idea that they wanted
the same thing. The evening had exceeded expectations.

18

Throughout his time in Moscow, Marcus had enjoyed the British embassy. Once or twice a month he would attend the parties there, many of them glittering, last-outpost affairs, full of music and frivolous chatter, arranged to give Moscow the color and joy that it was unable to give itself.

Each Wednesday he would pick up the milk supplies from the commissariat, each morning Cressida would attend the British playgroup. And there the contact ended.

Marcus had never been run through the MI6 station, because Foreign Office had never trusted it. "I have my own network," he said once, "so you can steer clear of the 'sugar palace.'"—a reference to the business transacted in the embassy before the Revolution.

So Marcus knew instantly that it wasn't the stupidity of the British mission that brought him a phone call at five thirty that morning, at least five hours before most of the press corps would even think of rising.

"It's Benny Scotland here. How are you old chap? We met at your mother's cocktail party last summer. Good Lord, is that the time? I haven't woken you, have I?"

"Of course you've woken me." Marcus lay back on his pillow, hearing the overbearing voice, only half certain where he was.

"Look, I'm just in town for the day—lots of early business—but your mama gave me the number and insisted I look you up. What about lunch?"

Marcus would have declined on principle. "Can't." And then as an afterthought, "Sorry."

"Oh well, not to worry," the voice breezed on, "I'll probably be back in July. Should be nice then, with the trees out around you. You could take me to that super restaurant outside the city—the Russkaya Izba, went there last time. Lord! I better go. See you soon then. So sorry—bye."

In the darkness Marcus turned over and tried to sleep. He was tired enough, worried enough. But now there was something else.

"Back in July," the man had said. Maybe it was like a crossword puzzle. Was that a clue? Down or Across? "Back in July"—the seventh month—seven o'clock. What else? Trees will be out. Nonsense of course. Trees don't come out in July. Trees around you—the rendezvous—Park Dubki—the little oak tree park by the old apartment. Seven o'clock that night. Bloody hell!

Even as he laid it all out, Marcus didn't like it, didn't like the tone of the man's voice or the implicit order to meet him. In fact he disliked it so much, he considered not turning up.

You don't go out for breakfast in Moscow. The best breakfasts are the ones you make for yourself. From packets and tins you've imported and cornflakes you bought on your last trip to the West. To Marcus it was time with the child.

"She's missed you, she has." Doreen came into the kitchen in her dressing gown, Cressida followed, a panda doll in her arms. "All this work," Doreen went on, "place seems to have gone mad. I don't know."

Dear Doreen, he thought. May you never know. May you see only the sunlight, the clear of heart, the laughter. Don't ever peer into the shadows, for there's nothing good to be found.

He took the little girl into the courtyard, pushing her on

the makeshift swing. Several of the Russian maids stood talking by the garbage containers. They pointed at him and shook their heads. Sad, they were saying. Sad to see a child without a mother. Sad to see a man on his own. It never varied. They'd been saying it since he got back after Helen's death. The women of Russia with hearts as large as their continent, still crying the tears of history.

He smiled and one of them came over to him. It was Masha, the longest-serving, a chubby smiling figure with gray hair trapped in a colored scarf. No one had ever put Masha down. All the foreigners knew her, recalling the time she had faced off with the KGB in the early days of Brezhnev, shouting and screaming abuse at them as they had dragged an American correspondent out of his flat. Masha had never had time for subterfuge, for the propaganda, for the petty hierarchies of Soviet life. She was natural justice, she was the core of Russia, the fine, fearless core, thought Marcus, the kind they could never humiliate. She had survived because she and the others like her were timeless. They simply outlived repression.

She looked up at him, her head level with his shoulder. "Mr. Marcus, the little girl, she has not enough clothes on."

"You always say that, Masha—it's summer."

"Please, Mr. Marcus, the sun can also be harmful, some stockings, a shirt with sleeves—this would be good. The child has pale skin. You must take more care."

He put his arm on her shoulder. "How many children do you have, these days?"

"Ah, children." She rolled her eyes. "I don't even think of children. It is grandchildren, Mr. Marcus. Everywhere I look, there is another baby. I say to my sons, 'Can't you do anything else?' "

He was about to say something but changed his mind. She could feel his discomfort. Over in the corner one of the nannies was holding Cressida, tickling the back of her neck. The child was laughing hysterically.

Masha leaned closer to him. "Be careful. I just tell you that. Whatever is going on—be careful."

"What does that mean?"

"It means nothing. Words, Mr. Marcus. That's all."

"You haven't been reading the coffee grains again, have you, Masha?" He grinned at her but there was no answering smile.

"I know what I know." She had begun to whisper. "You should understand this . . . Russia is like a river. It can change course. It can flow fast or slowly, but always it is the same river. Like now. These are bad times and bad times here have always been bad for journalists." She shook her head. "I could tell you stories . . . Ah, I talk too much. But some things don't change, Mr. Marcus. Anyway, you look after your little girl. She is beautiful. One day she'll be President."

"And me?"

"You? You won't be President." And Masha was looking away, avoiding his eyes, hurrying back into the building.

There was little sense of time in the newspaper office with its old front pages, framed along the walls, old stories, old memories of the days when Russia seemed caught in an endless death struggle with itself.

And yet it was pleasant enough with the view over the courtyard, the double doors open onto the balcony, and the hordes of resident cockroaches more or less at bay.

When he'd first moved to Moscow Marcus had employed a Soviet translator to help wade through the newspapers, but the Foreign Ministry had since withdrawn the woman and refused to supply another.

Maybe no one was available, maybe it was an act of petty harassment. In the end there was no way of knowing. So often in Russia the search for knowledge would terminate in a brick wall.

And yet now, at least some of the walls were coming

down. Marcus flicked through a pile of his old stories. The best were always the profiles: not of stars, but of those who had never shone. An interview with the seventy-year-old woman sweeping outside the Kremlin at six A.M. on a winter morning, a lone fisherman dangling a line through the ice on the Moscow River, a young army sergeant in a psychiatric ward after his return from Afghanistan. The new Russians, willing and available to talk. Unlike the one he wanted to reach most of all.

In the late afternoon he picked up the telephone and dialed Anastasiya's office number. It was the same man who always answered. Briefly, Marcus considered hanging up, but changed his mind.

"Anastasiya?"

"Moment." A bad-tempered grunt. Marcus didn't dare to hope.

And then there was the voice—throaty, muffled, quick. "Hello. This is Anastasiya."

"My God, I don't believe it."

She laughed. "Believe it. How are you?"

"I'm fi . . . Wait a minute, I've been trying to get you for days. Where've you been? I mean can we meet?"

"Of course, Marcus. I've had a migraine. I often get them." So matter of fact. Not a trace of pressure. Like nothing had ever happened. She was amazing.

"I . . . what about dinner?"

"What time?"

"Eight thirty. The Berlin . . ."

"Good-bye, Marcus."

He got up, not knowing whether to be glad or fearful. Was it an act? Could she just blot out parts of her life one moment, and then bring them back the next? With Anastasiya each road led to a junction. Some turnings led onward, others led back—or nowhere at all. Hard to know in advance.

He waited an hour and then drove out along Dmitrov-

skoye Chaussee, past the building sites, the blocks, the boulevard that swings right in a great arc beside the railway station. The sun no longer perched center-sky, a dusty breeze
along the pavement, the first of the home-goers on the
streets, white high-heeled shoes, ice cream cones, a day of
chaotic labor almost at an end.

Odd that they should pick the little oak tree park. Odd
when they find a piece of your jigsaw.

Once you leave the main road it's a sleepy district. A
baker's shop, deep into its evening siesta, a dairy, an empty
newspaper store with dirty windows and bric-a-brac. A few
people turned and stared at the Western car.

He'd only been back once since Helen's accident. Just to
pack up, move out, because he couldn't have stayed there on
his own. Good of the Russians to find him another place. A
gesture of sympathy from the awkward little man from the
Foreign Ministry, who'd come around in black tie with lots
of long words and euphemisms for death, and who'd had
genuine, unofficial tears behind his spectacles.

Marcus had moved in a day, quickly and cleanly, as you
almost never can in the capital of the Russians, determined
to relocate his life on the other side of the city, as if, somehow, his mind would follow.

He parked half on the grass and made his way toward
the wood. Lots of human traffic, he thought. Tiny children
with the grandparents who always look after them. Very
young next to very old. They sat and laughed at each other
under the trees. A relaxed kind of guardianship. None of the
tensions born of closeness between child and parent, but
plenty of caring all the same.

Beside the pond he could see the brighter, whiter summer clothes of the foreigners. They had to have come from
the compound, close by. Some of the children had taken off
their shoes and shirts and were dangling their feet in the
water. As he sat on an empty bench, Marcus looked for a
single person but there were only groups or couples.

A middle-aged man sat down at the other end of the bench, his legs wide apart, stomach fighting the shirt buttons. As Marcus watched, a woman in her forties came from behind him, put her arms around his neck, and kissed his bald head. She joined him on the bench, but they didn't say anything, just held hands, watching the evening crowd without interest.

"You must be Marcus."

He swung around, for the voice seemed to come from nowhere. The couple were smiling at each other.

"You probably expected someone else, from the voice I mean." The man was still looking at his companion. He turned and offered Marcus a cigarette. "We're here on business, actually. This is Anne, my wife. She'd never been to Moscow, so we thought it would be good to see." He screwed up his eyes in the sunlight. "You know, given the changes taking place, and all that."

"Nice to meet you." Marcus suddenly felt the situation becoming ludicrous.

"And you."

There was the inevitable moment of embarrassed silence, Briton meeting Briton abroad, unsure of the etiquette.

"Actually we've just been to see a friend in that place for foreigners—you know, Vish something, at the end of the road. He's the local rep for Barclays. Had a nice tea, didn't we, love?" He turned to his wife, who went on smiling but said nothing.

Marcus shifted uncomfortably on the bench. "I don't think I should stay long, you know . . ."

"Nor do I," the voice was suddenly much harder, more professional. "Thing is our friend feels you should work a little closer with our allies across the pond." He took out a handkerchief and wiped his forehead. "You know how it is. That nice Mr. R. at the embassy. Share a few facts from time to time, only our friend wants you to get to know him, delve a little. Apparently there are one or two question marks. You see what I mean, don't you?"

"What if I don't think that's such a good idea?"

The man screwed up his eyes again and stared out at the pond.

"You know, chum, I can think of a lot better ways of spending a bloody afternoon than sweating my nuts off in this piss-hole of a park. But it doesn't matter whether I feel it's a good idea, any more than it matters whether you do. You follow? I haven't come all this way to consult you. This is what our friend wants. All right?" He leaned over to his wife and kissed her cheek. When he spoke again it was as if he were addressing her. "All right and there's one last point . . ."

Always that, thought Marcus . . .

"The girl comes first in all this. What she's got we want. If she won't cooperate, squeeze a little—and we're not talking about under the sheets, right? Our friend made that clear in Helsinki, so get a move on. We want to know how the Kremlin fits together, the factions, the tensions, who's on the way up. In this period it's vital. Governments all over the West are falling over themselves to cut military spending. We have to know what the prospects are. Okay? So get what she knows and get it out. Her safety is not important. Is that understood?"

He wasn't looking for an answer. Marcus could see that.

"Right," he was still talking to his wife, "we're off. Pat me on the shoulder, say thanks for the cigarette, and watch us go. Then you can bugger off yourself. Okay?" They got up, his wife smoothing out the striped dress with its damp bottom, turning awkwardly, giving Marcus a jaunty wave, taking her husband's arm, stumbling a little in high heels.

They were an unlikely couple. Marcus watched the tiny gestures of insecurity, the quick look around, the hot palms wiped on the seat of the trousers, the animated conversation, where before there was none.

Why, he wondered, did he feel part of something rather tawdry and second rate? Perhaps because that's exactly what it was.

The Berlin had always been his favorite restaurant. Just as unfriendly as all the others, but at least the decorations had charm. An internal fountain, plenty of gilt fixtures, high ceilings and a chandelier. It was smaller than most of its rivals, so the service was better.

"I booked," Marcus told the doorman.

The fellow seemed unimpressed. He barred the entrance, struggling to consult his list in the dingy light.

Muttering to himself, he stepped aside, allowing Marcus to squeeze through. The band was playing rhythm and noise, the strobe lighting appeared to be on half power.

Anastasiya was sitting at a table in the middle, confounding his expectations. She would be late, he'd told himself, or she wouldn't come at all, or she'd only stay a couple of minutes. But by the look of the plates on the table she had even ordered.

"Zakuski," she announced proudly, "cold meats, vegetables, potato salad, and two hundred grams of vodka."

Marcus laughed, feeling the tension ease. "How did you know I was so hungry?"

"I didn't. Most of it's for me." She put her hand on his. "Besides you're always hungry."

There seemed to be an unspoken agreement that they would talk about nothing until later. But everything in Russia is sensitive and when they found themselves in a delicate road, they had to double back and look for another.

"You've returned to work?"

She was chewing a cucumber.

"I was working the whole time." She put the cucumber down and helped herself to cold sturgeon.

"But you said you had a migraine."

"I took work home with me. Really, Marcus, must you question me, like one of our old apparatchiks?"

"I'm sorry. I was concerned about you . . ."

"Well don't be. That is a burden I find very difficult to support."

"Why is it a burden?" He could feel the knot tightening in his stomach. Did he have to care so much?

"Really, Marcus. Leave it alone, okay? Just hear what I tell you. This is dinner—nothing but dinner. Don't read anymore into it—all right?"

Anastasiya poured herself vodka. "You are not a very good host, Marcus—and you're not eating." She poked her fork into a mound of salami. "It's really quite good. A bit fat. But what can you expect?"

She was as good as her word, eating most of the food, turning around much of the time to talk to strangers at other tables. Marcus noticed that she couldn't keep still.

Encouraged by her antics, a short, dark-haired figure arrived at the table and asked her to dance. "But of course, darling." She allowed him to kiss her hand. "Marcus, why don't you order the coffee?"

She was playing with him so openly that he could sense the unhappiness that lay behind it. But she didn't just want attention—she wanted distraction. Even as she twisted on the dance floor in a series of exaggerated gyrations, something immovable seemed to be lying in her path.

Midway through one of the slow numbers, Marcus shut his eyes, feeling the tiredness come down like a screen in front of him. He missed the man who slipped into Anastasiya's chair, picked up her vodka glass, emptied it and sat quietly staring at him. Later he was to attempt to explain it away by coincidence—the kind for which Moscow was famous. Only after a day like that, it really did seem more than a little over-organized, stretching belief and credibility beyond realistic bounds, making him wonder if any part of his life were still his own.

David Russert put down his glass and offered the familiar handshake, as if it were a salute.

Of course, Marcus reflected later, Anastasiya had been charmed. Well she would have been, wouldn't she, once she'd unstuck herself from her dancing partner. It was simply wonderful to meet Russert and his two colleagues from the American embassy. Poor sheltered thing that she was in the European department, she so rarely got to meet anyone from the U.S. It was, she said looking at Marcus, just a case of the boring old Brits and French, and they hadn't changed much for centuries. But Americans: so young, so inventive . . . she gushed and gushed, till even Russert, who had admired both her body and the way she dressed it, began to wonder if she had a mind to match.

Oh and of course Russert's colleagues, a first secretary and his wife, had to leave early to release their baby-sitter, so Russert was left without a ride home. "We'll take you," Anastasiya had declared, loudly enough to stop the music. But by then it had stopped anyway, most of the patrons had left, the waiters were clearing away the chairs faster than they could vacate them. Out into the summer night. Out along the Ring Road to the only building in Moscow that flies the Stars and Stripes.

"Just drop me here," said Russert superfluously.

"We will see each other soon"—from the front seat Anastasiya offered her hand for kissing—"and have a long chat. Here is my card."

They joined the sparse evening traffic. Marcus said nothing. Only when they turned onto Vernadsky Prospekt did he look at her.

"You are not pleased with me, I think?"

He could tell she was tired. Her English was the first thing to go.

"How did you guess?"

"I make no apologize."

"Of course not."

"If I upset you, I am sorry." She wound down her window. "I feel sick. Tomorrow I think I stay at home."

"Good idea."

She smiled, her face pale and shadowy from the passing streetlamps. "A very good idea, then you can visit me and we'll have tea party."

"Why do I care so much about you?" he asked.

"Don't." She ran her fingers through his hair, turning to look out of the rear window, watching the city disappear behind them.

The envoy saw Russert enter the embassy residence. He sat on the low wall beside the underpass, and you would have thought, like other Muscovites, he was simply smoking a cigarette, enjoying the cool of the late evening, whiling summer away.

What a city of contrasts it was! Violence one night, tranquility the next. Above him the flies and moths buzzed angrily around a streetlamp.

The surveillance teams had spotted him an hour earlier as he knew they would. The embassy was in a "sanitized zone," stretching for a quarter of a mile around the building. Anything that moved in a suspicious way, anything that stayed longer than it should, was scrutinized and assessed as a potential threat. They had looked at the envoy, with his dirty clothes and his pudgy face and concluded rapidly that he was no danger to anyone.

They barely noticed him leave the area, nor did they spot the trigger that seemed to release him.

But his dejected walk might have given something away if only they had been looking. He felt hamstrung, weak. After so many years on the inside, he was out, powerless to act. The night had been a failure. The contact out of reach. He would have to wait a day or two and try again.

He caught a late bus that took him to the grand, pillared

entrance of Gorky Park. From there he walked to Leninsky Prospekt, turning into the darkness of the side streets. He would talk to the teacher, drink with him. Something might emerge. The man had shown himself to be wise beyond his experience. A good sounding board. No allegiances or affiliations. He could see things for what they were.

The envoy quickened his step: an automatic reflex but for a moment he didn't know what had triggered it. Somewhere behind him he could feel a presence. Maybe one person, maybe several, maybe perfectly innocent. A few feet farther on he stopped and listened hard, realizing just as suddenly that he was alone. Whoever it was had passed, just a little way from him, in among the trees, but headed in the opposite direction. Whatever they had come to do had been completed.

And then he began to run, because the odds were being tipped against him; there was a sudden chill on his skin that he hadn't noticed before—and you don't want to call it fear, don't want to give it its name—even though you've known it for so many years.

He must have been a hundred yards from the block of apartments when he heard the siren—but he was determined to get there first, sprinting as he hadn't for more than twenty years, taking the dismal stairs two at a time, seeing the teacher's front door half open, knowing they hadn't even bothered to disguise their visit.

He stopped, because it was clear he didn't have to hurry and he didn't much want to see what was there. And yet if you go in you could have a moment of quiet with your friend. That's what his mother had always said: Whatever the turmoil, the disaster, or panic, seize yourself that moment. It may be all you have.

The teacher was lying on his side between the sofa and the coffee table. Everything around him was tidy, the way it had always been. He hadn't even struggled. And that was when the anger hit him. For the gentlest of men, who had

come to Russia in search of solace and friendship . . . and
they had smashed in his skull, even as he would have sat
there, looking at them with his pained, quizzical expression,
understanding nothing of their purpose.

In silence the Russian knelt beside his friend and cra-
dled his broken head—in which position the two officers of
the state militia, summoned by a nameless informer, discovered him.

Three hours later the envoy was released. He had refused to answer any questions, and referred all questioners
to a number in the Kremlin.

In the corridor he had listened to the militia commander, ranting into his telephone. No, he would not be
pressured by bureaucrats, a murder had been committed,
and he didn't care if it was the pope or Jesus Christ taking
responsibility. If the General Secretary wanted his man released, they would have to get off their fat arses and pick him
up.

All of which brought no less a person than the private
assistant to the General Secretary, striding blue-suited and
immaculate into the headquarters of the militia's criminal
investigations division, furious at having his arse discussed,
described, or invoked in any way at all.

"My name is Krichenkov," he told the sweaty, over-
weight commander as they stood in the corridor. "I had no
idea that scum like you were still employed."

"We'll see who's employed in a month or two. Looking
forward to sweeping the street, uh?"

The militiaman spat on the floor and returned to his office. Left alone together the envoy and Krichenkov looked at
each other with distaste.

"You shouldn't have come yourself." The envoy shook
his head.

"I merely carry out my instructions." Krichenkov

straightened his jacket. "Not everyone can manage that these days."

They were outside the militia station. It was four o'clock in the morning. A black Volga sat by the curb, its lights on, engine running.

"You better get going." The envoy looked up and down the street. All four lanes were clear.

"My instructions are to bring you with me. After that you can go where you like."

"Instructions from whom?"

Krichenkov smiled. "I think you know."

They got in. The driver didn't look around. Quickly, expertly, he swung the car through the side streets and onto the broad stretch of Kalinin Prospekt. Barely a light shone from the high-rise blocks of apartments.

They turned right by the movie theater, past the Defense Ministry and down the narrow slope toward the Borovitsky Gate. And you don't get stopped in this car, thought the envoy, not with these plates. The traffic light on the Kremlin Gate was green. He could hear the familiar swish as they glided over the cobbles, and then he was outside in the cool of the morning, with the crosses of the Kremlin churches away in the distance, black against the clear dawn sky.

My friend died this night, he thought to himself as the sadness took hold of him and the tears came again.

Andrei Krichenkov watched the envoy disappear into the Kremlin offices and ordered the driver to take him home.

He didn't live far away. Nowhere in Moscow is far when you have a Kremlin limousine that stops at no traffic lights, and plows its way through all intersections oblivious to pedestrians or other cars.

At the main door to the building, he stopped and thought for a moment. Then, as if making a hurried decision, he walked over to his own private car and got in.

There was no one about. In the darkness a hundred

yards away a militiaman was supposed to keep guard over the courtyard twenty-four hours a day. Krichenkov could see the outline of the box but could not make out if anyone was inside.

He wasn't scared or apprehensive, but it was useful to be reminded of the surveillance. The building was reserved for high-ranking civil servants: the middlemen of the Soviet Union. Powerful and unseen, they were the underground that the party leaders feared most. They decided who attended what meeting, which issues of policy came to the fore, which internal reports were circulated or died in the shredder. They managed and manipulated.

Krichenkov looked up at the windows. A few of them were illuminated. A few of the occupants would be rising well before dawn. He didn't have long.

The drive took him about three kilometers west of the city center, along the Moscow River. Behind a fence was a low wooden *izba*. From the chimney the barest suspicion of smoke.

"You're very late," an elderly voice greeted him in the doorway. But he didn't reply.

Along the far wall, perched on a sofa were two men, smartly dressed, professionals, just like the ones who had been there the night before and on so many nights before that.

They were party functionaries, like himself. But they came from the outlying republics, these two from Moldavia, others from the Baltics and Central Asia.

Every time such officials visited Moscow, they were sifted by his staff and assessed. Were they reformists or orthodox Marxists, did they have guts, were they players or watchers?

For some time Krichenkov and his friends had been building up their own network of like-minded sympathizers, communists who felt the reforms had gone too far, that discipline had broken down, that Russia should be saved, while it still existed.

He had a few more opinions to canvass, and then, they would be ready.

"Have some tea," he said to the men. It all seemed so civilized, so responsible, so much the right thing to do.

19

You can't master the skies without feeling pretty confident about the things left back on earth. This pilot was confident. More than that, he was bored.

For over three months he had shared the Arctic training missions with an officer from one of the other Moscow bases. But he had carried the major burden. He—Vitaly Bovin, twenty-seven, and in his own estimation, supremely handsome. More importantly he had seen combat service in Afghanistan—so he could pull a trigger. Even more importantly, he came from a small town in the Transcaucasus called Shelepin. He was the envoy's nephew, seconded to the third district flying school, outside Moscow—from where he flew the envoy's missions.

Vitaly had left his quarters soon after dawn that morning, hitching a ride in a staff car that was going to the city for repairs. So he was early for the meeting, sitting contentedly in the small park on Tverskoy Boulevard as the morning sun warmed the streets around him.

Wait until eleven, then go, his uncle had told him. Till then just sit quiet and try to leave the girls alone.

A dry old stoat, he was, thought Vitaly—but what a survivor! He smiled at the ground. Power impressed him: whether it came from the throttle of a Sukhoi fighter or the hands of a Kremlin official. But he had never sought responsibility for himself. Life, he felt, was for enjoyment, even when it came to that bleak air station inside the Arctic Circle.

As the weeks had gone by he had sometimes broken the rules and stayed over for an hour or two, to talk to the people up there. Once, bad weather had delayed his takeoff. Another time the female duty officer had invited him to her room for coffee, that they both knew she didn't possess. He had looked appreciatively at her boots and the ample swell of her blouse and decided he wasn't in such a hurry to get back to Moscow after all.

Now the next time . . .

His thoughts were interrupted by the envoy who slumped on the bench beside him, rubbing his eyes.

"You're looking well, uncle."

"Crap!"

"That's what I mean," replied Vitaly good humoredly. "Lousy night in the corridors of power?"

"I don't think joking is appropriate."

"No, of course not." The young man rubbed his hands together. He wasn't going to buy depression this early in the day. "Let's see, I've got a much better suggestion. Why don't we buy a couple of shovels, dig some graves, and go and lie in them."

"You wouldn't even . . ."

"Wouldn't what? Understand? Of course I would." Vitaly looked around at the early strollers. "There isn't a person in this park who wouldn't understand . . . things like, who fucked up this country, who robbed them of all the things they should have had. The question is which of us will do something about it."

"You know the answer to that."

"Yeah, well we've had enough half measures in this place. Maybe it's time for something more concentrated."

The envoy was about to leave. But there comes a time when you can no longer fight your tongue, or cower behind your shadow, when you stop believing that silence can ward off bad luck.

"I saw the General Secretary," he told Vitaly, and he wondered how the young man would remember this moment in years to come. But he couldn't look at him, couldn't stand to see his eyes or the disappointment he knew he'd read there. "He's decided . . ." The envoy glanced across the park. An over-orderly group of schoolchildren was on its way to school. "I mean, the man has had enough of all the arguing, the fighting, the disloyalty." The envoy's face was cold and expressionless and he pronounced the words with evident pain. "He wants to leave the country."

Teatime at Anastasiya's was as loose an invitation as coffee in the Arctic. Of course she had been in bed in any case. So it made perfect sense for Marcus to join her there for the afternoon.

"It will do me good," she proclaimed. "Help my circulation."

For a long time afterward they lay without speaking. The apartment was hot, the windows had stuck. Marcus battled with the sashes, then gave up.

"I'm getting ready for winter," she told him. "Here we are always ready for winter. Regrettably we are never ready for anything else."

There was a loud bang from the neighboring apartment. Marcus raised an eyebrow. "That's Pyotr," she explained. "He keeps dropping his paintings. He's an artist, you know."

Marcus snorted. "Everyone here is an artist. The three most overused words in the Russian language are—*Ya tozhe khudozhnik*—I also paint."

She didn't smile and he could tell that her mood had changed again.

"D'you want to talk?"

"Why should I talk, Marcus?"

"Because you know what's going on."

"Well, maybe I don't like what's going on. Maybe it's all going to shit and I don't want to tell you about it . . ."

"I might be able to help . . ."

"By writing in your stupid newspaper? Who does that help? You? More money at Christmas? Extra thank you from the bosses?"

"The outside world can help by applying some pressure."

She laughed. "You're too late, Marcus. Things are moving too fast for that. Russia doesn't want the outside world anymore. They're closing the doors, barring the windows. Don't you see what's happening? The future of this country will be decided over the next few days. What happened in Gorky Street is just the beginning. The killing has started in earnest . . ."

"What d'you mean?"

"What do I mean? I'll tell you, Marcus. I mean that a radical group has killed the first of a series of targets in retaliation for the people murdered by troops in that march."

"This has to be crazy." He turned away to the window. "Who are they claiming to have killed?"

"No one important."

"But you said they were going for . . ."

"I said targets. The man they killed was a teacher. He taught English to the General Secretary's son. That," she said quietly, "was supposed to be a signal."

"And you support this group?"

"What does it mean, support? Are we to go backward or forward? Does this end justify these means? We are finding out . . ."

"By killing people?"

"What would you have us do?" She was pounding the bed with her fists. "Let them drag us back into the cage and slam the door? Who the hell are you to judge us?"

Marcus got up and put on his clothes. "I'm just surprised that you feel so little, that it's fine to start killing anyone you want . . ."

"Listen, my friend," and her voice was quiet, almost calm. "I have already cried enough over this country, these people. Everything. To tell you the truth I don't know how to cry anymore."

20 _____

He flew almost due north from Moscow, nothing fancy, nothing creative: textbook flying, where the sky was a deep dark blue and the clouds three miles below.

From Vologda they passed him to air force controllers in Archangel, and he talked himself through the coordinates and the radio frequencies, talked out loud, because that was the way to double-check instructions, to make sure.

For the way he felt now Vitaly needed some safeguards. Otherwise his mind might wander off, replaying his uncle's words, each time more shocking than the last.

He caught the eastern tip of the Kola peninsula, arcing away from the sun, heading out toward the giant island wedge of Novaya Zemlya—new land. A route to nowhere in the empty skies over Russia.

Vitaly knew he was carefully monitored. His own people did that. But from listening posts around the world and in space, America would also be tracking his flight. To them he would be a dot on an orange screen, flagged by an identity number, just one of ten thousand comings and goings across Soviet airspace. Odd, he thought, that even out here, someone could find you, someone could destroy you.

The base cleared him for immediate landing, and he hit the runway faster than he'd intended. I'm tired, he thought, tired of doing nothing, except flying in straight lines. And yet this time the orders were different. Stay over, check it one more time, make sure the place is quiet, and the staff can be handled. As if it were easy.

He taxied toward the hangar. The whole area seemed deserted. The snow had long gone, to be replaced by mud and brown grass. No wonder they got their pleasures where they could. As he clambered down the side of the plane he had a mental picture of the duty officer, the way she had arched her back on that hard, narrow bed of hers, like a cat waiting to spring. Come again, she had said, and we'll fly a little more. You didn't find many invitations like that inside the Arctic Circle.

Stiffly he made his way to the command center. Of course, he reflected, air force control in Moscow would be on the radio within an hour, asking why he had not filed a return flight plan. But then they didn't know about the damaged navigational circuit board that he carried in his jacket. The one he had damaged himself before leaving the cockpit.

It was like being welcomed by a guard dog. You were never sure if the beast was going to snap at your ankles or jump up and lick your nose. The old timers at the base, shunning the world, ignored him because he represented it. The others, who had simply pulled short straws from the authoritarian hand that posted them, greeted him with exaggerated warmth.

As always he had brought a handful of music cassettes from Moscow, some cigarettes, and chocolate, and about ten of them gathered in the neon-lit canteen, like children at Christmas. Vitaly ate his fish soup as they asked their questions. Probing, penetrating inquiries, about events and trends and politicians. No small talk in Russia. They wouldn't waste his time or theirs. They knew a lot and wanted to know more.

Vitaly examined their faces. He could read the change. They were no longer the generation of young unhopefuls, born into Soviet tedium for decades on end, with no hope of improvement. Now, it seemed, they were involved, pushed this way and that by opposing forces, but still engaged. Soviet politics had ceased to be just a black car with curtained windows. It had been transformed into a bus that could take the bright and the capable all the way to Moscow.

She had come in and sat down without speaking, her face flushed with expectation. The other men saw it as well. Valya Belayeva, duty officer, was sharpening her claws, and it wasn't for one of them. She crossed and uncrossed her legs as they wound up the discussion. Darkness had fallen. Some were going to bed, others back to their screens and their radio monitors. He noted the general lack of enthusiasm. No one seemed to care about arriving on time. They trouped out in twos and threes, chattering, and it wasn't long before Vitaly and Valya stared at each other across the white plastic table—completely alone.

"I don't suppose you have any coffee." He allowed himself a half smile.

"Where would I get coffee, up here?"

"Sometimes there are visitors. A kind gentleman might have brought it."

"I don't know any kind gentlemen."

"I can introduce you."

They made their way to her room, but once inside she didn't come to him. Instead she sat down on a stool beside the bed.

"Are you tired?" He locked the door behind them.

"Why should I be tired? Just because I don't leap into your arms and tear my clothes off."

"You did last time."

"And this is this time." She let out a big theatrical sigh. "Vitaly. Listen to me. You cannot imagine how boring I find this place. Ten months I have been here and the most exciting thing was an air crash."

"Thanks."

She shook her head. "No, but you know what I mean. You are different. You come from the big city. How would you like it?"

He sat on the bed and reached out an arm to her.

"No, Vitaly. I want to talk. I have made up my mind. If I can't get posted somewhere else, I will just go missing. It's the best thing. Many people do it, and they don't even bother to trace you. Someone was telling me, they lose five percent of all officers that way. Just disappear. So what? It's a big country, after all."

Vitaly leaned back against the wall. "Stay where you are, just for a little while longer. Who knows what may happen. Things are changing fast in Moscow. There is much tension, many rumors. Be patient for a week or two . . ."

"But . . ." She shrugged her shoulders and sighed again. "It's useless. You just don't see it. Wake up here, work here, eat here, sleep here, if you get lucky fuck here as well. Like the sound of it so far?"

"Just a week or two, I promise you. Things are happening here. You may even get a top-level visitor, and you didn't hear that from me."

"Promises."

"I know how you feel, really." He put out his arm again. This time she took it.

"Sure you do." And she scrutinized him in the dim light from the bedside table. Really he was very handsome, and surprise, surprise there was nothing else planned for the evening. So what the hell! She would give him what he wanted and maybe he'd do something for her. And if he didn't the world wouldn't exactly end there.

He had to have been really tired. He had fallen asleep very quickly. Valya ran a hand through his black hair. Nice boy, good in bed. But he talked a lot of bullshit.

She got up, put on her dressing gown and sat on the stool, watching him. Top-level visitor indeed! Who the hell would bother to come out here, unless they were posted or had gone completely insane? Pilots always had big mouths.

And yet the base was important, even with all the new agreements between Moscow and Washington. She well remembered the lecture they'd been given on arrival—don't drop your guard, don't fall asleep, don't forget the enemy is alive and well and wearing a big smile. Now was more important than ever.

So who was the visitor? And then she had a thought. She wasn't a fanciful person, she told herself. Not a dreamer. And yet the thought wouldn't seem to go away.

When she woke up in the morning it was still there, weighing on her mind, blotting out everything else. So much so that she decided to share the notion with her direct superior, the base commander.

Half an hour later Valya returned to her room to find Vitaly already awake, curious about where she'd been.

"I went to see my boss," she told him. "I wanted to ask about a different posting." It wasn't hard to lie, she reflected. Not hard at all.

"What did he say?"

"Nothing, of course. He's like all the other old farts in uniform. Only a good deal unhappier than most. When people get posted here, they usually leave their wives at home. His insisted on coming as well. She probably thought the old devil would have a fling with an Eskimo. Anyway he seems to have had one. He's chosen today to tell wifey he's booting her out and sending her home." She recalled the image of the tiny, jittery little figure, shaking in anticipation. That much was true.

"Why doesn't he just murder her?"

She laughed. "Hasn't got the guts. Anyone else would have. Besides he doesn't like decisions."

That afternoon, a new circuit board was flown especially from Leningrad and installed in the Sukhoi trainer by a mechanic who sang Orthodox hymns to himself. Vitaly was overjoyed.

He couldn't resist visiting the commander's office, ostensibly to pay his respects, but in fact to catch a glimpse of the wayward bureaucrat. By that time, though, the officer was in his apartment on the outer perimeter, watching his wife destroy most of her crockery.

From the office secretary Vitaly gleaned that the boss was an idiot who deserved everything his spouse was about to take.

He flew to Moscow, quite certain that the base was ideally inefficient. As he cut through the clouds into sunlight, his worries turned into outright amusement.

21

It's funny, she thought. The extraordinary things of life never surprise you. The real shock is the ordinary appearing in the wrong place. Like the General Secretary riding the subway, or the pope on a motorbike. Or the phone call from the security office downstairs to say that David Russert had arrived to see her.

"How formal is this?" Anastasiya, looking tiny in the foyer of the Foreign Ministry, as the lines of dark-suited officials milled past her. A marketplace for diplomacy.

"Not really formal at all." Russert spread his hands in a this-is-me gesture.

"We have a department dealing with U.S. affairs."

"I know."

"The normal procedure is to direct your questions there."

He ushered her toward the vast front door. "But these are not normal times."

Outside she found herself dazzled by the sunlight. He led her across the road, down toward the embankment. She examined his clothes: a blue seersucker suit, dark blue tie. Neat, clean but almost over-preserved. Had to be at least fifty-five, she reckoned, but he would spend plenty of time trying to look younger.

He bought her Pepsi from a stand.

"I'd buy you lunch, but I don't have time today."

"You're very direct." She put the bottle to her mouth and took a long drink.

"I don't want to waste your time."

"I have half an hour."

They leaned against the embankment wall. Anastasiya counted the boats on the river. The water seemed to sparkle all the way to the Lenin Hills.

"I'm new here." Russert didn't look at her.

"Of course . . ."

"So I don't know all the ins and outs."

"Nor do I."

He looked amused. "I need someone to tell me what's going on."

"What makes you think I know?"

"You have newspaper friends. They don't waste time either."

She walked on, leaving him where he stood. He shouldn't feel he was making the running, doing it his way. He caught up, moving in front of her, forcing her to stop.

"What is it you want?"

"I told you—information. Besides I might be able to help."

"Oh God. Not you too."

"What d'you mean?" He seemed to have been taken by surprise.

"Suddenly everyone is offering help. It's as if my country has become a vast charity. Everyone wants to give."

They walked on. The traffic had jammed in both directions. A driver leaned out of his cab and shouted an obscenity.

"You see," she turned to Russert, "the people are impatient."

"I was hoping for more detailed information than that."

"So you want me to spy for you." She was grinning broadly.

"No, of course not."

She saw him redden. He wasn't confident enough to joke about such things. Took himself seriously, she thought.

She sat on the low parapet and stared down into the water. She could feel him close behind her.

"Could I see you again?" He sounded like a small boy.

"What for?" Her eyes remained fixed on the river.

"Just to chat. I'd like your opinion on the situation."

"Perhaps." She turned back to him. "Perhaps not. I have to return to my office now. Otherwise they will think I have disappeared."

She began walking back the way they'd come.

"Your English friend Marcus"—Russert hadn't moved—"do you trust him?"

She wanted to keep going, but something made her stop. She wanted to ask what business it was of his, but she wanted to hear the answer.

"Why?"

"Doesn't concern me really."

I'll play his game, she thought.

"Good-bye then."

"Anastasiya!" His tone seemed to carry with it a sharp hook. "Just be careful. That's all. These are strange times. People do strange things."

She looked at Russert for a second longer than she'd wanted to, long enough for him to see that his words had surprised her, caught her off guard, hit home.

Deep inside the Arctic Circle the wife of the base commander locked herself in her bedroom, with the same feelings of hurt and hatred as any number of other wives in places less remote, less windswept, less primitive. For a while her husband listened to the radio, read a book, then dozed on the sofa.

He awoke an hour later feeling cold and angry. All the blankets were locked away in the bedroom and he was damned if he would ask for any favors. Through the thin walls he could hear the occasional pitiful whimpering—well, let her cry. For years she'd been an argumentative bitch, carping, moaning, changing her mind—never satisfied with anything.

Of course she had hated the Arctic—but then no one had made her come. On the contrary he had provided all the inducements he could to keep her where she was. Even to the extent of joking to a few younger officers that if they had a free afternoon they could do worse than take her out, lay her on the backseat . . . "and you know, all for the motherland, and no questions asked." But none had obliged. He could hardly blame them.

If only he had listened to his father's premarital advice, things might have been different. "Look at the mother," the old man had warned. "If that's the kind of creature you want to live with in thirty years time, go ahead. If you listen to me, you'll look elsewhere."

Well, he hadn't, had he? Damned fool! Anyway who could blame him for casting his line at that female supply officer, who came up twice a month from Murmansk. No oil painting either—well, she wouldn't be, in the army, would she?—but no less willing for all that. And there was no messing around. No commitment. No lovey-dovey nonsense. They just got on with it. Did the business, had a bloody good time over it, and then went back on parade. If only they were all like that!

God, she was still crying. He got up and went over to the bedroom door. "Look, why don't you come out, have some tea. Let's talk. Maybe we can work something out." Anything to quiet her down.

The response was muffled. She must have been yelling through the pillow. "Fuck off and get out of here," said the strangled voice. "Now!"

Obligingly the base commander reached for his jacket and retreated to his office. He was about to lay his head on the blotter when he noticed the jottings he'd made earlier. The Belayeva woman had been in, that tart of a duty officer spouting some silly story, told her by a pilot.

He turned the pad upside down and reread his scrawl. Only what if she'd been right? What if the bloody man did turn up here? What sort of hellish trouble would he be in?

He looked at his watch, determined to get a call through to his friend at the Air Force Academy in Moscow. Of course it was far too late to telephone, but he went ahead and did it anyway.

22 _____

They had traveled separately: the envoy and the pilot, reaching the muddy settlements of the Transcaucasus midway through a rainstorm. Along the dirt-track lanes, smiling and gawking as if in some tribal ritual, the entire population seemed to have turned out to greet the deluge.

An ancient Volga taxi took the envoy from the railway station through the tumbledown streets of Shelepin. Wooden huts side by side with concrete squares, a supermarket with iron bars on the windows. I had to leave, he told himself, leave this place where thought and action never meet. People here died in the same houses and on the same tables where they were born, unaware that a world had gone about different business in between. And yet it was good to return. Strangely, you could travel the world and still take pride in a muddy street and a troubled gray sky.

At the Sunrise Hotel a porter shambled out to meet him. "I can't take your luggage. Got a bad back," he mumbled. The envoy wasn't surprised. "Go back to sleep," he said gently.

"You're very kind," replied the porter.

The envoy examined the foyer. It was empty. A handful of flies transcribed lazy circles around the light bulb. A long way from the cutting edge of Soviet power, he thought. More like the blunt end of it. The pimple on the bottom of humanity, someone had once said. So rarely did it see daylight.

He left his suitcase beside the front desk and pushed his way through the glass doors of the restaurant. There was no sound of chatter, no clink of glasses, no clatter of plates. Over by the window he could see his nephew, sitting in total isolation, bent over a bowl of soup. Beside him cold meat, chicken, and potato salad.

"I hope I'm not interrupting." He pulled up a chair.

"Uh-uh." Vitaly had his mouth full. His hands gestured to the food. "Eat, uncle. Today is a good day. Fresh supplies."

A young thin man with a mustache appeared through swinging doors, wearing a waiter's jacket. It was at least a size too small.

"A drink for my uncle," Vitaly declared. "Five hundred grams. You'll drink some vodka, won't you?"

The envoy nodded. As soon as the waiter had gone, he looked around the dining room, checking it was empty.

"Look," he told Vitaly. "We haven't come here to flash money around and hold a party. We come in quickly, pay the visit, and get out again. Try not to draw attention to yourself."

Vitaly broke a roll and put half of it in his mouth. "That's a little difficult, I'm afraid. We're the first visitors they've had in a month. Besides they couldn't help noticing us. We're alive and they're half dead. We stick out."

Vitaly paid. Outside the hotel they turned sharp right, moving behind the building. It was a narrow alley, overgrown with weeds and moss. They knew where it led, but the smell of dampness confirmed they were heading for the river. It was getting dark.

After a hundred yards, the envoy stopped and listened. "From now on," he told the boy, "if you've something to say, whisper it."

Vitaly clutched his arm. "Listen—this old woman. Are you telling me she isn't guarded?"

"She used to be. But she insisted she didn't want anyone around. Made a hell of a fuss. We stopped it about a year ago.

Now all she has is a panic button, connected to the local militia, in case something frightens her."

Vitaly shrugged. "But any lunatic could come out here and finish her off."

"This is Russia, remember?" The envoy began walking again. "She's a grandmother. We don't kill grandmothers."

They crossed a wrought-iron bridge, black, stark and elegant, belonging it seemed to another world, far away. The hard gravel track disappeared as they made their way through long grass, already wet from the evening dew. They skirted a tiny settlement of five or six houses. Vitaly could see lights in some of the shuttered windows. From somewhere came the identity signal of Moscow radio.

"Nearly there." The envoy stopped for a moment as if suddenly disoriented, but Vitaly could see he was listening. A long straight stretch now, the track sloping downhill. It was a tiny street that ended in a circular clearing, and in it a single house, unremarkable, with green wooden facing, a garden with shrubs, smoke came from the chimney.

The envoy didn't waste time. He pulled Vitaly up the narrow path and knocked at the door. For a moment all they could hear were the birds, the crickets, the sounds of the countryside at dusk. Maybe, thought Vitaly, the old woman had gone away, or gone out, or chosen this night of all nights to pass away.

But after a few seconds the door opened almost without a sound, and a tall figure clutching a black shawl stood there, old and unwelcoming. You could tell she was strong both in mind and body for she projected a presence that would never cower from the world but would meet it head on. Her eyes must have got accustomed to the light for as she looked at the envoy a smile of unexpected warmth and radiance reached her face. Vitaly was certain he could see tears. And he didn't know why that should surprise him. There was no reason why the mother of the General Secretary shouldn't cry as much as anyone else—in fact, these days, probably a great deal more.

She sat them down in her kitchen. An alarm clock ticked noisily on the table. In a corner Vitaly could see piles of newspapers and old photographs tied in bundles. No hint of luxury.

She drew up a stool beside the envoy and ran her hands over his face.

"So many years," she told them. "So many. You have always been such a good friend." The voice was stronger than Vitaly had expected. In the light from a single bulb he stared hard at her, searching for family resemblance. The same fleshy nose, the same wide peasant features, but the woman had a harder edge than her son. The eyes were cool and gray.

"You will have tea." It wasn't a question. She got up and went over to the metal samovar, steaming on the sink.

"We don't have long," the envoy told her.

"Who does?" She asked sharply. "We all have our duty. The country is in chaos. Even out here, we know that. Tell me what you want." Even in the warm kitchen she hugged the shawl closer to her.

"I want you to come to Moscow." The envoy took the cups from her and laid them on the table. "Your son . . . Mikhail has many problems. You know that. We are going to do something special for him. We need his family around him—yourself, some of the nieces and nephews, your other son, Eduard. We need a show of unity around him in Moscow. His birthday is in four days—come then."

The old lady seemed suddenly more weary. She kicked off her shoes and settled back onto the stool.

"Come to Moscow. Show of unity," she spoke quietly but her eyes were blazing. "My friend. Do not lie to me. It is the only thing I have ever told my children. If you cannot tell the

truth say nothing. You"—she pointed at the envoy's face—
"you of all people should know better than this."

The envoy looked down at the floor.

"Ever since Mikhail went to the Kremlin I have been
visited by idiots. At the beginning, there were some from
television, all velvet jackets and hair spray, wanting to make
me into the mother of Russia. Huh! I got rid of them. Then
the newspapers, and the stupid little boys from security, who
pretended I had a problem with my electricity." She opened
her mouth and grinned cunningly. "I have never had electricity. See"—she pointed to the ceiling—"kerosene lamps. Much
better. Much more reliable. All they wanted to do was poke
around, put in microphones, or some such nonsense. Waste
of state money, I told them. Buy tractors."

She sighed. The outburst seemed to have tired her.

"I don't know why you want us in Moscow, and I doubt
you'll tell me." She raised an eyebrow. "If it's that important,
we'll be there. I'll get them all together. The nieces are lazy
little chatterboxes, it'll do them good. As for Eduard, he's
always talking about going to Moscow and acting the big
statesman. Perhaps a visit will finally shut him up."

She got up. "You had better go." She took Vitaly's hand.
"You were a baby when I last saw you, young man. You
didn't know that, did you? Look after your uncle. He needs
you."

They were at the doorway, Vitaly already on the path.
For a second she grabbed the envoy's arm, in that instant
more frail, more vulnerable.

"My son," she whispered. "He'll be all right?" Her
strength seemed to have seeped away.

In the darkness his eyes found hers.

"I don't know. I don't know what will happen."

"He has never believed in God, but I do. I will say a
prayer for him, for all of you."

She shut the door behind her, so that no one should see

them against the light, and she waited on the path till the two shapes were lost among the trees.

The envoy caught up with Vitaly and motioned him to stop.

"You don't go back to the hotel . . ."

"What the hell are you . . . ?"

"Listen to me. Go to the central bus station and get yourself to Tarakhanov. From there you can pick up a train to Moscow at midnight. I want you on it."

"What's this all about? What are you going to do?"

"I don't know. Maybe nothing. But it strikes me this has all been too easy. We didn't exactly make a quiet entrance into town. Sometimes when a place is too empty it's more dangerous than when it's too full." He drew an envelope from his pocket. "Take this and give it back to me in Moscow. You know the way, now get out of here." He slapped Vitaly on the back and watched him disappear along the path.

For a few minutes the envoy didn't move. He knew there was no hurry. Tomorrow morning if all went well, he'd catch a plane to Moscow. That would be early enough.

He walked slowly back toward the town, letting the memories return. The smell of the woods brought him the sounds of voices, of games and laughter.

As he thought back he could see himself with Mikhail, listening as they walked along in their ragged school uniforms, blue with red neckerchiefs. Little pioneers, they had been, singing about the building of communism, long before they could spell it.

Even then Mikhail had been the one with opinions. He remembered him drawing in the mud with a stick. "Say this is the Kremlin," he would declare, "and we're right out here." The stick would mark off two sections well away from each other. "As a matter of fact, we're in luck," he would say. "All the leaders since Lenin have come from the small villages, never from big towns. You don't get noticed in big towns. But the mistake they've made is taking too long and staying too long. You can't arrive owing too many favors, because then you spend all your time paying them off. And you can't keep the job too long, because people get fed up waiting in the power line and throw you out. . . ."

He could recall the speech almost word for word: it was their game of make-believe, how they would mold the planet to their own mud and stick designs. At least the envoy had treated it as a game. Only much later did he find out Mikhail had been serious.

At the edge of the town he stopped again. That was all there was to Shelepin, he realized. Memories, some old speeches, tracks in the dirt. Real life, hard and gray. You should have stayed here and died here, said the voice in his head, instead of going to Moscow.

23 _____

The meeting was like no other she had ever attended. In her student past there had been poets and dissident poets—and Jewish refuseniks and they had all got a thrill from sitting around, drinking coffee, discussing how ugly Brezhnev was, knowing the gatherings were illegal. Russia had *really* been fun.

But Anastasiya knew it was over. You only had to look around the apartment. A large communal affair, with the beautiful high ceilings and the dilapidated walls, unpainted and uncovered for decades—and stuffed full of clerks, doctors, teachers—the serious-minded professionals of the new state. Not for them a cup of coffee and a joke, a police raid or a night in the cells—they were playing for much higher stakes. They weren't content just to taunt the beast—they wanted to kill it.

From habit, perhaps, she sat close to the window, glancing every now and again at the street, half expecting to see the black Volgas and the faceless clones from the KGB moving in. Always the regulation raincoats for the important swoops, or the casual Adidas track suits and sneakers for the rubbish. Whatever else they had done, they had always dressed the part.

This time, though, the street was empty. The KGB no longer cared. Maybe they spent their time watching videos of the good old days. And yet, she recalled, every state had its pain threshhold, and it wouldn't be long before they found it.

For a moment she stopped listening to the monologues. Not because she didn't agree with them, but because she sometimes got tired of the ceaseless political diet, the constant requirement to be passionately involved. In the old Russia you could always switch off for a day or a year, and come back to it later. Nothing ever changed. But now each day brought a fresh tremor, a new boundary, another era-ending sensation.

Yet the new Russia, she reflected, transmitted mixed signals. Some demonstrations were allowed, others, like the one in Gorky Street, were brutally suppressed. On different days different factions would win different battles. And the war just went on and on.

She hadn't told them what she did. Not the real thing. They believed she was a clerk in the Foreign Ministry, with access to nothing and nobody. It was her cousin who had introduced her. He'd had no idea what she did either. He was a young doctor who spent his life working or sleeping—and in the end he had given up the movement because he hadn't had the time.

"You look after the politics," he had told her. "I can't even keep up with the dying."

Suddenly the meeting was ending. Anastasiya got to her feet. She had not been looking forward to the next event. They would go out into the summer evening, walk away down the streets, some to buses, others on bicycles, a few to their cars. Only six of them would go on to another meeting place on the other side of Moscow, to a rendezvous two hours later.

Not everyone was trusted with the knowledge of these extra sessions. They were restricted to the few and the proven faithful. She, herself, had waited nearly three years before being invited to attend. For this was where they made the real decisions, where the battle orders were given and received, where they would settle their own fate, and that of many others.

As she got outside Anastasiya felt a shiver, despite the warm evening. Tonight they were to draw up a plan for further action. And she knew what that meant. After all the doubts and the tears she didn't know if she could face it.

The taxi dropped her close to the subway on Gorky Street. Stage one of three travel stages. You have to take your time, they'd said. Make certain you're alone.

Finally she found a telephone that worked. She dialed his number.

"Marcus! It's me."

He'd been having supper in the flat. She could hear music in the background, some voices.

"Hold on." He was shutting a door. The voices quieted. "That's better. Where are you?"

"Meet me. Now. All right?"

She put down the phone. Surely he would know to go to the Puppet Theater, the nearest rendezvous, the old favorite. There wasn't anywhere else, was there?

He came in the car, sliding over to open the passenger door, saying nothing, just letting in the clutch, taking off along the Ring Road. On Kalinin Prospekt he turned right toward the river, then right again, as if heading for the Trade Center. Good, she thought. Very good. A Western car wouldn't stand out here. He parked near the hotel entrance and took her hand. He seemed somehow more confident than the Marcus she had known before. Now he was the one in command, leading her, knowing what to do.

"Just talk," he told her. "Anything you want."

Anastasiya tightened her grip on his hand.

"I went to a meeting tonight. It's a radical unit. They're professionals, leaders of the new political groupings. They're not interested in just marching, they want power."

"Go on."

In the distance, along the river, they could hear a barge, sounding its horn.

She looked at her watch. "In one hour, I have to go to a second meeting. The leaders of these groups will be there. We have to draw up a list." She looked at him, wanting him to understand. "You know what that list is."

"No. I have no idea."

"It's the people they have decided to kill. Friends and associates of the General Secretary. They will kill them at intervals of a week unless he moves forward on reforms, unless he sacks the remaining hardliners and renounces the leading role of the party. He's always refused to do that."

She stopped, expecting him to speak.

"Marcus, say something. For God's sake."

He turned away and looked back toward the Trade Center—cars were pulling up, foreigners arriving for a party.

"I thought this was the group you supported. I thought this was what you wanted."

She took his arm. "Marcus, don't you see, we're being swept along by our own rhetoric. They tell us: 'Revolutions are like riding bicycles. If you go too slowly you fall off.' More rhetoric. But there's one question they won't answer. Is someone out there going to live better, because someone in the Kremlin dies? Are we sure of this? Because if we're not, shouldn't we stop here?"

"What d'you think?"

She didn't answer. Marcus could see sweat on her forehead, the red fringe damp and lank.

"If I were you, I wouldn't go to that meeting."

"I must." She released his arm.

"You could step back . . ."

"I can't afford to. D'you realize, I'm just about the only moderating voice there is, and I'm not that powerful either. I'm only there because I've been in from the beginning. The others are all intellectuals, and writers—just like the rest of

Eastern Europe. Because they've written a play they think they can run a country. . . ."

"You seem to have changed your view pretty suddenly."

"I'm just talking out loud."

"It's more than that, isn't it?"

"I don't know, Marcus. I don't know."

He drove her back to the subway station.

"I could take you closer if you like."

"It's better like this, but you can do one thing for me. Meet me at my apartment after midnight." She got out of the car but put her head back through the open window. "You should know your friend Russert came to see me yesterday."

"Christ! What for?"

"He said he wanted information."

It was business, and nothing else, he told himself. Just for now. Business that took him to the apartment on the outskirts of Yugo-Zapadnaya, that made him wait in the car until she arrived at two in the morning, exhausted, too tired even to weep.

Business that allowed him to sit her down, give her tea, open the door to draw in the fetid air of the city so she could breathe. Business that let him help her onto the bed, and stay with her, holding her tight until he felt her breathing take a different more steady rhythm, and knew she was sleeping.

Business that made him pick up the list she had left for him on the table, surely the most sensitive piece of paper that night, anywhere in Moscow.

Just business, he said again as he drove back to the office to send a story, with a code, that would wake Foreign Office from his slumbers well before morning.

24

The message hadn't just woken Foreign Office, it had sent him into the frenzy of London's early morning traffic in a car spattered by rain, with a radio phone bleeping and shouting at him, and cutting out behind tall buildings.

A man from the Cabinet Office had been forced to meet him in a cafe in West Kensington, because he couldn't penetrate the West End, and a public official, whose name had never appeared in any newspaper, rendezvoused for a ten-minute chat at Heathrow's Terminal Four, because that was on his route from Oxford.

The madness, Foreign Office reflected, was broken only by the takeoff for Washington of the British Airways Concorde, a flight so expensive that it would need at least three signatures to justify it to Accounts.

Once again he checked his briefcase. That *would* justify it.

At Dulles Airport he amused himself by ignoring the CIA driver, who was holding up a card reading Mr. Sampson—the name the Company always used for MI6 personnel. Instead he took the Washington Flyer taxi service to the Four Seasons on M Street and waited for them to come to him.

It didn't take long. Forty minutes after his arrival three black cars pulled into the hotel's tiny drive-in and sealed it off. The men at the wheel wore charcoal suits, red ties, and reflecting metal sunglasses.

One man in gray, short and suntanned, looking to all the world as if he'd just returned from vacation, went straight up in the elevator, found the room he wanted, and entered without knocking.

Foreign Office was in his underpants, drying his torso.

"Fuck you." Fox told him. "You were supposed to come direct to Langley."

"Good morning," Foreign Office replied. "Thank you for asking. I had a very pleasant journey."

They had gone to Langley in the end, because the American had taken one look at the material, and called for the drivers.

It had seemed to Foreign Office more than a little conspicuous, emerging at high speed into the sunny heart of Georgetown and screeching at breakneck speed toward Key Bridge. But it was one way of beating the traffic.

And then the papers had gone off around the building and he had sat in an office, leafing through the personal ads in *The Washingtonian*, feeling like a traveling salesman, anxious for his commission.

Fox returned with the one question he wasn't going to answer.

"Where did all this come from?"

"I can't tell you."

"We need to know to establish its authenticity."

Foreign Office got up and stretched his legs. He felt tired, but the constant injections of coffee had rendered him hyperactive. "Look, that's not my concern. I brought you the material. You've seen it. Do with it as you will."

Fox took off his jacket. "Do you want more coffee?"

"That's the last thing I want."

"How accurate is this thing?"

Foreign Office managed a yawn. "I don't know. I would think it's accurate. I just pass it on as it is."

"But that's not why you came."

"Last time we met, you asked that Marcus work with your man Russert, or at least stay in contact . . ."

"Right."

"Well for practical reasons, there hasn't been time . . ." His voice trailed off. "Apparently, though, he's been to see one of Marcus's contacts. A kind of fishing expedition. Highly irregular, but maybe that's what you asked him to do. Anyway I should be grateful if you'd pass the contents of my material on to him."

"Why?"

"That should be obvious."

"Does it come from Marcus?"

Foreign Office smiled for the first time that morning. "If it did, I wouldn't tell you."

25 _____

Jim Tuckerman did more than just control the CIA station in Moscow, he did lunchtime bar duty in the embassy club on Saturdays. In winter it was crowded, in summer there was barely a soul.

In times gone by the U.S. embassy had been the center of life as they'd known it. A refuge from "out there," the place where you lived, shopped, ate, worked, and socialized. But not anymore.

Moscow was freedom city, full of restaurants and people to talk to, places to go, things to buy. The diplomats went out happily with their families and their cameras, and got to know Russia—or thought they did.

Odd times, Tuckerman reflected. Often the Agency people had least to do when everyone else was at their busiest.

Who needed covert reports, when it was all in the newspapers? Who needed secret projections of the Soviet economy, when the Russians themselves were coming clean? Who, some voices in Congress were asking, who in the age of *glasnost*, needed the Agency at all?

He had made himself two rum punches, and was actively considering a third when the duty officer rang down for him. It wasn't so much his tone, but a single word that he used at the end of the sentence that made Tuckerman close up shop without hesitation and take the staircase at, what to a man of his build, must have been life-threatening speed.

"Where's Russert?" He read through the cable.

"He's out," replied the duty officer.

"I said where?" Tuckerman was shouting.

The officer began searching through a sheaf of papers. "Let's see now . . ."

"Oh give it here." Tuckerman pulled the logs toward him and scanned the paper for Russert's name. "Oh Christ. He's gone to the Bay of Joys."

"Lucky boy," said the duty officer and scowled at Tuckerman's departing back.

The Bay of Joys was everything it said it was. A lakeside resort for the city-weary, about forty-five minutes drive from Moscow.

It could have been relaxing and pleasant to drive there, thought Tuckerman. You could have stopped in the pretty farming villages, picnicked in the pine woods, lounged in the gentle, dry heat of the best summer Moscow had seen for years. But no. He had to drive like a suicidal maniac because one of his officers had decided to sun himself on the beach.

He parked about a mile from the water. There was an endless stream of cars, both Russian and foreign, and in his city slacks, he stood out among the shorts and T-shirts and swimsuits. He began to look like what he was—a hot, harassed official chasing his subordinate—and he didn't like that at all.

Down by the lake the bodies were thick along the sand. A few sailing boats were across on the other side. Closer inland people had hired pedalos. There was laughter and catcalling as he strode awkwardly across the beach.

He found Russert sharing a picnic rug with a Russian girl in her early twenties. It was probably jealousy, he reflected, but the situation struck him as awkward.

The girl seemed to sense that she wasn't wanted, and went off to the cafe.

"Isn't she a little young for you?" Tuckerman inquired.

"Local color, Jim. I think she's one of theirs, attached herself to me the moment I got here, all but asked for my rank and serial number. I didn't think these people were employed anymore."

They rode back in silence to the embassy. Cars were still streaming out of the city. But it was always like that. Working for the Agency, Tuckerman realized, you were constantly traveling against the flow, awake when everyone else was asleep, thinking thoughts that wouldn't enter a normal person's head.

In his office, Tuckerman recited the gist of Washington's message.

Russert looked incredulous. "Where did the Brits get all this?"

"I hoped you were going to tell me. You know the MI6 people at the embassy. Who has that kind of access?"

Russert bit deep into his lip. "Until a short time ago I'd have said no one. Their station here has been very average. No special contacts or insights. No one inside the new movements . . ."

"Till now." Tuckerman leaned back in his chair. "This is either very high class or it's bullshit. Which is it?"

"I don't know."

"Well Washington wants to find out, and it doesn't want to hear it from London. If this place is going to blow apart, we need to be in there with the new groups, not lining up outside next to the Nicaraguans. Okay?" He fumbled on his desk. "Oh and there's this list you should look at. Take it with you and bring it back later."

Russert made for the door.

"Just one thought, David. What if this comes from your friend Marcus?"

"I'd be surprised . . ."

"His contacts . . ."

"Low-level, from what I've seen . . ."

"Think about them. If you need assistance, ask for it. I mean that."

Russert went to his own office, put his feet on the desk, and looked out at the courtyard. Of course he hadn't enough of his own contacts. That's what Tuckerman had meant. And he certainly hadn't made the one contact he needed. But when things are moving so fast . . . Maybe he could sound out Anastasiya. Maybe it was worth . . .

He had picked up the list, and was idly flicking through it. And then he drew in his breath, and his feet fell to the floor. Right at the top of the page, the first of the targets, was the only name that meant anything to him. The one name he'd been certain he wouldn't find.

26 _____

A safe house. So inappropriately named. Because once they've been blown, they're the most dangerous houses of all. The ones they watch and go on watching till they wind it all up, move in, rip the network apart, human being by human being.

You think that because there's a thing called *glasnost*, because Eastern Europe went down the tubes, that they've filled their coffee mugs, and put their feet up. But they haven't, have they? Because no one trusts anyone else—same as the old days. The only difference is, now they have to say they do.

And these are the most dangerous times of all, times of change, when it could go one of a hundred ways, and all the different factions are out there on the streets, touting for business. And when it gets nasty you can easily find yourself caught in crossfire that has nothing to do with you, wasn't meant for you, wasn't going your way.

The confused bag of thoughts, as he headed out east of the city.

What had the Russian said? "Such a man would help us, such a man would wait for the time when we might need him." Well, he couldn't wait any longer.

The roads were all but deserted and dark, so dark. Every now and again a token attempt at street lighting, but mostly they didn't bother. And cars were supposed to drive on parking lights. Only the big official limousines shone their headlights. But who was in them? By what complex thread did anyone still cling to power?

He passed a police checkpoint. City limit. But they wouldn't stop him. He had taken the old Zhiguli with Soviet plates, stolen two days before.

It all looked the same, same as he'd known it in the fifties. Just as dismal, just as distant, blocks of gray, unknown and largely unknowing souls, still so far away from the rest of the world.

In Europe they'd imposed it—the system that had sent the Red Army into battle and taken it all the way to Berlin. But even there it hadn't lasted. The people didn't want discipline or repression. They wanted to be different. Here in Russia they wanted to be the same.

Another suburb, a row of shops, boarded up, empty. Day or night, it made no difference. There was nothing to buy. Elsewhere the economic mess would bring down the government. Here it was prosperity that was dangerous. The new envy—some with money, and some without it. Weren't they happier when no one had a thing to call their own?

Now I'm out here, how much do I tell him? Am I a friend or a traitor? Why is everything so hard to define?

If the directions were right, Russert thought, I should be almost there.

He swung across the railway tracks. In the rearview mirror he could see a red hue back over the city, a suspicion of light. Even when quiet, Moscow was never at peace. A place of troubled consciences, bad dreams.

He stopped the car and got out. There was no other vehicle in sight. But the lights had been turned on in the middle entrance. He was expected.

Through into the stone corridor, and you stay on the ground floor, fourth apartment along. You can't miss it.

It seemed so ordinary, so matter of fact just to slip in-

side, and say hello, as if it were only yesterday you saw each
other halfway across the world, and you've come just to talk
about the weather. But you know you haven't. You have only
to look at the Russian to know he's been suffering, mentally,
physically. His face is pale, the cheeks carry three-days stub-
ble, suit filthy. And you can't see the rest.

"What was so important? Why did you need to meet?"

It was unreal, standing there in the deserted little apartment so far from anywhere, talking about . . . you know,
things like that. And you remember this fellow from the old
days, not the brightest, but certainly brimming over with enthusiasm. What took it all away? The revolution? Was it
worth it?

They went into another room and sat on dusty chairs.
This is really where it all changes, he thought. Oh, I've done a
little for them—this and that—and maybe a courier died because of something I told them, but this is altogether a new
phase.

"You're here," said the Russian. He must have seen his
confusion. "That tells me something." A soft voice, not a ral-
lying cry. "I was going to contact you myself in a day or so."

"Why?"

"Time passes."

All at once it seemed, he was out of breath, but he hadn't
been running. He sat in one of the armchairs. "Maybe you
should open a window," he told the Russian. The air was
putrid, stale.

"I came here because you're in danger," he said. "That's
fact not conjecture. Your name's on a hit list. A reformist
group—extremists, more like. They're aiming to kill
you. . . ."

The Russian raised his hand dismissively. "It is of no
consequence. This I know. There have already been inci-
dents. What I have to tell you is more important." He rested
his elbows on the table. "You want something to drink, eat?"

Russert shook his head.

The Russian sniffed and wiped his nose on the back of his sleeve.

"My friend, this is a long story. We could talk all night, but I will make it short. And I will start with the ending. The whole process of reforms that we started is finished." He held up his right hand. "It's finished for us. Someone else may be able to handle it, but we can't. Look . . ." He rubbed his eyes. "We forgot our own lesson. In 1917 the Revolution was brutal and tremendously successful. This time, we thought, take it gently, step by step. Do it thoroughly, get the people with you. The result? No one is with us. Some say we go too fast, others—not fast enough. We please no one . . ." He spread out his hands. "So there you are, my friend—once again Russia has missed the boat. We tried and failed. Now there are plots and splits and killings. No one agrees on anything. And in the end the beloved men in uniform will take it all back and nothing will change for another sixty years. You don't agree? Just take a look at what is happening."

"You can't give up now."

"It's not we who give up. It's they. We were ready, we did all we could. They didn't want it. They give up . . ."

"For chrissake . . ." Russert got up and paced around the bare floorboards.

"My friend, let me put this more clearly. Mikhail must leave the country. He knows this. But he needs help. He doesn't wish to go to America, but only America can protect him. He wants to be left alone to pursue a private life. Not paraded like some dancing bear. No talk shows, no criticizing his country."

Russert sat down again. He spoke slowly and with difficulty. "I don't know . . . I just don't know. Maybe this is above me . . . I . . . I have no idea what the reaction would be . . ." He clawed at the air with both hands.

The Russian was watching him intently . . . "You have to sell the idea . . ."

"It may be better not to give them time to think . . ."

"How d'you mean?"

"Something like this would cause unbelievable panic in the White House. There'd be committees and consultations. With this President it could take a year to get any response at all . . ."

"We don't have a year."

Russert sat forward. "I know."

"Do any Western intelligence groups know what is going on?"

"For now," Russert told him, "the British are the best informed. And they handled the thing in Murmansk."

The envoy raised his head. "What about their Soviet contacts?"

Russert passed him a sheet of paper—a single name printed on it. "That's all I know. Maybe we should scare her off."

The Russian looked thoughtful.

His guest stood up. "Are you still flying the training missions?"

"It's the safest route we have."

"Then keep it open."

The envoy pointed a finger. "You keep it open. Do something about the British."

Before they left, the Russian found himself unexpectedly presented with a hand to shake. It seemed such a formal way to end such an informal encounter—even if it was the hand of the U.S. diplomat David Russert, stretching out to the General Secretary's envoy.

27

The base commander on Novaya Zemlya had moved back into his apartment, because his wife had moved out. She'd done more than slam the door. She had packed enough things to fill a suitcase and had then cried and whimpered her way onto the Thursday transport plane to Murmansk, with an onward connection to Kiev. Pinned to the kitchen wall was a note inviting him to insert his head where it was never meant to go, so he didn't expect her back.

But that wasn't the cause of his anger. It was the failure of the military radio operators to raise his friend at the Air Force Academy in Moscow. First the man was said to have been on holiday, then to have been transferred. Finally he was reliably reported to be having a bath. Such an important state occasion, his assistant implied, could hardly be disturbed.

The commander slammed down the phone and prepared to fly to Moscow.

It wasn't until he reached the capital that he remembered why he'd left. The dirt, the noise, the chaos at staff headquarters, and all the smiling, fawning mediocrities you could ever hope to meet. The problem, he reflected, was idleness. Promotion came slowly in peacetime. Only America ever seemed to go to war. And in Moscow you had no alternative but to wait for the officer above to die or be informed on—or else do it yourself.

It was some time before he could attend to business. First there was politics—a gift of caviar to the general, a bottle of vodka to his adjutant, some cans of shrimps here, a flower there—he felt like all the Soviet diplomats who returned from the West, obliged to shower their office with presents. They well knew that those who sit at home don't like those who go away. They become peevish and resentful and it's only the gifts that prevent them sharpening their stilettos and ramming them into your reputation, once you've shut the door. All this, the commander knew.

After an hour his jaw ached from smiling, and his back felt bruised from all the people who had slapped it, few enough of them in friendship. Inevitably there had been questions about his sudden appearance. Was he having hallucinations, had he screwed up, did he have designs on those delectable Eskimo dogs? Of course, he did, he told the grinning brigadier from Minsk—didn't everyone?

Midday found him over in his friend's office, exhausted and wishing he had never come.

"I'm very busy," the colonel told him in welcome.

"I know. I could never reach you on the phone."

"Difficult times." The colonel sighed. "Budgets are being cut all over the place."

The commander looked at his friend. His burgeoning gut showed no sign of economic stringency. On the contrary he looked redder in the face and more prosperous than ever before. Probably ripping off the *kommandantura* like everyone else, thought the commander. If they weren't buying guns, the money had to go on something.

"Well say what you've come to say." The colonel wouldn't even look up from his papers.

The commander didn't take long about it. As he pointed out, there wasn't much to say. The simple untrusting nature of the duty officer Valya Belayeva, the unexplained routine of a training flight from Moscow. And then the doubts, the risks, the implications if it were true. He wrung his hands. Maybe it did sound flimsy.

"Why should the man visit your base?" The colonel stood up. "After all there's nothing to see, and nothing ever happens." And then he sat down, for in his own mind he'd begun to answer the question, and he wanted to work it out.

In Russia you start backward. Always consider the consequences of failure before the benefits of success. And in this one the colonel didn't have much doubt: failure was too awful to contemplate.

When the commander had gone, he rang an internal number and then descended two flights of stairs. The door was unmarked, so was the man behind it. Tall, clean-shaven, immaculate—far too young, it would have seemed, to be a major in the GRU, Russia's military intelligence.

The two of them went down farther to the car pool and talked for about fifteen minutes. No one saw them. In any case it was known they were school friends. They often ate together in the canteen.

Which was where the colonel headed after the short discussion. He was much heartened. His GRU comrade had been sceptical, but had taken it seriously. Anyway, he reflected, the matter was now out of his hands and he could forget it.

Lunch that day was better than usual and so it was with a pleasant warmth in his stomach and a feeling of relief that he decided to enjoy a few moments in the sunshine.

It was only when a car drew up at the steps of the ministry, two guards emerging to grab him from both sides, pushing him roughly into the backseat, the vehicle already moving forward, that it struck him, his relief might have been premature.

The message came to Marcus, buried in a curt and argumentative telex from the newspaper. Why was he ordering new furniture? Why did he need a new bathroom? And in any case the estimates were too high. Shop around, it suggested. Get another quote.

Marcus read it a second time, his anger mounting, even when he realized what it was.

Typical for Foreign Office to hit the spot. For months Marcus had been disputing expenses with the Foreign Editor. But they never had a clue about Moscow. Shop around! The nearest shop was Helsinki. There were no choices. You paid what it took or got out of town. Moscow was not a bargain basement, despite the efforts of the newspaper to treat it as one. God, it made you sick! The editors all came out for the cocktail parties in the summer, stayed in hotels that had food and went to the embassy that offered hospitality. Looks fine to me, they all said. Can't see what the fuss is about. But then they didn't have to buy a loaf of bread or fasten a diaper!

And into all this, Foreign Office had the cheek to inject his own instructions.

Marcus took the telex back to the apartment. Doreen and Cressida were playing in the dining room. On the floor they had spread out at least a mile of Lego.

It was comforting that part of his life never changed. He took the little girl in his arms. Each time he looked at that smile, with the whole face engaged, the eyes and the heart, he could see the resemblance to Helen. But something, he realized, had changed. Cressida was no longer a link to the past. She was part of the future, part of a new life that would keep him in Moscow until he was blown or became worthless. A future that had nothing to do with Helen.

It was an hour before there was peace enough to decipher the code. He needed a dictionary for that. And when he'd finished Marcus didn't know whom to dislike most—the paper or Foreign Office.

He walked out into the courtyard to clear his head. Diplomats were leaving for dinner parties, reporters were returning to file their stories. The wealthy and privileged of

Moscow were on the move and he, Marcus, had his instructions.

Whatever you see, however unpleasant—keep out of it. And if anyone else tries to influence the course of events, you are authorized to stop them. In his mind he could picture the expression on Foreign Office's face as he would have drafted the message. What does "stop them" mean? he asked the face.

You know what it means, the face replied.

28

And one day, she thought to herself, this is how it will end. With no warning, no explanation, no one to go and see.

For the third day running the black Volga from the Foreign Ministry pool had failed to pick her up for work. The first morning Anastasiya had waited a half hour, the second ten minutes. Today just a glance from the upstairs window was enough to assure her that the chauffeured car was a thing of the past.

In Russia the little things have enormous importance. Tiny drops, her mother used to say, come from huge rivers. And so someone of extreme importance in an office way up high in the Gothic towers of the ministry had decided to clip her privileges. There would be no recourse.

She hadn't been consulted when the car was allocated, she wouldn't be consulted now that it was being withdrawn.

In the mirror she checked her curly red hair, the white formal daytime suit, the alligator brooch on her collar. She was far too well dressed for the area she lived in, but when you mixed with diplomats, you didn't turn up wearing a sack.

Anastasiya took a look along the street in both directions. Plenty of sacks that morning. It didn't give her a sense of superiority, but she couldn't help noticing envious glances from the women, the way some of them stuck their fingers under their noses as she went past, the dim, bovine inability to understand that not everyone needed to be the same: socialism didn't have to consist of dragging everyone down to the lowest and dirtiest. It could even attempt to raise them up to the best, show the people some standards, give them a reason to try.

At the bus stop the ancient, uncomprehending faces gave little cause for optimism.

The first bus was more like an overloaded delivery truck, so full that the doors could barely open. She caught a glimpse of agonized faces behind the dusty windows. Not a soul managed to squeeze on. And when the old tin box limped away, it was leaning crazily, its body low on the wheels, barely clearing the ground.

Thirty minutes later Anastasiya pushed her way on a bus. It was too bad about the suit. She was immediately shoved against a building worker, with a foul cigarette hanging from his mouth, but at least she was beside the window. Which is how she came to spot the presence of a gray Moskvich with four people inside that followed the bus all the way to her stop at the Kuznetsky Bridge.

When she emerged at lunchtime the car was outside the Foreign Ministry, but two of the passengers had gone. In the evening, soon after seven, the car was full again. Anastasiya decided to walk.

Many Russians know what it's like to be followed. For a long time, it seemed, their government did little else. Informers might be staff or part-time, might work weekends or nights, but there was no shortage of volunteers. Surveillance was part of the price you paid for an ordered society; and while on some days you could be the instrument of it, on others you might expect to become the victim. It no longer meant instant banishment, but it indicated at least passing official interest. You were warned.

These days, Anastasiya told herself, the interest might not be so transient. To carry out surveillance, the KGB now

had to show reasonable cause. And that meant much more
than an anonymous phone call, or the complaint of an angry
neighbor, or a chance conversation about politics on a train.
You needed the suspicion that national security was at stake.
And they didn't have time for jokers on that score.

As she walked back toward the bridge, the sun was descending over the other part of the city—and she was more
worried than she cared to admit.

On the second day the car returned with the same occupants. Anastasiya called Marcus from a public phone across
from the Foreign Ministry.

"Come to the office. There is to be an announcement
about Anglo-Soviet trade."

"You're very kind."

He was over within half an hour. She came down to the
foyer and led him to one of the meeting rooms, reserved for
foreign visitors.

"The microphones here are broken," she told him, as if it
were of no consequence. "I myself signed the order to repair
them."

Marcus drew in his breath.

She produced mineral water from a cabinet.

"This is the second day I have been followed, the second
day I have no official car. Upstairs my supervisor refuses to
return my calls. What does that tell you?"

"Nothing good." He perched on the table. "But it's very
crude. These days, if they have evidence against you they
pick you up, or they follow you discreetly. They certainly
don't advertise, like these guys in the car. I don't know what
to suggest . . . maybe it's your contacts with me."

Anastasiya shook her head.

"Why not?"

She smiled. "Because, my dear, I've been reporting on
you for months. They know all about our meetings . . .
about every meeting I have."

"Christ almighty, you never told me . . ." He got up, his eyes wide open.

"How d'you think I could go on seeing you the whole time? You imagine everything here has changed? Are you mad? We still have to report every single contact with a foreigner—particularly me! I have access to the General Secretary. I get to see God himself."

"Yes but . . ."

"Don't be naive, Marcus. This is still Russia. Okay? In Britain, they do the same, and they've never had communists. You should try to grow up."

He reached for a bottle of the mineral water, opened it, and drank it down.

"Then how do I know what the problem is? Something else must have happened. Maybe one of the Europeans is in trouble. Maybe there's someone you've come across who . . ." He stopped suddenly.

"What is it?"

He nodded. "Remember when you were getting out of the car the other night? You were going to that meeting. You said you'd had an unusual visitor."

"David Russert." She made a face. They both looked at each other. "I don't know. Why Russert? What difference would that make?"

"Can you think of anything else?"

She shook her head. She didn't want to think it. Didn't want to believe that she herself was the target.

Anastasiya had the good fortune to have a friend, who had another friend. She, Nina Alexeyevna, was senior records clerk in section four, the section that deals exclusively with the United States.

They met for coffee in the ninth floor canteen.

"I will take a look at the file, but you can't." Nina was helpful, but there was a price. "And you say you will have the tickets for *Spartacus* for Friday. Uh? Kremlin Palace?"

Anastasiya nodded.

Nina gleamed in anticipation. "You know it must be five years, no wait, six at least since I was there. *Swan Lake*. It was very disappointing. Half the corps de ballet had defected. The swans were like elephants. You never heard such a noise."

"His name is Russert. . . ."

"You afraid I forget?" She smiled, once again in a trance. "But to think of it! Baryshnikov back again in Moscow, dancing for us." She took a mouthful of sandwich. "Let's hope he is still fit. Uh?"

By mid-afternoon Anastasiya had received Nina's scribbled notes. She went to the rest room to read them. She scanned the first page. Really though! The woman was barely literate. And then there was all this drivel about his title in Washington and some wife he'd once had . . . it barely seemed worth the tickets. She sighed crossly. They'd been sent to her specially by the Swedish ambassador, who always made a point of smiling at her during receptions.

For a moment, she sat listening to the traffic far below, staring at a blank wall. Then she turned and read the last page of Nina's notes.

Russert, it seemed, had been an exchange student in Moscow, back in the fifties. Nothing unusual about that. Nina had quoted from the security check, done at the time. "High probability that subject is intelligence operative—but may have suspended activities temporarily." Anastasiya smiled. In those days they wrote that about everyone. She could feel the disappointment in the writing. Some oaf of a Stalinist had most likely followed the young Russert for months, learning nothing. He himself had probably faced punishment for incompetence. Thank God times had changed. If they had.

She went back to her desk and sifted papers. So Russert had been at Moscow University in the fifties and read Soviet law. Interesting time. He might even have studied under that

Grand Old Man of Soviet Justice: Igor Karpov, in and out of controversy for decades. Several government figures must have also been students at the time.

For a while she thought no more about it. But then she remembered the gray Moskvich outside and the worry returned. Maybe she should try another way. Maybe someone else could help. Anastasiya waited until everyone had left her office, then called the switchboard.

"Give me a home number for the lawyer Karpov. And try Moscow University as well. He still teaches from time to time."

She put down the receiver, not knowing what she had done.

Like many people of great learning, Karpov kept his own extensive library. He called it his reserve, his backup. But the bulk of his knowledge lay in the head he had carried into courtrooms for nearly sixty years. He had a voice so quiet and gentle they called him the "whisperer." He used to say it was his greatest asset. While his colleagues ranted and waved their hands and the judges stopped listening, Karpov would speak in a tone so barely audible, that everyone was forced to concentrate.

Once a week a car would take him from his apartment on the Lenin Hills and drive him the three hundred yards to Moscow University, where his office was maintained, along with his books, and a female assistant two years older than he was.

According to university legend they had last spoken to each other in the late seventies, but then mutual dislike had set in and created the perfect working atmosphere. Gone was the need for pleasantries, for silly birthday presents, for the ritual of office flirtation. When they had to communicate, they wrote notes.

"He's in there," the old woman pointed Anastasiya to a

warped gray door. "If he's asleep, wake him up. There's a lesson in half an hour."

Karpov did, indeed, appear to be sleeping. A head of full white hair had fallen forward onto his chest, as he sat painfully upright behind his desk, looking as if he were in church.

"Welcome, girl. Please sit down." The head rose. The voice was soft and provincial. Raised along the banks of the Don, she remembered reading. A Russian country gentleman. "I am certain that the creature out there did not think to offer you refreshment. In most offices assistants assist, mine however is a personal gift from the devil: just a foretaste of what is to come in the afterlife." He smiled, but the eyes were not laughing. "You will drink tea?"

He got up. Over by the fire he placed a kettle on the gas burner. "China tea." He held up a tea bag. "Old age has its compensations, and my friends are good to me."

She looked around the room: nothing to suggest it belonged to an old man, no piles of papers, no dusty files, everything clean and bright. For a moment they drank in silence. "We have never met," he told her, "why is it that I feel you have so much to tell me?"

It was Anastasiya's turn to smile. "I came because I wanted your help, maybe also your advice."

"I fear the world has moved on and I have not." He switched on his desk light.

"But you know the Russian people. They haven't changed, have they?"

"It's hard for me to say. The students who come here have so much more freedom than in the old days. They can say what they like. A boy of nineteen walked in here this morning, telling me the kinds of things that would have got him shot thirty years ago." He lifted his hands off the desk and put them back again. "My dear girl, there are so many who died for nothing. Sometimes I see their faces, sometimes I hear their voices. All sorts you know, big tough rebels, tough all through right to the end, others, frightened, withered, dying long before their executions. I . . . I wonder sometimes if this is the same country, the same planet. Is it possible that we could have practiced such cruelty?" A look of immense sadness came over his face. But then he smiled. "I don't know why we talk of these things. . . ."

"They are not so far away."

"Maybe not." The elderly eyes fixed hers, clear, strong eyes. You didn't want to face them for long.

"I work in the Foreign Ministry"—she stopped suddenly —"that's not why I came. I met a man, an American diplomat. He was a student here in the late fifties. Maybe he studied under you. I don't know why, but it could be important."

"His name?"

She told him.

Karpov said nothing. In the outer office Anastasiya could hear the old woman shouting at someone.

"Russert," he whispered. "The name is not familiar to me. But then I have forgotten so many. Wait, let's look in the books. No, they are in the other room. Let's see, 1959 was the year we had most foreign students. . . ."

There was a knock at the door. A young girl put her head round the door. "I am early, Igor Viktorovich. I'm sorry. I have to go to the doctor later."

"Then we must not keep the comrade doctor waiting."

Anastasiya stood up. So did Karpov. He took her hand.

"Why don't you come back tomorrow?"

"May I?"

He beamed at her. "I would strongly recommend it." Karpov leaned forward and grasped her hand, holding it for a few seconds, warmly, almost desperately, she felt, as if he thought it might be his last chance. "But you wanted advice," he remembered suddenly.

"Tomorrow," she told him. "Tomorrow."

29

Back at the base, he felt better. The Arctic air was clear after the summer stench of Moscow: all that cheap perfume, all the crowds, the chatter, the forced smiling.

And it was good to be on his own. "She" wouldn't be returning. And it was funny, he thought, but he couldn't remember any good times—although there must have been some—just the moaning and carping. Instead of building things together, they had simply gone through the years dismantling each other's hopes and dreams, each wishing the other were someone else. In the end both had admitted defeat. Finally the war was over.

The commander didn't dwell long on his broken marriage. After all, the supply officer from Murmansk was due that afternoon, and he had spent half the morning cleaning out the apartment. For once they wouldn't have to lock the office door and take the phone off the hook, they could do it in a decent, well more or less decent bed, and take their time.

From Moscow he had brought chocolates and a bottle of Crimean champagne. He hadn't had long to shop, but there'd been a turquoise necklace in a market near the staff headquarters and he'd bought that as well, so he'd win himself a few smiles. Maybe she could even arrange to get posted here with him . . . hold on, he thought, don't go too fast. It's only her body that's keeping you awake at night, don't let's get serious about this.

He chuckled to himself and left the office. Already two o'clock and the sun was weak and watery. Never much of a day in the Arctic, even in summer. Another month or so and the cold would set in, and then they'd be locked up again for seven months, staring at the radar screens, while peace broke out in the rest of the world.

But at least he'd done the right thing, he told himself. Even if his friend had looked at him as if he were mad.

The commander had nearly reached the main dome, when he turned back and looked at the runway. Above the wind noise he thought he heard the drone of a plane. Not the jet—it wasn't the trainer—and too early for the supply plane. He stared hard at the horizon, but could see nothing.

And if it was true? Were things really that bad in Moscow. Was the General Secretary hanging by his tail? He raised his eyebrows. Of course, he'd been brought up believing the leaders were like gods. Well they were, weren't they, waving down a couple of times a year from the Lenin Mausoleum . . . what had his friend in Moscow said? . . . it was time they went back to that, time for some discipline.

Inside the main control room there were a dozen officers hunched over their screens and computer terminals. He couldn't see their faces. The place was in almost total darkness. At the far end he nodded to the supervisor.

"All quiet?"

"Yes sir, just the two planes from Moscow."

He stopped. "What planes?"

"We sent the clearance to your office about ten minutes ago, sir . . ."

"I haven't been in my office." He felt the sweat on his hands.

The supervisor switched on a small jet of light beside his console and read from a printout. "Two transport planes, sir.

Notification came in about fifteen minutes ago. Security clearance. No facilities requested."

"When are they due?"

"Now, sir."

"Not much of a warning, uh?"

The commander went back outside. So he hadn't been mistaken after all. Coming out of the clouds around two thousand feet, he could see the giant dark-green Ilyushin turbo-props. Thundering great beasts, he thought, burning up far too much fuel, older than most of the pilots who flew them.

The planes must have been about fifty yards apart on landing. As they taxied toward the hangar the noise was deafening, the grass flattened beside the runway.

There had to be some kind of aerial exercise, he concluded. They'd asked for no facilities, no refueling. Once or twice over the last year air force planes had come in for no apparent reason—look at the trainer! Maybe it had to do with surveillance or evading radar. He hadn't asked. As long as the clearance arrived from Moscow, you sat tight and said nothing.

The commander stood still as the propellers wound to a halt. He couldn't see into the cockpit: there was probably a protective shield over the windshield. And then the hydraulic cargo doors began to open on both planes in unison.

Of course he hadn't known what to expect: probably a few troops, he thought. A commanding officer who would saunter over to pass the time of day. "Just dropped in, comrade," the usual kind of air force banter.

But even before the cargo ramp had hit the tarmac, he could hear the revving engines. Suddenly they were out in the open: sleek, new armored cars, with machine gun emplacements, troops in full combat gear, maybe a hundred of them. His mouth opened in amazement. A group of six engineers were sliding a surface to air launcher onto the runway. In seconds it seemed they had come together into a unit. Six rows of troops. Half a dozen vehicles. The whole operation quick and faultless.

A soldier with blackened face made his way toward him, issuing orders as he went. The commander noted his confidence, his bearing, the strong educated voice. This would be an elite force. But what were they doing here?

"Forgive the intrusion, commander."

"No intrusion, major. This is state property."

"I have sealed orders to give you. It would be as well if you read them now."

He drew an envelope from his combat uniform. The seal was from the Joint Chiefs in Moscow. Inside—a single sheet, six lines of typescript, four signatures.

He groaned inwardly. What had he done? Strangely enough in that moment all he could think about was the arrival of the supply officer from Murmansk that would have to be postponed and the bottle of wine in his refrigerator that wouldn't get drunk.

Vitaly flew with a stomachache. High over Russia a series of terrible spasms tore at him with ever-increasing intensity. He took a painkiller from the first aid box on the floor of the cockpit, but it didn't help.

After a few minutes he descended sharply to 27,000 feet. Maybe some excitement would take his mind off it. The move brought a query from Archangel Air control. "Why the acrobatics, comrade lieutenant?"

What was he supposed to do? It wasn't like going down the highway looking for a lavatory.

"I don't feel well," he told them.

"How bad?"

"Painful. Stomach."

"Can you make it to the base?"

"I'll try."

"Get some ice up your arse. That should do it."

"You're very kind." Vitaly shut off the radio and checked

the computer. Another forty minutes would do it. Maybe there was a portable latrine they could wheel onto the runway.

He came in very fast, anxious to escape from the cockpit as soon as possible, screaming down the runway toward the hangar.

Over the radio the voice sounded nervous. "Head toward the main building. Do not, repeat not, approach the hangar."

Inside the dome, a medical orderly was waiting for him.

"What are your symptoms?"

"I'll tell you in half an hour."

Vitaly emerged from the lavatory to find the doctor waiting for him, but he wasn't going to bother with an examination.

"Here are some pills. Enough to cork up an elephant." He looked him over. "Should be enough, even for you."

"Can I sit down somewhere for a while?"

"Sorry"—the doctor looked flushed, awkward—"you have to get out of here. There's some kind of classified mission expected through here, any minute, and they want you on your way."

"Terrific. Can I drink some tea?"

The doctor handed him a flask and a brown paper bag. "I'm sorry. Really." He turned to go. "By the way your friend wanted to see you, but she's not been allowed to leave her post. We're all kind of on alert today."

"Don't worry. I'm leaving. Have you all got the plague?"

The man grinned. "You're better off back in Moscow. If I could, I'd go with you."

As he took off Vitaly put his radio on search. If there were any classified transmissions he'd hear them, even if the set wouldn't decode. He flew slowly, carefully, taking a wide circular route that kept him in the area as long as possible.

If there'd been any classified flights around, he'd have heard them. But the airwaves were clear for at least two hundred miles. and his radar showed nothing in any direction.

*   *   *

The commander and the major watched him take off.

"You got your planes out just in time."

The soldier didn't answer.

"Your men . . . they all right in the hangar?"

"They'd be all right on the icepack. They're fighters. Keep them cold, keep them hungry, and they'll perform. They're not supposed to lie in baskets."

"How long are you going to stay?" The commander began walking back to his apartment. The supply flight was canceled. Only the trainer would be allowed in until the army gave its agreement.

"Until it happens." The soldier's face showed no expression. "If it happens."

30 _____

East of Moscow the darkness seemed complete.

"Does no one ever come here?" Russert peered over to where the envoy was sitting. The generator had failed. The gloom seemed to match their mood.

The Russian ignored the question, substituting his own. "You've done what we talked about?"

"Yes, but it doesn't seem worth it. Five more days and it'll be over. . . ."

"It'll just be beginning." The envoy lit a cigarette. It was the first time he'd smoked in more than a year. "Besides this is where the snowball starts rolling, and when that happens it makes waves, people see it, hear it, you can't avoid that. Already they've started asking questions about you . . . your past . . ."

"Let them."

"I can't. When you've worked so long, when there are so many details, you must watch them all. A tiny thing can tear the whole operation apart. You should know this."

Russert sat listless, toying with a pencil. "I should get back. I have another trip wire to pull." He slapped his hands on his knees. "You staying here?"

"It would be better to go somewhere else, but I have no choice. That's what happens in the final stages. The alternatives run out. Streets that you thought were long and wide become narrow alleys, large houses turn into cells, where there was freedom and unrestricted movement, you begin to feel trapped." He tapped his chest. "Believe me, this I know."

Igor Karpov discovered the first of the morning's shocks. He had taken one look at the sunshine and decided to walk to the university. Besides, the car was only booked for the normal one journey a week. It would have taken, he suspected, something approaching a parliamentary decree to order another.

Of course the girl was the reason to go in again. An unusual type, he reflected. Beautiful, certainly. But she had something else as well. Allure.

He walked slowly, coming out of the shade, pausing on the wide balustrade that overlooks the city: the tourist trap, the place of pilgrimage for the newly marrieds.

The girl might have been married, but he doubted it. She had about her an unattainable quality: never belonging, never committing, giving her time, but not herself, holding the key deep down and out of sight—and not just one key. She would change and change again and when she was old, she would sit down in a park much like this one and ask herself: Who was I? How could I do the things I did?

All this Karpov saw in her as he stared out over Moscow.

In the corridor of the Law Faculty, he nodded at his assistant, surprised that she was almost running—and were those tears in her eyes? He didn't really stop to consider it: after all he had disliked her for years. But for a second he turned and watched the elderly bundle scuttling away on the lino, and raised an eyebrow.

He opened the door to the outer office and halted in mid-step, unsure where to focus his eyes. The scene was of the kind of chaos he had never witnessed at close quarters. Bookshelves pulled from the walls, files torn open and scattered, pictures strewn on the floor.

Karpov took a step back into the corridor and leaned

against the wall, breathing heavily. When he was younger he had coped with much worse—threats, robbery, physical harassment, standard fare during the Stalinist years—but now it seemed hard to grasp. And suddenly he didn't feel so well, or so confident, and the strength in his elderly legs must have filtered away. For he slid gently down onto the floor, unable to stop himself, unable to rise.

In which position, anxious and afraid, Anastasiya discovered him.

She led him outside and they sat on the well-tended grass strip, the pride and showpiece of the state university. A gentle sun and a cool breeze. For several minutes neither of them spoke.

Karpov opened his mouth but checked himself. "What does it matter?" He shook his head. "You asked me yesterday about the Russian character." He laughed without humor. "You were right: it doesn't change. Now—even now. We are capable of the utmost barbarity. No, worse than that—stupidity—actions without sense or justification."

"Why do you say 'we'?"

"We are all responsible. All of us, myself included. We allowed the thugs to hold on to power for so many years. We acquiesced, we were silent. We refused to admit that the revolution had taken away one corrupt regime and replaced it with another. Already in the party, they are questioning the legality of the Bolsheviks, Lenin as well. How long before they burn the whole edifice to the ground? Ahh!" He shut his eyes. "I'm tired of it. I have lived too long and now I don't want to see anymore."

Anastasiya could see his hands shaking. She helped him to his feet. "I'll walk you to your apartment. You should rest. You've had a shock."

The old man smiled, the color returning to his cheeks. "Shocks are good for me. You want me to die of boredom?"

She took his arm, a gesture so warm and so natural that

they might have been father and daughter, drinking in the sun after breakfast.

Anastasiya turned to face him. "Igor Viktorovich . . . in the old days, the fifties—it must have been so hard for a lawyer. Were you not afraid they would come for you? How did you manage to avoid being shot?"

"Simple, my dear. The lawyers were the lucky ones and you know why. They were trying each other and killing each other so rapidly, none of them knew when they might need our services. We were the untouchables. One day we defended the oppressed, the next day the oppressors. Like most tragedy, there was an element of farce in it. We were the narrators, the prompters in each terrible production."

They reached the entrance to the block. It was new, but better finished than its suburban counterparts. Trees and shrubs decorated the front garden. The privileged lived here, she thought, the elite, both ancient and modern.

"You will come up with me. A glass of tea?"

Anastasiya shook her head. "I have taken too much of your time."

Karpov moved closer as if he were about to kiss her.

"My dear, the American that worries you, must indeed be an interesting man. I have searched my memory to think who he might be. There were several American students in the fifties. I taught them myself, but none of them sticks in my mind. I remember"—he chuckled—"we thought they were very unserious, frivolous people."

She shook his hand.

"It may be nothing at all"—Karpov's voice got quieter—"but our present General Secretary is supposed to have shared a room with an American student, when he studied law. You know all the foreigners here were allocated minders, party members, agitators to discover their opinions and then influence them. I have no idea if this is the same man." He winked at her and returned her hand. "But the attention lavished last night on my office may perhaps tell you something. Good-bye, my dear."

She watched him shuffle through the main gate. Inside the hall he turned for a moment to wave. In that moment he made up his mind that he would not go again to the university.

31

For the third time that day the telephone went dead when Marcus answered. The fourth time he was treated to standard sixties provocation.

"All Western correspondents are filth," announced the disjointed voice. "What you say about that?"

"I agree," Marcus replied equably and put down the receiver.

It rang again thirty seconds later. A deep female voice dripped with sexual melodrama.

"You don't remember me, darling?"

"Tell me your name and I might."

"Maybe my husband can remind you. He very much wants to speak to you about the things that we did. He's very angry . . ."

And so it continued. By the eighth call Marcus had stopped answering. By the ninth he had pulled the socket from the wall.

He sat down in the sitting room and put on a folk record for the benefit of the microphones.

Maybe it was his day for petty harassment. Maybe his name had simply fallen from the hat. Screw Marcus. The word had gone out to the little men with the sallow complexions and sweaty palms. Too much indoor work, too much time at the keyholes. But now it's Marcus's turn. Have fun. Make a day of it.

And yet that didn't seem likely. Much *more* likely, they wanted to see if they could upset him, and if they could, what would he do next.

Good on the one hand, because they don't yet have a case, or they'd move in. Bad because they think they'll get one. Otherwise they'd be off annoying someone else.

The little straws of doubt that blow in on Soviet winds.

It was enough to make him go downstairs to check on Cressida. She wasn't in the courtyard. Nor was Doreen. He could feel his temperature rising.

"They went food shopping at the Gastronom," a nanny called out.

"D'you know which one?"

"Trade Center, I think." The girl smiled. She couldn't have been more than sixteen.

He took the office Zhiguli. And now they've done it, haven't they? Forced your hand, unnerved you. Didn't take much, did it?

It was coming up to midday. Traffic was heavy. The Ring jammed as ever, all the way to the underpass. He turned off and took the side roads through the Arbat. Moscow old and yellow-ochre, from the days when they built real houses for people with names.

He found a space right outside the center, but he couldn't see the Volvo, not the green one with the child seat and the stickers on the rear window. Cressida's work. Life's early achievements.

Running now, because you just want to make sure—and he rounded the swinging doors and all but fell into Doreen's bags, weighed down with fish and imported orange juice, and the big chunky bars of Toblerone—almost as old and hard as the Swiss mountains.

Marcus laughed and leaned against the wall, trying to get his breath back. "I was wondering where you were."

"Why?" Doreen rough and abrupt. Was her conduct in question?

"Oh nothing really. Nothing at all."

"Good. You could help me then with these bags."

He smiled. Cheeky kid. But she was all right. They both were. Maybe it had been nothing at all.

32 _____

The procedure for arresting a foreigner in the Soviet Union is complicated and time-consuming. Mostly the matter is referred by the KGB to the Politburo or a secretary of the central committee. There the international implications are weighed and decided.

By that time the file has grown fat and heavy, passing as it does through several government departments for comments and suggestions. Harsh and ruthless as it may be, the Soviet security machine is seldom slapdash or arbitrary. They don't just build cases: they cement them.

The second European department of the Foreign Ministry has, in its time, reviewed the arrest warrants for five people. It was required to open its own files on the citizens in question and to supply information, acquired through its own sources. No detail is considered too trivial or irrelevant: attendance at parties, behavior at parties, habits on weekends, sex on weekends (or other times), styles of dress, foreign friends . . . the list goes on and on. And someone has observed it all.

Hour by hour the warrant to arrest Marcus was gathering momentum. It didn't just come to an office and lie there waiting for a stamp. It was taken by a KGB messenger from destination to destination. It never left his sight.

Without any hesitation Anastasiya knew who the man

was and what he was bringing. That "I-am-charged-with-authority" look had been cloned and cultivated by the KGB for years. This fellow must have been in his forties, pushy, sweaty, the world of ordinary mortals laid out at his feet.

"All you have to do is read the summary and sign." He pushed the file toward her. "Although it won't teach you anything new, will it?"

And how do you contain your shock, when you see the name there, the man they've tailed, the man they've watched, fact piled on fact. Black and white and clinical. Your own reports in there as well. And yet nothing here should surprise you. Nothing! Somewhere in the haze a distant half-memory clawed its way to the surface. She pushed the file back to the messenger.

"If I have questions, I don't have to sign."

"Just sign it. Everyone else has."

"I'm going to read it first. . . ."

"I'll have to report that you decided this on your own."

"Wonderful, but as the representative of the Foreign Ministry I have the right to ask for further details, even to question a witness . . ."

"Believe me, this is not necessary."

She inclined her head, but her eyes bored into him. "Believe me," she replied, "it is."

As she read, the scope of the investigation appalled her. But there were gaps. Even now, she noted, they had relied on the evidence of an unnamed informer, although the Foreign Ministry had given some circumstantial evidence.

It was Marcus's trip to Murmansk that had been dissected: lists of everyone he'd seen and talked to, travel arrangements, hotel bills, a conversation with a waitress. She gasped. The detail was extraordinary. A separate folder contained notes from one of the Foreign Ministry press spokesmen: Yuri, something or other. The signature was difficult to decipher.

Anastasiya knew how to work the bureaucracy, how you

can play one level off against another, how you can trap it in its own procedures, slow it, divert it, make it serve. She pushed the file back to the messenger and pointed to Yuri's name. "I want to see this man, immediately."

It took nearly an hour to find Yuri. Yuri hadn't much wanted to be found. He had left work at midday, complaining of headaches, and had chosen to say nothing about the shame and disappointment that drove him to his one-room apartment off Prospekt Mira. There he pulled the curtains, lay down on his bed, and tried to forget he was a Russian in Russia.

Not, of course, that he had been offered a choice. It's when they take you into an anteroom at the press department: three of them, sit you down with your file, tell you what you could do with your life, and would do—if only you did your duty first.

Three of them from the old days.

All about Murmansk, wasn't it?

"But we've been through that," he told them.

"Let's go through it again."

Only this time it was different. The nice English journalist. You know the one. You saw him leave the hotel that night, saw him slip and sneak his way around the streets, saw him head for the football field, saw him wait for a rendezvous, saw him retrieve a message, saw him carrying out the duties of the foreign spy *you* always knew he was. Didn't you?

A sheet of paper was pushed in front of him.

"You saw it—so sign it."

And he had looked around at the cheap plastic furniture, the cheap carpet, the cheap suits of the men gazing down at him. Yuri felt just as cheap as he signed the paper, knowing full well he had seen nothing at all.

*   *   *

They brought him to Anastasiya's office, dressed in a hurry, his mind, like his hair, wild, standing up in all directions. Not another prosecutor, he thought.

She wasn't what he'd expected. Cool, professional, competent. Not a desperate, back-watching apparatchik. She was the new breed. Yuri took in her makeup, the long painted fingernails, the denim dress.

She didn't greet him, didn't offer him a seat, but he took one anyway.

"I've read your declaration." She pushed it across the desk to him. "There are no times, no observations, just . . . 'He went there and did that and came back . . .' How did you happen to see all this?"

Yuri hadn't expected questions like that. Who was the woman? How much power did she have? The KGB messenger seemed to answer the question for him. "Tell her," he said, "tell her the way you told us."

She flashed him an angry glance. "Quiet. This is my office. If I could have you thrown out, I would."

Yuri's eyes traveled from one to the other.

She turned back to him. "What sort of night was this—when you saw the events you describe?"

"Dark, cold."

"How unusual. Many people on the streets?"

"A few."

"What's a few? Ten, twenty, fifty?"

"I don't remember." Yuri felt his face reddening. "Ten maybe."

"You know Murmansk, do you?"

"No. That was my first visit."

"And yet you followed a foreign journalist through the streets, and then hurried back to the hotel, without losing your way?"

"I had to ask someone . . ."

"Who?"

"I'm not sure . . ."

"Man, woman, child . . ."

"Man, I think. Look . . ." he swung his head around to look at the messenger. "These questions I have answered already."

"You have answered nothing," Anastasiya told him. "Go back to the beginning. What made you follow this man into the streets?"

"I was in my room. I heard a noise outside. I saw the British journalist going down the stairs and thought it was my duty to follow."

Anastasiya took a guess. "But your room was on a different floor."

Yuri looked as if someone had stabbed him. "I . . . I had been drinking in another room with some of the journalists . . ."

"But you said you were in your room."

"Look, I may have been confused. I have headaches . . . I'm not well."

"I can see that. Answer one question. Why has it taken you all this time to report the incident?"

"I thought it would look bad for me. I was the one who organized the trip. But in the end"—his voice was a whisper—"my conscience . . ."

"You did the right thing, comrade," the KGB man interrupted.

Anastasiya ignored him. "Your conscience," she told Yuri. "Your conscience—you don't know what that is." She looked at him sadly. "Get out of here."

The messenger stood up.

"Ready to sign now, comrade?"

She laughed without humor.

"I'm ready for nothing, comrade," she mimicked the last word. "Bring your file back here this afternoon and I will read it again to see if there is even the tiniest grain of truth. And then we shall see whether I sign a paper against this

Englishman"—she looked at him and raised her eyebrows—
"or against you."

In the canteen she found Nina Alexeyevna staring out of
the window, a plate of cheese and salami in front of her, a
half-eaten cucumber in her hand.

"I was just thinking of the performance," she turned
wistfully. "In my life I have never seen anything quite like it.
You know, the audience and the artistes . . . I would not
have missed it."

Anastasiya fetched a glass of tea.

"I'm going to give you an envelope. Nina—listen to me."
The woman faced her. "You have to take this to the foreigners building on Kutuzovsky Prospekt. Deliver it to a man
there. The name and apartment number are written down."

Nina emerged from her trance. "Now I know you are
mad." She sat up stiffly. "I shall do no such thing. A file, well
that is one thing. Of course that is just communication between departments, right and proper, but what you ask now
is quite impossible." She pushed her plate away.

Anastasiya caught her arm. "It is not impossible. It's vital."

"I can't."

"You must, Nina. If there was any other way I would not
ask it of you—but there's a note in my bag that gives details
of our arrangement. If I have to I will send it . . ."

"This is outrageous . . ." Nina Alexeyevna looked dizzy.
She turned around to make sure no one had heard her. "Why
are you doing this to me?"

"My dear, I'm so sorry. I did not wish it, but you have to
take the letter. Now. There is no other way. Believe me: this
is not against our country." She softened her grip. "We will
laugh about it in weeks to come."

Nina looked unconvinced. "You had better get me some
more tickets to the ballet," she said tartly. "I fancy the Bolshoi next time."

* * *

Marcus discovered the letter when he came in from the courtyard. He had been playing with Cressida and needed a drink. In the mid-afternoon heat someone had set up a splash pool and she would stay there until the water had gone.

The blue envelope lay on the mat, pushed under the door. It was odd. Normally mail was shoved into the box downstairs. He took it through to the sitting room and tore it open.

And then for the first time in his life—he surprised himself. It was really just a question of making your decision and carrying it through—fast. He looked for a pullover for the little girl, took all the money he could find from his desk, and put it in Doreen's handbag.

Then he descended in the elevator, with the objects in a shopping bag.

"Let's go out for a drive," he told the nanny. "I brought your bag. You can get us some ice cream."

Doreen made a face. "Do we have to? Cress is pretty settled now. She'll have to go to bed quite soon anyway."

"No, it'll be fun," he told her. "Get a bit of fresh air."

They bundled the protesting, crying girl into the Volvo's child seat, put the windows down and headed onto the wide, crowded avenue.

"Listen," he told Doreen, "you're leaving now. I'm driving you to the airport with Cress and you're getting on the BA flight to London."

She was speechless. Even the baby stopped crying.

"I'm sorry about this. I can't even explain. When you get to the other end go to my mother in Hatfield—you've got the number—and stay there."

Doreen tried to say something.

"Look, I'll send on your things as soon as I can. Meanwhile buy anything you want. D'you have a credit card?"

"Yeah, but it's only got a hundred-pound maximum." Finally the trivial had brought back Doreen's voice. "But I don't get this. I mean I live here. You can't just pick me up and chuck me out. I . . . is this a game or something? And what about her?"

"She goes with you. I know . . . I know . . . it makes no sense at all. But just accept it—please. You have to get out of here. It's a question of your safety: that's all I can tell you."

At Sheremyetyevo Airport, he bought the tickets, and took the little girl in his arms. Don't make a scene, he thought. Don't attract attention. Just get them through customs and immigration and out of the bloody place.

She smiled at him. In a month or two she'd be speaking. In a year or two she'd ask questions. Would there ever come a time, he wondered, when she'd want to know what the hell was going on that hot June day in Moscow?

The BA manager was by the desk. "Make sure they get on, will you?" he told him. "Bit last minute. Sorry."

The man nodded. He didn't ever ask questions. It's why he had survived in the job for so long.

"Wait here," he told Marcus. "I'll be back when the thing's gone. About forty minutes."

He returned in just over twenty. "No problem." He smiled. "The kid was laughing all the way to Club Class. Flight's just taken off early. Relax."

Relax, Marcus repeated, as he drove back into the city. When am I going to do that? He'd traveled half the distance before he remembered he couldn't go home.

Yuri lay on the bed, knowing he wouldn't sleep. They'd brought him back, not saying a word, no threats, no promises—just silence. The weapon of Old Russia. We'll find you when we want you, it said, more eloquent, more pointed than any words.

I thought we'd left all that behind, said a voice inside him. I thought we had a chance. I thought there was a life to look forward to, instead of just years to survive. All my child-hood we had nothing, and still had to pay.

He got up and went to the window. The evening traffic was sparse: the grand boulevard half-lit, dim and dusty six stories below.

His head began to hurt and he went into the bathroom. In among the old razor blades and shaving brushes he found a bottle his mother had got from the doctor three years be-fore. Heart pills. She had died before she could take any—and, well, you never threw anything away. Not in Russia where bodies scarcely went cold before you divided up the leftovers in the ritual family bazaar.

He remembered the ghastly scene. Chairs to cousin Ivan, cutlery to the nephews, plates and a picture to Natalya who was getting married, carpet to mother's long time "friend" who was the only one who refused. And he, Yuri, had got the photographs and the pills.

He emptied them into his hand—old now, useless and probably only aspirin. That's all the doctors had anyway—lies and aspirin, Russia's diet over the decades.

Yuri sat on the bed and thought about the days ahead: and then the fear hit him, and fear is all right if you can share it—but his life was pretty empty of friends, and the family didn't ever visit. He thought of work: the cutthroat little office and the news conferences—Soviet truth offered up to the world like a lousy meal. And in a day or a month or a year, the three would be back again, wheeling him into the anteroom, listing his deficiencies or asking for something else.

Marcus. He shook his head and said the name aloud. Was he already under arrest? What had he ever done? Maybe the woman could help him. But what if she couldn't? Would the Englishman go to jail because he, Yuri Khaldin, had lied? What about the man's family? Oh God, didn't he have a child, and a wife and relatives to cry over him? He wrung his hands in desperation and moaned into his pillow.

Something told Yuri that he should get out of the apartment, breathe the outside world: but he hadn't the strength to
move. How easily you can shut out the rest of your life, he
realized. When it comes down to it there's really just you and
the room—nothing else. You and the white walls that don't
offer excuses and don't accept them. All the friends you once
had and the family that brought you up are suddenly part of
another life—past or pretended—now inaccessible. There's
really only this room, and when you've had enough of it, you
have to go.

And it wasn't, perhaps, a conscious gesture, looking at
the pills from mother's bottle. But if you were going to take
two or three, you might as well take them all, since they were
only aspirin—and God alone knew where you'd get any more
in Moscow.

For a few minutes afterward he lay on the bed feeling
nothing at all. It was only when the light dimmed and a steel
girder seemed to descend onto his chest that he knew what
was happening. Even then he could have got to the telephone, a foot away, and called for help—but the fact was that
he really didn't want to. Not now, not during the night, not
when he had the prospect of peace and stillness for the first
time in so many years.

Anastasiya held the file for as long as she could. It was
long after the rest of the office had gone home and the messenger had lapsed into sullen silence and the office reeked of
his cigarettes.

Even after she'd read it through three times, she couldn't
fathom the source of the information. The bulk of it seemed
plausible, perhaps even likely. But where had it come from?
Not Yuri. He wouldn't even get accepted for street theater on
the Arbat.

She took out a pen, initialed the page, stamped it with
her own personal imprint, and pushed it over to the messenger.

"The whole thing stinks," she told him.

It was nearly nine o'clock, long after the last plane to the West had left—and if Marcus had wanted to get away, he'd had the best chance she could give him.

33

First sunlight, then shadow, then darkness, and under the branches of the cedar tree they had gathered up the tartan travel blanket and taken the little girl inside. Marcus's mother, trailed by a quieter and sadder Doreen in borrowed clothes.

Together they bathed Cressida and put her into Marcus's bed. "Bit rough and ready," the old lady whispered, "but it'll do for a couple of days. 'Spect my son'll be home by then, and we'll know what's what." She smiled comfortingly in the certain knowledge of a safe and ordered world.

They put trays on their knees, piled high with defrosted chicken dinners, and watched television and tried not to think of Moscow.

Only later did Marcus's mother forget they had already covered the subject.

"My dear, did he not say anything about where he was going?"

And Doreen, cross anyway, now thinking she wasn't believed, tired and brittle after the journey.

"I told you, didn't I?" Words harshly delivered. And the son's mother sat, so light and so frail in front of the television, not seeing or hearing, only imagining darkness and dread.

In the end the thoughts became sounds, whispers at first,

then sentences, not caring if Doreen was there. "I expect that man from London will come and visit, you know the young one with glasses, who came before." She poured herself a glass of sherry. "Would you like one, my dear?"

"I'm going to bed." Doreen stood up. "I was invited to a dance tomorrow at the Canadian Embassy," she said lamely.

"I know, dear, I know."

"I haven't got any clothes," Doreen added, almost accusingly.

"We'll go into Hatfield in the morning, find some things for both of you. It'll be all right. I know it will."

On her own she sat for a long time, reliving little sections of Marcus, his days at school, a prize-giving, a holiday by the sea: the patchwork of a childhood, with a mother as comforter, friend, player, and guide, through the clouds and the sunlight of ten thousand days. Marcus, where are you tonight? Be safe my son, take care my son, go well. Far away she could see a sports day at his old school and Marcus running way out ahead of all the others: she at the finishing line, willing him on, striving for him, the way she did now.

We'll get you home, Marcus, somehow we'll get you home.

She was climbing the stairs to bed, when she heard the knocking, knowing it was Foreign Office. But he might have come earlier, and might have called in advance. It was pretty rude even by his standards.

She hurried to the front door and pulled it wide open, scared suddenly because it wasn't Foreign Office at all, not even someone who looked like him. Altogether a different type.

If you don't make it, the note had said, if something goes wrong . . . and she had chosen a meeting at one of the most crowded subways: Revolution Square, right up against the Kremlin, full of tourists and first impressions.

He had left the car, way out to the north, past the television tower at Ostankino. A bus took him back into the city.

At least he'd got them out: Cressida and Doreen. Done his duty. And you could have gone too, he realized. Think about it, Marcus. Better still—don't think about it.

Anastasiya had said after eleven. He sauntered toward the exit by the National Hotel. A group of teenagers were catcalling, two of them had guitars on their backs, much joking and horseplay, the crowd looking on bemused. You could see they were still puzzled by freedom, still expecting the police to muscle in and spoil the fun, to send them all back in a box to the bad old days.

And somehow she had fallen in beside him, taking his arm, just above the elbow, locking him to her, as she always did.

"Beautiful night." Her eyes were shining with relief. A group in dinner jackets were on their way to a reception. Marcus had lost count of those drink-in-hand, talk-about-nothing events that he'd attended. Russia had always spread around its champagne and caviar for the foreigners. In the past it was to cover up the problems, now it was to seek help for them.

"This way." She led him along the north side of the square toward the Lenin Library. "We can walk, we're not in a hurry."

"What d'you mean? I've got nowhere to go . . ."

"Don't be silly, Marcus. I'm taking you somewhere. Besides I'm going there myself."

Suddenly all the questions seemed to come at him. They sat on the steps of the library, the gray stone edifice with its pillars like sentries.

"How did you lose your friends in the Moskvich?"

She looked tired suddenly, running a hand through her thick hair. "I think they're just for show. I went out one of the side entrances, and there was no one in sight. They were not serious."

He looked at her quizzically. "Everything is serious. Somewhere there's a reason."

She took his hand. "Your baby—she got out okay?"

He nodded. "So what was it then? What was the danger?"

She was looking at the ground, saying nothing.

"I have to know."

She breathed in deeply. "It's Murmansk. The trip you had there back in the spring. They've put a case together, saying you were involved in an intelligence operation that went wrong. They got the Foreign Ministry press man to make up some nonsense about you"—she waved her hand dismissively—"but the truth is that something happened that night—and you looked as though you might be involved." She squeezed the hand. "You weren't, were you?"

"What do you think?"

She looked at him sharply. "Don't play games with me, Marcus. You're a foreigner. In the end you can go. But I live here. I've already gone too far. I risked a lot to hold up the arrest warrant. So when I ask you a question like that, I want an answer."

"I wasn't involved."

She didn't respond, simply shut her eyes for a moment, as a light breeze came up, raising the dust and the candy wrappers, ruffling the trees beside the Kremlin wall. It seemed to revive her.

"Come on, we can go now."

For a moment, Marcus let go Anastasiya's hand. It surprised him how easily he could deceive her, when the choice came, when it seemed like the thing to do. Till now there had been no lies, no half truths. In this relationship, for the first time in his life, he had wanted to be honest and open. He of all people. He with his two lives, feeding and distorting each other for nearly a decade. Honest! He wasn't even sure any longer what it meant. And yet, he told himself, if it came to a choice again, he'd tell her the truth.

* * *

"You don't know me. I'm a friend of your son."

Confusion on her face, but he knew he had pushed the only button that would get him inside. They stood for a moment awkwardly in the hall.

It was strange, he thought, how British reserve and shyness made him feel ill at ease.

She showed him into the drawing room. "Forgive me, Mr. . . . You're American, aren't you?"

He nodded. "Harry Fox. I'm sorry, I should have said. I work on the Foreign Desk. Live just down the road."

She gestured to an easy chair.

"Excuse me for visiting so late, but have you heard from Marcus in the last few hours? We're a little concerned. He was supposed to have been in contact about a story. And it's a couple of days now, since we heard anything . . ." He looked up from the carpet, unsure what else to say. There was really no nice way of doing this.

"Why should he contact me? He's a grown boy." The old lady smiled. "Mr. Fox, I regret I can't help."

"May I ask when you spoke to him last?"

"Let me see . . . it would be last week sometime. Tuesday perhaps."

"I see." Harry Fox got up. "If he calls please ask him to contact us urgently. I know you will."

They went into the hall. From upstairs he thought he heard a noise. The old lady had caught it as well. She turned, embarrassed. "Please show yourself out, Mr. Fox."

"You've been very kind."

She took a look at the small suntanned face, the uncreased gray suit and thought how unlike most other journalists he was.

Harry Fox pulled the door shut, smiling. He hadn't got all he wanted, but he had heard the child. So Marcus had sent the little girl out. Russert had been right after all. The Englishman was bent.

* * *

Half Moscow seemed to have taken to the streets. Even though the sunshine had gone, the warmth had remained behind. Children were out late, dancing around the feet of their parents. In the shadows the giant water-bearing trucks lined up to spray the streets and bring order and discipline to the hours of night.

They crossed the square in front of the Borovitsky Gate and walked along the river, away from the Kremlin. To the right a maze of side streets, low white houses squashed on top of one another, the homes of former noblemen, now divided into communal apartments.

Anastasiya led them into a cul-de-sac that had no street-lamps. A wooden door creaked open and they were descending two or three steps to a hallway. Still no light but she knew her way. Sure-footed, he thought, this daytime diplomat.

Only when the door opened did Marcus realize the building contained life. For a second, half a face appeared and then a hand seemed to sweep them inside, closing the door rapidly. Marcus was instantly aware of the dimmest lighting, a wall covered in dark oil paintings and icons, the sound of a violin from another room and a young figure pale and blond, a man no more than twenty-five, looking, oddly enough, as if he had found something hugely funny to laugh about.

For a moment Anastasiya clung silently to the man, not in passion, but as if she were seeking to share his strength.

They moved farther into the darkened room. The man held out his hand to Marcus. "I'm an old friend," he said. Marcus could feel the steel in that grasp. A practiced hand, confident, well used. The kind of hand you would want on your side.

The three of them sat awkwardly on a chaise longue.

"Can we talk?" The Russian waved a hand in the direction of Marcus.

"Of course." Anastasiya dismissed the question, delving a hand into her bag. "Here: your papers, money, a ticket."

The young eyes took it all in, but he didn't check, just shoved the pile into a breast pocket. He smiled again, as if to say it looked right, felt right, everything in order. To Marcus, he seemed like a man who could make quick decisions.

"You will have something to eat." The Russian got to his feet. "Not my place, of course, but they left things in the refrigerator. Considerate, I'd call it. There's beer too."

"Not for us . . ." Anastasiya pointed a finger, "and not for you either. No drink, I said that before . . ."

"You worry too much."

"And you don't worry enough." She rose to her feet. "I should get going . . ."

Marcus touched her arm. "Where to?"

"Home, Marcus, where else, what did you think? You stay here. Our friend"—her eyes glanced toward the fair-haired Russian—"our friend is a soldier. Only now he's our soldier. You'll be in good hands. He may come and go, may appear and disappear, but you have no reason to fear him. Am I right, Mr. Soldier?"

The man grinned and tapped his inside pocket. He was examining the paintings and icons along the walls. Maybe it was show, but he seemed alive, interested in his surroundings. The eyes were quick and intelligent.

Anastasiya pulled Marcus into the hallway. She was whispering. "You'll be okay here. We'll move again in the morning. I trust this man. Don't ask why but I do." And she kissed him suddenly, a rare gesture to come so quickly and with such intensity. And it seemed to Marcus that his heart rose up to meet her, just as she slipped through his grasp, found the door and vanished through it.

As ever, she had taken both questions and answers with her, handling neither.

For a long time Marcus sat up, talking to the young man.

A photographer, the Russian said, breaking out from the happy snaps of the seventies and early eighties, trying his

lens on the unfortunates, the cripples, the no-hopers of Soviet society, pushed out of sight for so many years.

"In the old days I photographed one country and lived in
another." He poured vodka from a fresh bottle. "In my pictures, smiling faces, flowers, beautiful babies, and works of
art. On the streets lines, trucks, drunks with their trousers
hanging open, tears and hardship. I used to ask myself—
where am I? I must have been very creative."

"And now?"

"Now, everyone is crying and it isn't just the drunks with
open trousers."

He laughed, but it died quickly. "Maybe we sleep now.
Who knows? Maybe we just give it try."

But Marcus wasn't tired. Too much adrenaline had fed
its way around his system. "Why did she call you a soldier? Is
it a propaganda war? Do you keep photographic records? Do
you document the daily events?"

"Really, my friend," the man looked away. "You don't
want to know."

"No, but I do. It'd be interesting. You see I'm a . . . I
mean I used to work as a journalist."

The man wouldn't turn around and his voice was barely
more than a whisper.

"If you really want to know—the day after tomorrow—I
kill someone."

34

The envoy put down the cardboard box and stowed it in the corner of the sitting room.

"What's that?" Russert looked anxious.

"He won't leave without it. Some pictures, books, personal things that belong to the family. He doesn't want them to be found and ridiculed by those who come afterward."

"I can understand that."

"I'm surprised." The envoy began checking through cupboards. "You Americans have not had to live like this."

"We've had our civil war . . ."

"Yes, and now it is all so"—the Russian seemed to search for a word—"so secure. You know even when things looked stable in our country, it was chaos. Take the years of Brezhnev. You know why nothing was done? They couldn't agree on anything. The same time the newspapers were talking about the complete unanimity of views of the leadership, they were shouting at each other and slapping faces inside the Kremlin. Boys in school. Stupid boys too, with no ideas, no skills—just more ruthless, better manipulators than all the others." He laughed without humor. "Sometimes all they talked about was Western cars, Mikhail told me this; which model was faster, how big were the engines, how they got them into the country and kept them secret. Brezhnev and his sports cars!" He snorted with derision. "He was so senile he couldn't get into them, and if he did he wouldn't have known how to turn on the engine. What a spectacle!"

They tried some packages of soup, dried raisins, bread that tasted of cardboard. Army rations. Foul but edible. The little flat had begun to fill with the mechanics of transit. Piles of clothes had been laid out on chairs, there were maps and other documents, forms and passports, envelopes with foreign currency. A crate that Russert knew to contain small arms and ammunition had been laid in the bath.

He whistled softly. "You've been busy."

The Russian shrugged. "Not just me. You seem to have done as much." He sat at the table. "They were apparently impressed by the information on the Englishman—even if it did arrive from an anonymous source . . ."

"Yeah, but where is he now?"

"He will find it very hard. Not like the West. Even now Russia is far from being open. Besides people have been taught to fear foreigners. That doesn't go away so quickly."

"But the woman . . ."

"I doubt there is much she can do for him. The surveillance will prevent that. It will put a ring around her. She knows she has to be careful."

Russert said nothing for a moment, got up, then went back to the table.

"What troubles you, my friend?"

"Just the girl—that's all. You wouldn't think of taking certain steps . . ."

"Like killing her?" He shook his head. "Killing is always a mistake. Mikhail used to say that. You know what he told me last time I saw him: 'The reason I'm going is to prevent killing, not to provoke it.'" He shook his head. "If more people are to die, we will not be the ones responsible." He looked sharply at the American. "I hope you understand this."

* * *

"Harry Fox?" A voice above the midday London traffic. "Who are you?"

But they didn't answer him, the two of them advancing fast from different sides, almost on the steps of the U.S. embassy, linking arms, leading him so quickly he could have fallen, bundling him into the car with the darkened windows, the engine already in gear.

They sat on either side of him, early forties, expressionless, and he knew the doors were locked and it wasn't worth talking to them. He had broken the rules, and now they were breaking them again to show they didn't care a damn for him, and could get him wherever they wanted.

For such a slick maneuver, he reflected, there was still nothing they could do about the traffic. They were crawling west, he reckoned, through light rain. He caught a sign for the airport, and then they had left that area and were into the streets of tiny terraced houses, behind the BBC's Television Center. He didn't bother to look at the road names. It would be a drab, instantly forgettable, use once and throw away building—and not much hospitality on offer.

They pushed him out into the narrow street, the cars double-parked on either side. One man indoors leading the way up the bare stairs into a room with striped paper, half-ripped from the walls. A house between owners. They would have a dozen or so like it around the city. Fox looked around for somewhere to sit and realized the room was totally empty. They had shut the door on him and he was looking out over the low rooftops, through windows freshly barred, the wood shavings still on the floor.

He had promised himself he would keep his temper, but when the door opened after an hour and a half and Foreign Office walked in, Fox had to restrain himself from lashing out.

"So sorry to keep you waiting," said Foreign Office with total insincerity. "Mr. Fox," he added, as an afterthought.

"Let's just get this over with," Fox told him. "I have things to do."

"I already consider it over. In fact I've come to give you a lift. Please . . ." He gestured to the door, past the two raincoated figures from the car.

Out in the street the rain had stopped, the sky already brighter, a few rare moments of sunshine in prospect.

"You can take me back to the embassy." Fox settled back in the car, Foreign Office beside him.

"I'm sorry that's quite impossible. You're leaving the country. You've been summoned home. Please treat this as your taxi to the airport."

"What the . . . ?"

"Harry Fox," Foreign Office said smiling benignly, "we are a tolerant and often overtolerant society, but you went a little too far last night. And before you start threatening the wrath of the White House, there've already been phone calls about you—and I understand your President will not, after all, be at Andrews Air Force Base, to welcome you back."

Fox smiled wryly. "Aren't you being a bad loser?"

"What d'you mean?"

Fox relaxed visibly. "Your man in Moscow slips the leash, goes free lance, sends his family back with a one-way ticket. Our suspicions were justified all along. He's bent. Face it, fellah."

"There's no proof of that. There may be perfectly good reasons why he broke cover . . ."

"That's not what our station tells us."

"And how do they know?"

"They've been watching him—what d'you think?"

"I think you're going off, as you always do, half cocked."

"Please yourself. Kind of a British tradition to tolerate traitors. As long as they have the right accent, went to a decent school, they've earned the right to piss on you all from a great height. Terrific. Don't expect us to go along with it."

"I long since stopped expecting anything from you people." Foreign Office looked out at the passing traffic. "But unlike you, we don't condemn people without evidence. There's a certain loyalty involved, if you like . . ."

"Loyalty." Fox laughed. "Like Philby, Blunt, uh? That kind of loyalty. Good public school stuff—support the team. When are you people going to grow up? You think in a war there's time to sit down and hold a full-scale trial?"

"The war's over, or did you miss that one? Eastern Europe went democratic . . ."

"That's what you think. Some of us are going to wait and see. What the hell?" Fox looked pityingly at his traveling companion. "Why should we bother protecting Europe? I'm sick of it. Far as I'm concerned you guys can start paying your own bills." He waved a finger at Foreign Office. "Frankly I'm glad to be going home."

They didn't speak again. Foreign Office stayed in the car as a single escort took Fox through into the terminal and passed him to special branch. Within ten minutes he was on the plane. They waited with him until the aircraft doors were closed.

Later Foreign Office got out of the car and stretched his legs. In some ways, he knew the trouble was just beginning. There had been no transatlantic phone calls, no clearance from above—and he had no idea where Marcus was. And when he thought about it, how could he be sure that Fox wasn't right—and that if Marcus hadn't gone over for political reasons, might he not have sold out for a woman with curly red hair who had crept her way into his soul and taken it over? After all, he reflected, Marcus wouldn't be the first.

In the end all five of them went shopping for new clothes. Marcus's mother, Doreen and Cressida in one car—and the two others in theirs. "A nice little party," the old lady called it and patted her lap as if she'd been reassured.

Of course Foreign Office had been very nice about it too. The men were just looking after them: Charles and Robert, he called them. Quiet, well spoken, very grateful for their coffee, and no trouble to anybody.

"And what about the man who came here?" Marcus's mother had asked.

"Not to worry. He won't come again." And "No, there was no danger."

It seemed to her that they had tried to avoid talking about the main issue. Foreign Office had this way of slipping backward toward the door, not really saying anything, trying to get away with the minimum of damage. She could sense it, but she couldn't let it go at that.

He was almost in his car when she spoke up.

"I mean how long is all this going to go on?"

He smiled his automatic smile. "Not long, I shouldn't think."

"But a week? Two weeks—a month?"

"Hard to say, I'm afraid."

"Where's my son?" Such a quiet voice. Not a voice that would ever make waves or launch ships.

"I wish I knew," he told her. "But I don't."

35

Half a continent away, in the town of Shelepin, another mother packed her things into a tiny bag and assembled her family and friends.

Eduard had been the first to arrive and when she saw him she raised her eyebrows. He hadn't worn a tie for more than a year—more at home in baggy trousers and checked shirt—now he was strutting around in a jacket with hideously wide lapels, talking of cutting a swash at the Kremlin.

She was tired, as she knew she would be—and they hadn't even left.

"Yelena, Yelena!" They all called her that. "Thank God you're still here." A red-faced woman, fat and jolly, and as wide as a small car, forced her way through the door, flinging baskets and papers and all sorts of bric-a brac before her. Her entrance was like that of a minor hurricane.

"Heavens above." Yelena surveyed the woman crossly. "What in the name of the Almighty are you doing?"

"I baked these for your journey." She handed over a basket with small objects wrapped in paper. "Cakes and some pies. Such a long way you're going. . . ."

"We are going to Moscow, not to a small town in Africa." Yelena looked profoundly unhappy. "You should give these to the hospital . . ."

"But Mikhail might . . ."

"Mikhail has always eaten far too much. I have told him that many times." Yelena clicked her teeth in irritation. "However I shall take him one as a gift."

The woman beamed.

"The others you shall give to the sick children. We can only hope that your cakes do not make their condition worse." She turned to the others. "Now are we all ready?"

It was a ragged little group. Eduard and his wife Adriana, their two daughters, and a distant cousin, a sallow teenage boy who stood mostly on one leg. With the exception of Eduard they had never left Shelepin, and had only the haziest of ideas where Moscow was.

"Are you sure the tickets are paid?" Eduard looked worried. He had never possessed much money, and never been generous with what he had. But he felt sure the Kremlin dripped with rubles. "I'm not at all sure we could . . ."

He stopped talking. Everyone was looking at him.

"We will just be silent for a moment." Yelena looked around the room, at the bags and suitcases, and the worried, expectant faces. It was the Russian tradition. Before leaving on a journey, assess what is past, and pray for the future. But as she watched their faces, the lips of the girls, moving in silent supplication, she felt uncertain and ill at ease, as if she were stepping blindly into darkness.

Perhaps it was the sudden summons from the Kremlin, the coolest of official voices, the "you are requested" phrases, so distant from the language of the proletariat, from this their headquarters—but it made her feel important and powerful in a way she hadn't done for weeks.

As she emerged from her apartment Anastasiya caught sight of her shadows in their gray Moskvich. It was parked about a hundred meters down the street, enjoying the shade. She could see the windows were open. Lethargy seemed to have engulfed the figures inside.

But a much rarer sight was a militiaman, halfheartedly

directing the morning traffic, his cap pushed up onto his forehead, suggesting he had simply borrowed it for a while and was only doing the job as a favor. Anastasiya couldn't resist. She stepped out into the road toward him.

"There are some people over there—they've been following me for several days. And I'm scared."

The officer looked barely more than twenty and, at that moment, he seemed infinitely more scared than she was.

"What do you intend to do?" she demanded.

He drew a notebook from his shirt pocket, changed his mind, reached for the radio clipped to his epaulette and dropped his pencil. Anastasiya felt like laughing. The militiaman blushed at his own confusion.

"Over there." She pointed to the Moskvich. The officer's radio gave a squawk as if from a distant civilization, but clearly, any useful help was out of range. He looked both ways then strode toward the car. There was instant activity. The figure in the driver's seat was nudged upright, the engine started with a burst of blue smoke. Crazily, with its tires screeching, the overloaded hulk burped its way into the traffic, past the waving, whistling militiaman. He looked in vain for a rear number plate. It was missing.

Decisively, he spat into his radio microphone. There was no reply. A shrug of the wide, blue-shirted shoulders. A fresh country face. Not a glimmer of understanding for her plight and no wish to spend a day thinking of it.

"Zhalko"—I'm sorry. "You can make a complaint if you wish." He took off his cap and stared up smiling at the sun. "But maybe it's not worth it. Besides you're pretty," he told her. "Don't men follow you all the time?"

"Only idiots like you," she replied, watching his mouth open in surprise. He wasn't used to plain speaking from women, she thought.

In frustration she turned away from him, searching the traffic for a taxi. Only after a few minutes did she see it—the black Volga by the curb on the other side of the road. She screwed up her eyes and then the amazement spread across her face. It was a car she knew well. Her car from the pool, in it her driver Alexei—two of the most treasured possessions the Soviet state can offer. And yet she didn't feel good about it. They still gave things at random and took them away on a whim. How could you trust such people? After all the reforms, after all the promises, the real decisions were still made in secret. The same faceless team was making them.

"Wait here." Krichenkov stood blocking her path. He, the master of the outer office, guardian of the General Secretary's domain, marching briskly away down the corridor, as if he had taken umbrage at her presence.

Anastasiya sat in a leather armchair, surveying the scrubbed wood floors, the fresh paint. Krichenkov had become altogether too powerful, she thought, too arrogant. She disliked the precious, hairless white face, the effeminate bearing, the flaring nostrils. And yet you had to be careful of Krichenkov. That's what they were saying. A party secretary in his own right, a maker of deals, a troubleshooter, charming and deeply unpleasant at the same time.

"There's been a mistake. You've been summoned for nothing. He can't see you." Krichenkov emerged through double doors at the end of the corridor, turned and shut them carefully behind him.

He gave her a look that seemed intended to sweep her up and push her through the door, but she sat where she was.

"This is highly irregular."

"That's as may be." He smiled. "These are not regular times." He tried to disappear back into the inner office.

"So when should I come again?"

"How should I know? You'll be called."

"Please pass a message to the comrade General Secretary . . ."

"You have to write on a special form."

She lost her temper. "Enough of your obstruction, comrade Krichenkov. You either serve in this office or you have no right to be here. I have regular and legitimate business with the General Secretary, but if he is too busy with affairs of state—that is quite normal. However I have the impression that you are being deliberately evasive. Tell the General Secretary that he would do well to listen to what I can tell him about foreign reaction to events in this country."

She looked at him coldly. "You know where to find me."

Anastasiya turned abruptly and walked away. She had the sensation of Krichenkov's eyes boring none too kindly into the small of her back.

36

The decision had come to Tuckerman with almost paralyzing slowness, as the early morning sounds of the city reached him in bed.

His wife was in the bathroom, "painting," as she put it, flossing her teeth, watering herself, the way one nurtures a plant—so he had nowhere to go.

And he didn't know why he hadn't seen it before, the obvious imperative obscured by detail, the chaos, the tension. Already the excuses started to present themselves. And yet if he didn't move now, the excuses wouldn't count for a thing.

He banged on the bathroom door. "I'm in a hurry."

"Me too," she replied.

She would never know, he thought later, that she had delayed matters of national security. He imagined the cable —sorry I couldn't get out fast enough. Wife was in the bathroom, tricky new hairstyle, power lunch to go to . . .

The traffic didn't help. Tuckerman found himself regretting the Russians had become so prosperous. Only one in eleven of them had a car. But the full team seemed to be out on the streets that morning, and by the time he reached the embassy Russert was already there.

"Office," Tuckerman told him abruptly, the way people ask dogs to sit.

They sat across the desk.

"There's no nice way to say this, David."

Russert grinned. "You've forgotten my birthday?"

"No. You're leaving. You have to be out of here by the weekend."

"Why?"

"Why!" Tuckerman shot up from his seat. "Why d'you think? A British asset looks as though he's gone over. He knows your identity—therefore you're blown. Okay? End of story. I can't put it more simply than that."

"We don't know for certain that he's gone . . ."

"Christ, it was your report that made that the lead conclusion. Confirmed all your suspicions about the Murmansk deal, didn't it?"

Russert's grin had gone. "I need a few more days, Jim." He looked tired. Tuckerman could see deeper lines around the eyes.

"To let them get your cell ready? Don't be stupid."

"I may have something . . . the reformists are stepping up the pressure."

"What does that mean?"

Russert looked hard at the station chief, as if deciding whether to breach a confidence.

"I think the radicals will go for a coup."

"You think—or you're being told that?"

"It's what I'm hearing."

Tuckerman laid his elbows on the desk. "I think that's crap. The radicals don't have a prayer, no guns, no experience, no impact in the country. If things move anywhere at all—and I have doubts even about that—it'll be backward."

"Okay, if that's the way you see it . . ."

"We're dealing in probabilities, David. That's just not one of them."

Russert got up.

Tuckerman stayed where he was. "I'll drive you to the airport."

"And what if the General Secretary comes knocking at
the embassy door?"

Tuckerman shook his head. "Don't make me laugh."

They met in a line for toilet paper.

Anastasiya had got there first—Marcus and the photographer joined her, like family, laughing, chatting, as if there
were nothing else in Russia that families would want to do.

As soon as he could Marcus pulled her to one side.

"This man's a killer."

"Marcus, he's a photographer."

"And tomorrow night he kills someone."

"It's the last one—they promised me."

"There should never have been a first."

They moved behind a Pepsi stand, out of sight of the
line. She took his arm, the way she always did, but there was
no answering pressure.

"You talk about this as if it were of no more importance
than shopping . . ."

"We've had this conversation before." She looked away.
"You English can be so arrogant."

Marcus pulled her back toward him. "What happens
now?"

"The Kremlin is falling apart. Chaos. I was there this
morning to see the General Secretary—but they wouldn't let
me in."

"You think he's in danger?"

Anastasiya looked amused. "He is perhaps the only one
who is not in danger. But that doesn't mean he is free. Maybe
his hands are tied behind his back, maybe he really is the one
in control. Did you think of that?" She spread open the palms
of her hands. "It is possible he could have staged these problems, in order to trick his opponents. Marcus . . . I don't
know anymore. These people are capable of anything. Besides"—she held his arm tightly—"we should get you back to
the apartment. It's not safe here."

They caught the subway and walked the rest of the way in silence. Marcus's clothes were creased and unwashed, worn for the second successive day. But he wasn't out of place. Moscow was still for the shabby and down at heel.

And as they entered the cul-de-sac, it was Anastasiya who looked up to the first-floor windows. She, who started counting the faces, not one or two, but suddenly half a dozen, she who slowed them, knowing suddenly that the people would be watching for a reason, that something had happened and someone was in there and that all the residents *knew* a spectacle was on the way. As she stopped, an old lady raised an index finger from a second-story window and shook it quickly. And Anastasiya didn't stop there, aware then that the black security cars must have drawn up just a short time ago. Abruptly she pulled both of them around, saying nothing, the urgency only in her eyes, and then all three were around the corner, halfway to the subway. It wasn't till they had started down the steps, sprinting now, taking them three at a time, that they heard the sirens.

Duty Officer Belayeva had never won prizes at school, never excelled in intellectual pursuits or sport, or anything else for that matter, but she knew trouble when she saw it. You didn't have to be a member of the Academy of Sciences to realize that.

She had watched with alarm the arrival of the extra detachments, billeted separately in the storage complex, watched the comings and goings, the new unscheduled flights and instructions—and knew somehow that Vitaly was in danger.

In the old days, of course, nothing had been more important than your own career, the silent, secretive way that you advanced yourself and your prospects in the mother of all socialist states. A favor here, a little bit of informing, a bribe, a night in bed—each gesture an upwardly mobile leap on the communist ladder, a way of circumventing the bureaucratic monster, who would always turn a blind eye if you stroked him the right way. Nothing for nothing, Belayeva reflected. Those were the rules.

But there had been something about Vitaly. Sure he was arrogant; all the pilots were. If you defied nature and flew at suicidal speeds fifteen kilometers above the earth, you had to believe in yourself. And yet deep down, she knew he was a child, the way he held her, the way he gave of himself, the tenderness in him. Inside, deep down, there was a person, not an animal, just wanting to connect his body with hers. He cared. And so should she.

For the tenth morning in a row, the Arctic day came up gray and windblown and the earth was without color—and Belayeva decided this was the day she, too, would give.

In the control room she discovered the arrival time of the training flight, stayed there as they talked him in, straight, professional, so sure footed. Whatever else he was, Vitaly was an expert at what he did.

Even then she hadn't made up her mind how she'd do it. The idea had been poorly formulated. These days they tended to keep him at the far, north end of the runway. A quick refuel, sometimes a meal and a cup of coffee in the canteen. More often than not, they would deal with him out there. She had watched him stretch his legs beside the aircraft, drink from the thermos flask they gave him. So strange. A man who flew himself each day from one point to another, with no apparent purpose. From Russia to Russia and back again.

Belayeva headed for her room and pulled the parka from her cupboard. It wasn't cold but the extra protection gave her courage.

Habit made her look in the mirror, check her makeup, ruffle the black hair. She turned around and gasped in surprise.

How long had he been there, she wondered. The base commander. Watching her, just inside the door, with much more than a glint in his eye, letting his gaze drop gradually from her face, slide over her parka, down to her skirt and beyond.

"Going for a walk?" He smiled without warmth.

She pushed past him, hurrying into the corridor. In the old days, she might have let him stay, just to keep him sweet and get some extra days off. But you had to stop somewhere, she thought. In Russia you were forever buying people off with something. In the end you had nothing left for yourself.

37 _____

Perhaps Anastasiya had given it no thought at all—or perhaps it needed none. If there's really only one place to go, then your mind will tell you. It won't bother with alternatives and doubts and questions.

So smoothly she led them through the subway system, taking the green line out to the southwest, the cars half full, buffeting their way toward the suburbs—Kievskaya, Fili, Pionerskaya—she ticked them off in her mind, counting the minutes till the end of the line.

From there she knew her way so well. Her mother had lived in the district, before marrying again and moving to Leningrad. Long walks, long talks, she recalled. Even when you're running, your mind can wander.

But they didn't talk now. Marcus and the young Russian, accepting simply that she would lead them to safety. Her city, her politics. She would know the way.

They emerged at Kuntsevskaya, past the peasant street traders and the last of their produce. Some radishes, potatoes, and a handful of flowers that had died hours before. The women seemed to be gazing sightless in front of them, uncaring, unnoticing. Where were their thoughts, Anastasiya wondered. How old must you be before your mind and your body part company, before they no longer function together?

It was only when they reached the gray apartment block

that she could sense the fear, the first far-off tremor, the warning that you shouldn't ignore.

Into the elevator now. They could just make it, squeezing together, watching each other anxiously, realizing that all the roads they took now led forward. There would never again be any leading back.

Each floor they passed brought different sounds: the crying of babies, the hammering of a carpenter, a radio, a drum. No quiet to be had in the suburbs of Russia.

A moment of uncertainty as they hit the top floor. Anastasiya looked both ways and then remembered. "Wait here," she told them and pushed her way through the swinging fire doors. She knocked on the door. The reply was almost immediate.

"Who is it?" A woman's voice. Not old, not young.

"It's me."

"Oh God!" The door opened and the figure stood there, lifeless and sagging, as if her worst nightmare had just been confirmed.

"I'm sorry." Anastasiya took her hand.

"What are you sorry for?"

"For this . . ." She gestured to Marcus and the young photographer. "There really was no other way."

"That's what you said last time." Nina Alexeyevna, filling the doorway in a plastic housecoat, drew herself up to her full height and let out a big sigh. "I suppose since you've made me into a spy or a terrorist, or some such other nonsense—you better come in. Why did you have to remember where I lived?"

A full half hour later and Nina was no happier with the arrangement. "How can I put them up here? They'll be seen." She rolled her eyes. "There's an old man by the elevator, pensioner, keeps making eyes at me. Doesn't miss a thing. You know what it's like in these apartments. You can't even hide a toothpick. People will think I'm a bad woman, living immorally. Two men here! One would be bad enough." She paused to get her breath. "And where are they supposed to sleep?"

Anastasiya handed her a glass of her own tea.

"I'm only trying to do what's right."

"Right," snorted Nina. "The right thing would have been to leave me out of all this. If you want to be shot as a traitor, that's fine. Why do I have to go with you? I mean it's not even as if the job was going anywhere. I'm retiring in a year—didn't I tell you? But I had a bit of money saved. Who knows? I might even have got a trip to the West. There are some now, you know."

She swallowed her tea. Tears suddenly appeared in her eyes and she searched for a handkerchief, blowing her nose loudly, looking away from them as they sat around the kitchen, embarrassed, not knowing what to tell her.

No one said anything until the young photographer got up to clear away the cups.

"Why don't you call me Ivan?" he suggested kindly to Nina.

"That's not your name, is it?"

"If you call me by it, then it will be my name."

She smiled and blew her nose again.

"And you"—she looked at Marcus—"What do I call you?"

He shook his head. "Nothing." He thought for a moment. "After all, I was never here."

They barely noticed the photographer leave the flat. Nina had cheered up, found a bottle of wine, cooked some rice and dragged an old guitar from behind her cupboard. There were three strings that could still cope with a tune.

With Anastasiya she also found a voice as the darkness softened the edge of the suburbs, and they sipped the wine.

He went out across the city, losing himself in the subway, heading north to locate his brother—and more importantly, his brother's car.

Then east, skirting the city center, taking the narrow uneven byways, where the Revolution and its backers had so obviously run out of money.

The directions they'd given him carried no street or number. He navigated by landmarks—three streets right past the filling station, left before a church, straight on past the Victory of Socialism collective farm. And there it was, unlit and unannounced, the great, gray elephant, with the debris of a building site around it.

He parked a mile away, covering the remaining ground on foot. Dark T-shirt, jeans. No impact on the landscape. He was so sure, so confident. Day or night, it made little difference.

In a way it amused him to be back on a mission. We were all so good, he thought, checking the landscape, his senses on a hair trigger. We, of the special forces. We, of the Spetsnaz. We who did the dirty work of the nation before they all went soft and signed us away in troop reductions. It was funny to talk of being a photographer. He'd trained in that. He'd also trained in marksmanship, karate, encryption, communications technology—the list was a long one. And then, of course, there was killing. But not tonight. Tonight was just the groundwork.

The electronic lock to the apartment was easy. He'd done worse than that. Easy now. And he shone a small penlight through the crack in the doorway, looking for tripwires, or pressure pads, or infrared cells. And yet it didn't seem a high-budget affair. Good security, but nothing excessive.

He tiptoed over to the window and closed the blind. And it didn't take him long to see the preparations—the boxes, the clothes, the supplies—instruments of transit. And he knew all about that.

The job presented no immediate difficulty. But he was not trained to be slapdash. Believe in failure, and you'll work for success, had been the Spetsnaz motto.

After ten minutes he was satisfied that the groundwork had been done. The apartment checked and rechecked. He could return at will to complete the contract. He was the best of the new free lances. He would deliver.

It was just before midnight when he returned to the block at Kuntsevskaya. Marcus was asleep on the floor, Anastasiya on the sofa. Nina in her bedroom, where she heard him come in, but didn't think to ask herself until much later, how he had opened the door without a key.

By six in the morning Anastasiya was standing over Marcus, dressed, her hair brushed, the makeup applied. She leaned down and kissed him, but not long, embarrassed suddenly at the presence of the photographer, half asleep in the armchair.

"Where you going?" Marcus asked.

"To work of course. You think I dress like this to go swimming?"

"D'you think you should?"

"It will be a good day," she told him. "This evening, as one of the General Secretary's advisers, I am invited to the Kremlin to help celebrate his birthday."

Marcus looked hard at her face, but could see only excitement and expectation. Not the face of a woman involved in treachery.

She kissed him again. "It will be a big occasion," she confirmed, as if to convince herself.

"And you will be followed," he told her.

"I doubt it. At a party like that, it will be easy to get lost. Even you could come along." She laughed, her mood changing with the flick of an eyebrow. One minute sad, he thought, the next ecstatic. One moment adult—the next, a child, whose innocence had led her, almost blindfolded into chaos and danger.

He followed her down to the lobby. It was cold and bare. Through the windows he could see lights coming on in the neighboring buildings.

She kissed his cheek.

"You don't have to go," he told her.

"Don't be silly, Marcus. I have to talk to the man, make him see reason. Besides"—she hung her head—"don't you want to know what's going on?"

"It's too dangerous."

"Welcome to real life." She pulled away from him.

"Listen to me." For a moment Marcus could barely recognize his own voice. "Listen, the chances are that you're under as much suspicion as I am. If they don't pull you in tonight, it'll be tomorrow. Is that what you want . . . ?"

"I have to go, Marcus . . ."

"We could go from here, both of us." He caught up with her and held her arm. "You know how I feel about you. Some things are more important than politics. This isn't the first power struggle here and it won't be the last. You can't play in all of them."

She stopped and turned to face him. "Is that how you really think?"

"It's clearer to me than anything else."

"Not to me, it isn't." She touched his cheek. "I don't want to hurt you, Marcus, but this is something that comes first."

"And then?"

She opened the front door, the door back into Moscow. "You don't know the answer to that any more than I do."

38

They all looked older, but then Russian train journeys do that to you. The waiting, the poor food, the uncertainty as you crawl haphazardly across the map. Yelena had insisted there be no special treatment. So they had crowded into a single compartment, changing twice, invariably in the middle of the night, at the crossroads of an unworkable timetable, devised with only the railway in mind—not the people who traveled it.

Dawn had found them in a tiny station, some two hundred miles from Moscow, stranded, they ascertained, because a sick driver had failed to show up for work, and a substitute was without a telephone. The station master had been rude and offhand, but they had barely noticed, grateful, like all innocents, for even the most worthless of promises.

It wasn't till late afternoon that they reached Moscow, by which time their bread had grown stale, and the salami had been eaten down to the tough, skinny end. Eduard produced a tie from his suitcase and wound it solemnly around his neck. It was black with white diagonal flecks across it—the same one Mikhail had worn when *Pravda* took his first photo all those years ago—and still just as hideous.

As they got down onto the platform the bustle and the shouting seemed to daze them and it was a few moments before they could get their bearings. In bright sunlight

Yelena assembled them in a semicircle, brushing away crumbs, smoothing the children's dresses, counting suitcases among the long shadows.

Big cities are full of thieves, she had told them, as the train pulled into the station. And they had looked at her scarcely able to believe that the mother of the General Secretary could talk in that way. But they clutched their possessions tightly as they looked around at the confusion and chaos.

From nowhere, it seemed, the envoy was with them, his huge hands gathering people and bags, like a moving mountain, steering them toward the street. And it was only then that they saw the symbol of power and realized where they were. The ancient Chaika, all chrome and black paint, so excessive and ostentatious, with its bulbous body and long, sweeping fins. They all stood and stared at it.

"Welcome." The envoy bundled them fast into the car. "Welcome to our capital."

It was Eduard who noticed that they weren't heading for the Kremlin. "Hey, what's going on?" He banged on the glass partition. "This isn't right. We're going away from the river."

The envoy drew back the glass. "I'm sorry. Mikhail has been detained for a few hours. He asked me to take care of you. A little tour of the city. A chance to rest and wash. Some shopping."

The two nieces grinned at each other. They had both heard the magic word. And ever since leaving Shelepin had thought of nothing else. Moscow shops were a legend outside the city, even if they were a nightmare in it.

All afternoon they were shunted from special shop to boutique, admitted behind closed and curtained doors, simply for the card that the envoy held in his hand. At each place they found the kind of hallowed silence that had never featured in any shop they'd ever visited before.

Yelena shook her head incessantly. Such a long way from the peasant markets, she thought, from the dismal state enterprises in the big provincial towns. And what of the shop assistants, all in suits and uniforms? She resolved to speak sternly to her son about it all—because it couldn't be right and wasn't the kind of Russia *she* had fought for.

In the end she could stand it no longer, pulling the family out of the jewelery store where the gold and silver trinkets had gleamed at them behind polished glass cases, pulling the girls' hair, stifling Eduard's protests.

"What d'you want"—she cuffed him on the shoulder— "earrings? Are you suddenly a girl?"

He blushed.

"Isn't it enough to go around in that overheated tank, but you want to start wearing bracelets as well?"

They climbed back into the car.

"I want to rest," Yelena told the envoy, "before I regret coming at all. Besides the girls have to get ready for tonight."

They drove smoothly through the eastern suburbs and when they reached the gray lonely block on the outskirts of the city, they stepped out of the car to be met with such stillness and quiet and only the distant hum of the city to remind them where they were.

"What is this place?" Eduard turned slowly in a circle and stared at the envoy.

"It's a special apartment building, not yet inhabited."

"Special, special." Yelena clicked her teeth in annoyance. "Why is everything here so special? Is there nothing normal left in Moscow? Are they all so carried away with power that they can't live anymore like the rest of us?"

Inside the apartment they picked their way through the boxes, moved cases and clothes. Yelena found a kettle and boiled water for tea. "This is much better," she proclaimed. The nieces didn't look so convinced.

Outside in the parking lot the driver's door opened and Vitaly got out. This is where you watch and say your prayers, he thought. Even the ones you can only half remember, the ones they told you never to say in public, the ones you recited at your mother's knee for the day when you would so surely need them.

The office had been silent since early morning. And Anastasiya had waited for the messenger or the phone call, or the men who wore raincoats on the days when it never rained—but nothing had happened.

Her assistant had called in sick, the normal departmental mail had failed to be delivered. It was as if a notice of quarantine had sealed her office off from the rest of the world. Just as well, she thought, for she couldn't work.

Alone on the ninth floor of the building's southern steeple, the anxiety returned. How easy it had been to kiss away problems when others were with you. All it took was a glib retort, a smile, a bit of spirit, and then they took you for the calmest and bravest in the world. And there was always a chance they were right.

On your own, the jokes don't look so funny, the answers don't seem so right, and when you know you're running with nowhere to go it's not good to think of the future.

Always hard to make decisions, she thought. Always, I wanted others to open the doors or close them. That way I never had to choose.

If the world were in my hands for just a minute, would I spin it, plucking its treasures, or would I watch it go around, fearful, hesitant, unable to take anything for myself?

That night, though, the decision was hers. She would get to the General Secretary, and talk to him alone. She would warn him, persuade him, argue and remonstrate if that were necessary. Had he made up his mind to go forward or back? For herself—she had to know.

Exactly at five she took the elevator down to the main foyer. As usual the militiaman checked her pass. She had almost reached the tall wooden and steel doors, when a cheery male voice said her name—quietly at first, and then much louder when she appeared to ignore it.

She turned back. It was Shukhin, head of all the European sections. A ruddy-faced avuncular figure, always smiling, his front teeth burnished with gold. According to the gossip his smile was at its broadest when he sacked or informed on his staff.

"My dear Anastasiya. What a surprise. The very best of news . . ."

"Then don't keep me waiting," she replied in a mildly reproachful tone.

"There is an official meeting tomorrow at which the leading people of five ministries are asked to participate. We will have the chance to put questions about national security to the men charged with maintaining it . . ."

"But how fascinating . . ."

"Of course it is. And I have picked you to accompany me. Such a thing has never happened in all the years since I came here . . ."

"And where is this to take place?"

"The Lubyanka of course."

Anastasiya looked hard and tried to read his expression. It wasn't so much the smile of the expectant tiger, she reflected. This time the animal had opened its mouth and was positively salivating.

"David, hi. Can I come in?"

Jim Tuckerman pushed through the front door of Russert's apartment. He had a knack of making all barriers or obstacles seem irrelevant.

"You're in now." Russert made a face.

"Hey, I don't see much sign of packing . . ."

"Look, Jim, is this professional or social?" Russert, it seemed, had been taking a nap on the sofa. He got up stiffly and stretched.

"Er . . . social, in fact. I didn't mean to disturb you." Tuckerman's head seemed to be floating from side to side in embarrassment. Like many powerful men he was easily wrong-footed in his personal life.

"Sit down, Jim."

"What I wanted to say was this. We were going to make it a surprise, but a few of us felt it would be good just to have a few drinks before you left. So I figured if you came around to us tonight about nine, maybe we could do something. Short notice, I know. But hell, you've got to move when you can."

Tuckerman blushed as if he were bearing his soul.

All at once Russert felt acutely embarrassed for him.

"Jim, that's great . . . that's really nice of you." He smiled awkwardly. "But I'm sorry I can't make it tonight. You know how it is—last look at Moscow, dinner with a couple of Russian friends. I really can't break it."

"Oh . . . I see. Oooo-kay. Well I guess I'll see you tomorrow then. If you change your mind . . ."

"It's not my mind, Jim, it's a fixed plan."

"Sure." Tuckerman nodded. He walked crablike to the door and raised a hand in farewell.

For a few minutes after he'd gone, Russert sat motionless on the sofa. Then he pulled a sheet of writing paper from the desk and began to write Jim Tuckerman a letter.

Krichenkov had not looked forward to the party but he was ready for it. A coming-out party, he decided, embodying all the traditional ingredients of Soviet politics: the stab in the back, the ritual denunciations, the breast beating—and the final late-night transfer of power, every bit as slick and precise as the guard-change outside the Lenin Mausoleum.

He smiled to himself. Some things, he muttered, we do so well.

Of course they would wait until the guests had gone, until the General Secretary was tired, until the alcohol had softened him up. And then they would lead him gently into the corner and break him. By argument first and then physical inducement if needed. Before the night ended the man would be out.

Krichenkov's mouth turned down at the edges. If only the General Secretary would take a hint. But then Soviet politics had never been about hinting—more about bludgeoning a path through daily life. There were always sacrifices. Some involved principles and policies. More often, the sacrifices were human.

In the end it hadn't been hard to channel the opposition to the General Secretary—no shortage of it, either. Even Krichenkov had been surprised at the high-level personnel prepared to stand against him—men he counted as friends and allies. All they needed, they said, was someone to open the castle door and let them in. A Judas, ready to deliver his victim in a quiet place at a quiet hour.

Krichenkov got to his feet. The hour was close by.

39

"Are you ready yet?" The envoy stood in the middle of the living room, surveying the debris. All around him were opened bags and boxes, wrapping paper. The first family of the Soviet Union looked back at him in some disarray.

Yelena was encased in black. Dignity rather than elegance. And that was fitting. The nieces, despite their best efforts, still resembled wild hedges. You needed more than a body to wear clothes well, thought the envoy. Poor girls. They had the kind of irregular asymmetrical shapes, on which garments would always hang out or droop.

Eduard . . . well, he'd seen to Eduard earlier. He'd taken him aside, given him the dark gray suit and the French silk tie and brushed aside the protests that it was "far too dull" for the Kremlin. "You have to look the part," he'd told him, without ever saying what the part was.

He led them to the car. Vitaly had the engine running. Go, he told him, get out of here. You're on your way, on your own, and I'll never tell you, but I don't know how you'll make it. The margins for error are too wide. You're out there running between God and the Devil and both can act against you. Have a care, if you can.

"Aren't you coming too?" Yelena's hand caught at his arm.

"I'll follow you. Just a few things to sort out . . ."

"Nonsense." She got back out of the car. "There's a lot you haven't told me. You just say—come to Moscow, birthday party in the Kremlin, show of support. And we, the family, the simple people—we just pack up and come to the city. Why?"

"Because it's important."

"Just that?"

"Yelena"—the ruts in the envoy's forehead seemed to deepen—"there will be dramatic events tonight. They had to come. This has been building for months, maybe even years." He led her a few feet away from the car. "You may not like what happens. No. You won't like it. But I must tell you there was nothing else we could do. You will say that we used you. And maybe that's what we are doing. But only as one friend uses the help of another friend, given freely." He shrugged. "Forgive us now. Forgive us before you go."

Her hand was still on his arm. "You don't need my forgiveness. I'm an old woman, useless to everyone except myself. I have done nothing for my son since the day he left home to go to Moscow more than thirty years ago. I packed for him, gave him his meal, and sent him away with the blessing of the God I still believe in. He hasn't forgotten that." She sighed. "He forgets nothing. But"—the grip tightened—"a mother never stops wanting to help her child. To me even now that he's a man, even such an important one, he is still my boy, the one I held at night when he cried, the one who came to me when he had fallen, the one I brought into the world and gave to the world."

She got back in the car. "We will do what you want. All of us."

He watched the car head out across the wasteland, joining the highway, losing itself in the distant evening traffic. Whatever happens now, he thought, it's begun.

Marcus had never been good at watching, never been good at football matches, never stood on the sidelines cheering the home team. Always he'd wanted to be involved, play-ing, training, organizing. His father had once said: "Don't wait for life to happen to you, the way I did. You have to go out and do it."

Words, thought Marcus, just words, as he sat watching the photographer prepare to kill.

Nina Alexeyevna had gone to work. Just the two of them left in the tacky apartment, with the old theater and ballet tickets on the mantelpiece and the unwashed coffee cups from breakfast.

No good-byes as she had left. Strangely, thought Marcus, you only say good-bye when you're going to see someone again. When you know it's the end, there isn't much point. Just a nod and a shrug. Final comments on the time you spent together.

He watched the young man cleaning his gun. And where did you get that in Russia, he wondered.

The photographer seemed to read his thoughts. "Service revolver," he said. "Kept it after they folded us down. No-body bothered. Turned out they'd lost all the records of who had what." He weighed the gun in his hand without enthusi-asm. "Didn't think I'd have to use it again though."

Marcus tried to look straight into his eyes. "Maybe you don't have to."

The photographer got to his feet. "Doesn't work like that. Pity. No gentlemen in this place. Besides there isn't any other way."

"You all say that."

"Maybe it's right then."

"There's always an alternative . . ." Marcus was struck by the hollow sound of his own words. More than one road to Kiev, wasn't there? And yet when it came to it hadn't they been down most of them? Especially in the last three years: all the chaos and the violence, the slide into economic disas-ter. What road now to Kiev?

"I'm not a politician." The photographer seemed to make

up his mind. "Russia is full of politicians. All the lazy fuckers who sat around in the Kremlin and everyone else who sat around moaning about them. But what did anyone do?"

"Not much," Marcus agreed.

"Nothing. It was nothing. Really. Believe me, I have lived here. Lots of speeches. Long speeches. For the longer they talked the more important they were considered to be. How could a General Secretary talk for less than three hours? First, it would prove that he was too sick to stand up for that long. Second, people would believe he had nothing to say. A politician without words is like a gun with no bullets." He put the revolver in his pocket and made for the door. Casual. Unhurried. Just a man on his way to work.

In that moment, Marcus found himself moving fast toward the young man, determined to stop him, with no idea how to do it.

And in a strange way, it wasn't till much later that he could piece together the photographer's reaction, seeing the Russian's right hand come up in a chopping motion, angling toward the carotid artery, striking him even as he realized he'd never had a chance.

You wouldn't have known there was a crisis, thought Anastasiya. Not in the center of Soviet power where the grand authority lay sick and powerless. And yet that night it had sat up, got out of bed, and was dressed in all its finery.

As her car brought her past the Kremlin palace, she sensed some of the feeling of wild excess that had prevailed in earlier years—the time when the powerful had gorged the fat of the land, while the heroic proletariat munched stale bread and heard how lucky they were to live in a just and socialist state.

Guards were everywhere in ceremonial uniforms. Flunkies guided the guests into the main hall. There was noise and bustle, and as far as she could see the most beautiful women, and the most handsome men in Moscow wearing the finest clothes, were arriving for the party. She got out of the car and stood for a moment, drinking in the atmosphere as the sky darkened over the city.

A young woman came forward in an elegant black dress. Anastasiya caught the smell of her perfume. "May I take your invitation?" She led the way forward, the familiar path where the czars had once held court and into a room Anastasiya had never seen. Situated on the first floor, it seemed more suited to a family gathering than a state reception. The walls were paneled in wood, a few armchairs had been dotted about the room, photographs on a side table, a low ceiling that created the impression of intimacy.

Perhaps she'd imagined the large turnout. In fact there were probably less than thirty, but it was the catering staff that lent volume.

For a moment she panicked. Everyone *else* seemed to be there, stuffing in the canapes, spitting gossip and guesswork. And then she saw him, felt the presence across the room. For the first time he seemed fragile, his head bowed like a broken reed.

I have to reach you, she said silently, and crossed the room.

It was a shambolic entrance. Yelena led, striding purposefully from the car, assuming her family to be close behind her. But she'd counted without Eduard.

No sooner did rural shoe hit Moscow cobble than he twisted his ankle and folded in well-feigned agony to the ground. Yelena heard the yelping, stopped in her tracks, and turned around. An entire division of security men had rushed forward to help, and Eduard seemed to be making the most of his injury. At least three people were supporting him bodily, and he was groaning out a series of rhythmic "oh" noises as they helped him hop to the sidewalk.

"Pull yourself together," she told him crossly. "You're not dead yet, are you? Really, Eduard, you're supposed to have learned how to walk years ago." The nieces burst out laughing. Yelena gave them a despairing glance and launched herself into the great hall.

It wasn't, she told herself, that she had done such things before. In fact, she had been to Moscow only once in her life —when Mikhail had graduated from the party institute. She had come to see him receive his certificate, acknowledge the applause, and an hour later she had been on a train home. In the days that followed, she had told friends that if he'd wanted his mother around, he would have stayed in the village. It wasn't her job to chase around Russia after him. She had simply witnessed the event and gone away. Proud as anything, she had confessed to them all. Proud as a fox with two tails.

That night she had no intention of staying long. Moreover, she was genuinely horrified that the conversation halted abruptly as she entered the room, that everyone insisted on applauding her and the rest of the family, and that her son, whom she glimpsed on the other side of the room, seemed close to tears.

Even then she didn't move toward him, although everything inside her wanted to reach out and hug him. But she waited, suddenly embarrassed and awkward in front of so many people as he walked over to her, his hands outstretched, oblivious to the pretty girl with the mass of red hair who was trying so hard to get his attention.

In his mind the envoy counted off the unfinished tasks. Very few left, he realized. There would be space for just a single bag: a change of clothes and the barest minimum of mementos. He transferred a handful of papers and pictures from a cardboard box to a small leather suitcase and snapped it shut.

As for the family, he had no worries about them. Yelena would know instantly what had happened, she would gather them all together and take them home. He had a sudden image of the despondent little group, waiting somewhere on a deserted railway platform, trekking back across Russia with their hearts and their dreams broken wide open. And yet, he felt sure the storm would break around them. They would hear the thunder but the lightning would strike elsewhere. Almost certainly they would be watched, but they wouldn't be harmed. There was no reason for that.

The rest, he reflected, was mostly in Vitaly's hands. The boy had done well. He had been given his instructions. He had memorized the fallback position, the codes, what to do if things went wrong.

Of course they had both known what would happen if things went really wrong. In a crowded cafe off the Arbat, almost a week ago, the envoy had explained quietly and clearly the consequences of what they were doing. Things that had never been tried, he said. A move that would shock the world, but might still bring peace and unity to the Soviet Union: to the country they cared about, to the factions that were seeking to tear the nation apart and scatter the pieces.

And Vitaly had looked at him across the coffee cups, with a face, finally devoid of all expression. For there's only so much you can imagine, only so many end-of-the-world scenarios that you can picture, before the mind turns off and refuses to grasp the enormity of the enterprise.

They had sat for a while in the cafe window, not speaking, watching the faces of summer Russia pass by. After becoming the first communist country, he realized, they were well on the way to being the last. Eastern Europe had gone its own way, just as it should have done years before. Communism hadn't been for them. In fact he doubted whether a single system of any kind would bring them together.

Mikhail had always envisaged a federation of states across the continent—disarmed, neutralized—and therefore free to argue and dispute to their hearts' content. But that seemed a long way off. And anyway Russians were different. They still needed, still wanted, firm government. Not the ruthless, unaccountable sort of dictatorship of the past—but a benign, intelligent executive that could make decisions and yet wasn't hamstrung by petty regulations, that didn't have to take a vote each time it went to the lavatory.

The envoy put the meeting out of his mind, went into the kitchen and boiled water on the stove. Whatever the ordeal, whatever the pressures, you have to fill the rest of your life with the routine and the mundane. And that's how you make it through.

He made tea and took it into the dining room. He could hear the generator whirring away in the bathroom. Occasionally, in the distance came the creaks, rattles, and thuds of an empty building, badly constructed and uninhabited by humans. All that, the envoy heard and registered. But he missed the tiny click as the main door opened and the photographer crept inside, crouching like an animal in the darkened front hall.

David Russert had finished the letter and left it on his desk. He had removed all the other papers and books, so it would be easy to find. For a moment he thought Tuckerman might consider it a joke, try to laugh it off. But the empty apartment would speak for itself and Tuckerman, with an eye to his own career, couldn't afford to wonder for long.

It was a day he had thought about for many years. Not that he'd imagined quite the scenario that confronted him now. But the chance to see his friend again, to feel the power of that formidable intelligence, to track the man's vision and inspiration.

Russert had often wondered how a system so dead could have thrown up in its midst a mind so unusually alive. And yet, he thought, the old prospectors would find nuggets of gold in among the mud and filth of the rivers. So maybe it was the same. Just a few times in every generation, a genius gets to where he was meant to go. So it must have been with Mikhail.

Out of habit Russert went around the flat tidying and smoothing. Of course they'd be tearing it to pieces in a few hours, cursing him, branding him with all sorts of names and titles that would be so wholly inappropriate. But they wouldn't know that. To them he'd be "traitor," "renegade," "scum of scum." "A lousy little mole that had finally gone back home, after an unremarkable life underground."

And had it been so unremarkable? He looked at himself in the bathroom mirror. Gray and tired was the verdict. Well, what could you expect after a broken marriage and a handful of desks in the Washington area?

Thirty years of the same sort of thing, give or take a few major disappointments. From condo to Colonial and back to condo again. Start as you mean to finish. But that hadn't been the American way, had it?

Russert took a paper tissue and rubbed at a smear on the mirror. Back in the living room, he sat in the leather armchair and put his feet on the coffee table.

It wasn't that he'd ever been close to greatness. He hadn't even been in the same country. It was the boredom that had finally got to him. The unwavering equilibrium of Monday to Friday on the subway, meetings in, and the occasional lunch out, at which he ate but didn't speak. Years of being assistant for this or that, weekends out on the beltway heading for the Shenandoah or Ocean City, get-togethers with Bill and Sally, Dick and Hannah, a concert here, a movie there, life in the middle lane, life without passion or tears, and an unremarkable little death to top it off, when you finally run out of road.

But not today, he thought. Whatever happens in the end, today will be different.

He got up and toured the apartment a final time. The telephone rang, but he didn't answer it.

40

Somehow Yelena felt the pressure of his arms around her, ushered as she was past smiling, glistening faces, past the glasses and the music and into a tiny anteroom with a desk and two upright chairs. Somehow she seemed to hear a voice that sounded like his, but said words that she had never heard before, sentiments that could have come from almost anyone else—except him.

She listened but found it hard to concentrate, absorbing key phrases, aware suddenly that the life and the vigor had gone out of him—and that the monotone of disappointment reflected the way he truly felt. It wasn't a game suddenly, nor a show for the party or the public, but real, written in his face, and the stoop of his back, and the lines that cut deep around the eyes.

At some time during the little speech, the boy had come into the room—and she had nodded her agreement to take him home with her and care for him and protect him, until the world was a better place and the men of Russia came to their senses. He could have gone with his father—but he hadn't wanted to. He was sixteen. Like others of his age he was often morose and apathetic, but now he too had made his decision.

She remembered the boy, leaving his father's side, and symbolically walking around the desk to stand next to her.

And then there was a gap. For she found herself sitting in a chair, a glass of water in her hand, and her breath coming in deep painful waves. Her head hurt, and she thought . . . I must have fainted. Shame on me. After the war, and all that, the occupation, and I collapse because my son tells me he's going away. She reached for the handkerchief she always kept in her sleeve and wiped her forehead, thinking to herself . . . I have to hold on, have to be strong now, for all of them, the boy and Eduard, the girls and all the others left back home.

A final squeeze, and a prayer mumbled deep inside her heart where he wouldn't hear it and there wasn't time for tears. All at once she was back out again among all the people of the party, and another glass was in her hand—only this time it wasn't water.

The alcohol seemed to bring her around, for suddenly she was aware of the people crowding about her. "Wonderful party," they said. "So glad your son's looking well." "Difficult times," said another, scowling, and then his face changed into a clownlike smile, "but thank God we can still have a drink." Everyone seemed to laugh ridiculously loudly. Yelena wanted to go home, but she knew she couldn't leave yet. When the time came for it, someone would take her arm and lead her gently out of the Kremlin, and then it would all be over.

Anastasiya had watched Yelena emerge from the anteroom and had seen Eduard enter straight after her. It had all the appearance of a family council of war. Yelena's face looked like a battlefield.

Krichenkov, pale and proud and false, broke free from a large group and came toward her.

"You returned."

Statement, she noted, not question.

"Indeed."

"So good that you could manage it. We're enriched by your presence."

Play the game, she thought. "I would not have missed it. The General Secretary and I have much to discuss . . ."

"I hardly think this is an appropriate time."

"Then throw me out." She kept her voice even, almost friendly. "These are dramatic times, comrade secretary. Sometimes business is more important than pleasure, or did they not teach you that?"

"You are very rude, comrade."

"And you are very unhelpful." She looked past him, checking the door. Had Eduard come out? Was the General Secretary alone?

"May I perhaps suggest that you have outstayed your welcome at this party?" Krichenkov edged toward her. Suddenly she felt his arm on hers, the pressure none too gentle.

She leaned in close. "If you don't remove your hand from me this instant, I will scream and go on screaming until the General Secretary emerges. Do you wish to incur your master's displeasure?"

"That is a matter . . ." He stopped himself suddenly and she felt the pressure disappear. Roughly he pushed past her, heading for the main exit. She knew he was going for help. The next stage would be a slight accident with a drink, a pinprick in the arm, and they'd get her out that way, and she wouldn't be coming back. They were experts at that technique. Always had been. If she waited much longer she wouldn't stand a chance.

Anastasiya glanced hurriedly around the room. A few more people had arrived, but they offered scant protection. Mostly women. The men were drinking heavily. If she cried out they probably wouldn't even notice. Much more likely they'd all begin to laugh.

By the door she could see Krichenkov in earnest conversation with a security man. They glanced repeatedly in her direction. What had he been going to say? Did he not care

anymore about his master's displeasure? Had the malaise
spread so far inside the Kremlin itself? Was there no one the
General Secretary could trust?

Midway through the questions, a man in a white coat
joined the gaggle by the door. She had been right. An accident was about to cross the room and hit her. Even as they
began to move she took the ten steps to the anteroom entrance, shoving a waitress to the side, and all but colliding
with the grand piano. She heard a muffled shout, but didn't
look back, seizing the door handle with both hands, spring-
ing inside, and slamming it behind her. It must have been
reflex that made her look for a key and twist it in the lock. As
she did so the man leaning on the desk turned around. The
light was dim, so that for a second she thought she might
have been mistaken. And yet there was really no mistaking
Eduard, the General Secretary's brother, grinning at her,
amused, surprised—and yet willing, it seemed, to play whatever game she had in mind.

"Do you always lock doors behind you?" he asked.

Only then did Anastasiya look around the little room,
aware suddenly that the two of them were quite alone there
in the Kremlin, and that something momentous and unthinkable had just taken place.

"Get up, please, and put your hands in your pockets."
The photographer's tone was so matter-of-fact, he might have
been asking for a drink from the bar. And yet the envoy
couldn't quite believe that someone had entered so quietly,
so stealthily, as if from the air itself. For a moment he sat
where he was, quite unable to move, until the young man
rested the gun lightly between his shoulder blades, politely
almost, a gentle reminder that he was required to do as he
was told.

He stood up and only then did the thoughts begin to rush
in on him, seeing the young man's face: the detached, clinical
expression, without any trace of nerves.

"Please go into the bathroom and turn off the generator."
A whisper, not a trace of an accent.

The envoy felt the man close behind him. In the bathroom he had to kneel to get to the generator switch. As he flicked it, the lights in the apartment went out.

"Go back to the kitchen."

The envoy stifled a sudden desire to rush the man. For he realized that the intruder had taken several steps away from him, and was navigating simply and easily from the moonlight that shone through the windows. This was a professional. He had learned the tricks and the ways around them.

They both sat at the kitchen table.

"I don't have long." The young man seemed apologetic.

"You have your business and I have mine."

"Yours is dangerous . . ."

"For whom?" The envoy leaned forward.

"For the country."

"Is that what they told you to say?"

The photographer paused for a moment. "They didn't tell me what to say. No one ever did that. But it doesn't matter."

He looked toward the window and the envoy caught sight of a narrow pointed jaw in profile. The man was ex-army, a specialist, the very best of the very good. They weren't all Mongol conscripts, pissing their pants and digging pavements. Russia had plenty of elite soldiers—men who had spent years traveling the world, grabbing target practice for themselves in the dirty little wars their government financed.

"Is there anything you want to say?" The photographer dropped his gun arm to the ground.

"To you? Nothing."

"To anyone else?"

Only then did the envoy try to clear his mind. The man's quiet voice had seemed to lull him, hypnotize him, take away all drama. A killer who acted like a priest. And when he thought about it, sitting there in the kitchen with its shapes and shadows, it was better to go quietly. Better for the operation. Vitaly had his orders. Without a signal from the apartment the boy would head straight out to the military airfield. This was only a staging post. There was nothing to tell an outsider what it was for. All the essentials were elsewhere.

"Is there nothing you wish to know?" The photographer seemed to want to talk.

"I have lived a long time and met plenty of people like you," the envoy replied. "I didn't have much to say to them either." He breathed in deeply. "Although I do have one thing to say. It's a regret. Not for any of this. Just a regret that some human beings are thinkers and doers, while the rest are tools. Those who will do anything to live in a larger space, or put better food in their stomachs, or clothe themselves in finer fabrics."

The photographer said nothing.

"In life, if you learn anything at all it is that there are limits. Limits to what civilized people will do." Keep talking, he thought, you have to talk, but he didn't know why. "Everyone is capable of barbarism, of killing and cheating. That kind of ability, like everything else, is stored deep inside us all—our choice what we use. . . ."

"D'you want to die?" The voice was still quiet but it cut straight into the envoy's thoughts and he stopped for a moment, suddenly disquieted, his hands shaking.

"I'm just tired of living in a world full of people like you."

"Why don't you make a run for it?"

"And let you shoot me in the back?"

The photographer left his gun hand where it was. "I might not. I really haven't decided. Maybe you're right, maybe it's time to draw a limit."

The envoy got to his feet. "I've said all I have to. Perhaps it's time to go."

The photographer didn't move as the older man walked

slowly into the hall, pulled open the front door and stepped into the corridor.

Forty maybe fifty yards ahead of him, past darkened doors and empty apartments he could see the moonlight through the glass panels. And it didn't seem to matter which way it went. He'd done all he could, tied the knots, tested the rope. Now others could make the climb to safety.

But it was good to have had a friend. Better a friend than a cause, he thought, for causes change, causes go sour. They leave you and you leave them—and a friend never goes away, never dies.

There was a cool breeze in the corridor. Just a few more yards to the moon. The draft made him think of Shelepin and the cold, moaning wind that worried it through all the seasons, as if God had once looked down on the town, disliked it on sight, and decided there should never be peace on its streets.

Russia had thousands of Shelepins, he reflected: tiny mud-heaps across the steppe. Mostly they were no-hope towns, largely unaffected by progress or history or revolution. Sometime after the Bolsheviks murdered their way into power, a group of red guards had ridden into the place, torn down pictures, put up new ones, burned the schoolbooks, and replaced an enlightened local government with idiots who could barely remember the slogans they were told to promote. Such had been history's march in Shelepin.

He got to the door and paused. What a terrible legacy. And yet it was home, home to him and Mikhail and all the notions they had dreamed of to change it, to make it work. You should have stayed there and died there, said the voice, as way back down the corridor, his hand cast like stone, the photographer fired at the moving silhouette.

It was a most exceptional shot under the most difficult of circumstances—a last-minute impulse, the assassin realized. A hard decision. But you had to look after your interests. If you didn't kill when you received the order, sooner or later someone would be sent for you.

The photographer felt no sadness or remorse. A man had simply lived and then died. Even as he tidied up he knew the same thing was going on all over the world.

41

The two of them had stood in silence for several minutes, watching the storm clouds gather to the north, well out over the Arctic sea. The sky had been a gallery of color, mixed and remixed as the sunrays struck the atmosphere, subtle hues that formed and disappeared, never to be repeated. Novaya Zemlya had the power to enthrall you or drive you mad.

"And if he comes?" The base commander shifted his weight onto the other foot.

"We shouldn't discuss it." The major didn't take his eyes off the horizon.

"C'mon. I'm interested in what you think. We've been here for days, talking about all the old fuckers in Moscow and women and that sort of thing. But you must have your orders."

"This is Russia . . ."

The commander touched his arm. "What does that mean?"

"It's different from what it used to mean. These days the orders come at you from all sides. Oh maybe one group sends you sealed envelopes and the others take you for a drink and a whisper—but they're all orders. Each side pushing you in a different direction."

The base commander was clearly astonished. "Are you telling me you have to make a choice?"

"How else would you do it?"

"But for God's sake, there's still a central command."

"You think so?" The major laughed. "Yeah, they send out the paychecks—sometimes, cut the uniforms, but you're a bit out of date, my friend, if you think central command can even keep track of the paper clips!"

"I don't get it." The base commander seemed to have transformed into a sweating, agitated figure. "Who sent you out here?"

"That was the sealed envelope."

"And the rest?"

"The rest knew the contents of it before I did. Look, we flew in from Kiev. Just before takeoff I get a call from a man I hadn't seen since officer training. He actually finds me on a phone in a hangar. Here in Russia, for God's sake. *You* know the odds against that. Anyway, he's high up now in Moscow. Colonel—general, whatever . . . he asks me: You still in with the General Secretary. I say yes. What was I going to say? No, I'm a traitor, shoot me? So then he says . . . Well, stay in with him. He may need your help. Good luck in the north. And the phone goes dead." He looked at the commander and put a hand on his shoulder. It only needed a light touch. "If you repeat what I've said to anyone I'll first deny all of it, then I'll feed you to the polar bears. You understand, don't you?"

But the commander was too nervous, too excited to feel concerned. "If it happens," he mumbled, "if he were to actually step off a plane here"—he wiped his mouth on his sleeve and pointed to the ground, as if he feared he was making no sense—"how d'you decide what to do?"

The major looked at him with disdain. "There are some things that don't change, commander. Some things, maybe, that have stayed the same in politics all over the world, through all the centuries." He looked back to the horizon as the wind carried in the first drops of rain. "You back the winner," he added. "It's that simple."

* * *

There was an hour to go before her shift began. Duty Officer Belayeva rotated for work from 1800 hours through to 0530 the next day. Eleven and a half hours in the service of her country, she thought, lying back in the tiny room, with the fashion photos on the walls and the Dior poster she'd once been given in Moscow. And now this.

She checked once again in the only private place she possessed in the world—a hole in the mattress, feeling the automatic and the two clips of ammunition—taken just a week ago, because she'd had a bad dream and couldn't shake it off.

They used to joke about the overnight shift: played havoc with your social life, they said. All those domes to go to, and country to see, and coffee to drink. What a time you'd miss.

But she preferred the nights because when you finished work the tiredness forced you to sleep, and the noises of daytime were safer, more comforting than the silence of the night.

She checked the gun and the safety catch and returned it to the foam rubber mattress. She had no idea what to do with it. But if you could take something in Russia, you took it. For all the times when the unlikely came true.

Belayeva wasn't cold, and yet she clasped her robe tightly around her, trying to understand what it was she feared.

42

Anastasiya stood in the middle of the anteroom, listening to the thump of her own heart and the labored breathing as if they were coming from someone else.

"I'm sorry." She shook her head. "There's some mistake. The comrade General Secretary . . . I mean, I was to have spoken with him."

Eduard waved her to a chair. "My brother," he said with exaggerated grandeur, "has just stepped out for a while. Please wait here."

For a moment neither could think of anything to say. Eduard's eyes were swiveling between the two doors. He didn't fit the room. The suit hung badly at the waist and shoulders, the hair a little long for Moscow, the sideburns from the sixties—the green socks.

"Where did he go?" she asked casually.

"I . . ." He smiled as if to say, "In polite society we don't mention that kind of thing," but somehow the smile froze. He was losing confidence, the way a holed supertanker loses oil—fast. And there was something else: sadness, disappointment, Eduard's thirty-second stab at glory disappearing.

"He's left, hasn't he?" She stepped toward him. "You have to tell me . . ."

"No . . . I said . . ."

"Listen. I have to reach him. I have to make him understand. This isn't the way . . ."

The banging had begun again on the door leading to the
party.

"Tell them to go away," she whispered.

"Vsyo khorosho." It's okay, he shouted, louder than necessary. The noise stopped. She could just see the young men
outside, ushering the guests from the building, explaining
there'd been a minor family problem, someone unwell.
Maybe even drunk too much, said with a nod and a wink that
they'd all understand.

Anastasiya touched his arm gently. "What did he say to
you?"

Eduard didn't reply.

"Look at me." She stepped into the light from the standard lamp. The face was heart shaped, lightly freckled, the
jaw strong, the whole effect softened by the kindness of her
eyes. "I won't harm your brother."

He sat in a chair and turned away from her. And it was
only when she saw the shoulders heave, and the head bow
down into his hands, that she knew he was weeping, the way
the Slavs often do, their emotions open to all weathers, bare
and unprotected. But this was more. This was a man struck
in the face by events he couldn't understand. A strong man,
broken deep inside.

She took a handkerchief from her purse and put it in his
hand. A few moments passed and then he turned to face her.
"I'm sorry . . ."

"No need," she told him. And it was then that she was
going to prompt him, but she didn't need to.

"I have never seen him so upset," Eduard whispered. He
put the handkerchief in his pocket. "Always, ever since I was
a child, he was so tough. Tough with all of us. Mother as
well." He sniffed and looked around the room. "And yet we
loved him and we knew he loved us. He would always listen

to our problems, always offer a way out—even when he went
to Moscow." He shrugged and raised his eyebrows. "There
were times when I . . . well I would have liked things from
him—you know, a present here or there, some clothes. In the
country, after all, we don't have very much. And he knew
that. Of course he did. But instead of presents he would give
us something much more valuable—time. And when he tele-
phoned as he did, every week, he really wanted to help. Were
there problems in the village, what was the right way to go
about things? He never offered influence, never put in a good
word—just advice . . ." He stopped in mid-sentence. Anastasiya knelt in front of him.

"Go on."

"Tonight they took away his dream." She could see
Eduard's eyes still glistened. "He said it was time to find another way. Six years was enough. And then the demonstration on Gorky Street. That was the turning point, he said. 'If
they're dying on my streets, I have to be doing it wrong. This
has to stop . . .'"

"Do you know where he is . . . ?"

"I cannot say."

"Cannot?"

"He didn't tell me. Better like that, he said. They'll all
ask. They'll all find out in time."

"Not even a hint?"

Eduard smiled. "My brother used to close his mouth so
often, we sometimes wondered if he had lost the power of
speech. He can place something in his mind and lock it there
almost indefinitely, unseen and untouched. He's a remark-
able man."

She nodded and stood up. From the other room came
the treble notes of the piano.

"I wish I could stay for the party," she told him.

He pointed to the outer door. "Go out that way. I am to
keep them at bay for as long as I can."

"I can't quite believe this," she murmured, "any of this. Him, you, the party."

"Yes you can," he replied softly. "You have only to look around you. It had to end this way."

When he thought about it David Russert knew there was danger. But he entered the apartment, unprepared for the quiet sense of terror that hung there.

Nothing was out of place, nothing disturbed. The lights were out, blinds left open. A still summer night with no wind at all. Only the envoy was missing.

He could be late, couldn't he? Could've broken down. Could've changed the plan at the last moment. Could be taking out that one extra piece of insurance . . .

But it doesn't happen like that, does it? How many operations get altered at the last moment? How many people break down? How many just don't make it through the traffic when it's this important? None at all, my friend, none at all. Unless and only unless the whole thing has gone to hell by special delivery. Only when it's fallen apart and you all begin to run. And he isn't going to make it . . .

Russert began to walk around the apartment, trying to slow the mind, get a grip, think through the fallbacks. Only that too came back to him—when you play this high, when you don't just bet your shirt, but you throw in the house, the car, the wife, and kids, there's no one to catch you when you stumble. You've just staked the entire company, and the company's gone.

Russert tried a light switch. Odd the way the generator had stopped. He went into the bathroom and crouched beside it. The switch had to be somewhere. That was it . . .

And then without warning the lights came on, not one set, but all of them, it seemed, and Russert was looking at the envoy, propped up in the bath, and no longer wondering about anything at all, staring straight ahead, devoid of fear or pressure, quiet and very detached, as if in the moment of departure he had found serenity and had wanted to bequeath it as the signpost to a better world.

Vitaly had barely felt the car door open, barely sensed the downward give on the suspension as his passenger got in. He hesitated to look in the mirror, because in that moment all the self-control began to melt away and his hands were moist and trembling on the steering wheel. The shape was there all right, a light raincoat, a gray homburg pulled well down, and the glasses . . . Christ Almighty, Vitaly! Get him out of here. The Chaika went smoothly into gear, out over the cobbles, so dark in the recesses of the Kremlin, and you're just driving him out as if it were the mailman off on his rounds. No fuss, no ceremony, and for the first time in a decade there isn't a single person in the world who knows where he is—except me.

He checked again in the mirror. The shape was motionless. The face inclined to the window as the unlit city rushed by. Holy Mother of God! More terrifying than any spinning plane, more like a dive out of control—and there'd been one or two of those.

Think, Vitaly. Get it sorted.

Traffic was sparse along the Embankment. Keep going fast, keep your foot down. After all it's an official car—and you're supposed to force everyone else off the road. That's the way it's always been.

Out on Kutuzovsky, another glance in the back, and his spirits lifted. Fucking clockwork. Almost to the second. The envoy had been *so* clever, getting the party organized next to the anteroom with its passage to the private apartments, and the staircase straight out into the courtyard. Plenty of escape routes. Every one of Russia's rulers must have insisted on them, built and planned their own, knowing the treachery they'd had to use to take power, and the treachery others would need to remove them.

Swing it east now. Gently. The car was a pig. Squeaks

and thuds at every bump in the road. There at the intersection—the militia's control post, and they were out there beside it, three or four of them, watching, pulling some of the vehicles in, checking documents. Two of them saluted the Chaika—and they'd never know, would they?

Vitaly rubbed a hand through his hair. He was tempted to open the glass partition, greet the man, make a human contact. But the envoy had forbidden it. Not a social event, he'd said, you won't be graded for your manners. Get him there, get him out—and one day, who knows, you could be a hero.

He could see it now in the distance. First woodland, then scrub, and the block stood out way beyond. Lights suddenly behind him, then ahead, and his heart rate must have doubled, but the cars passed him and the darkness returned.

He turned into the parking lot and then for the first time in his life, his nerve went. It was a flash or a shadow that he saw first, a few feet to the side of the car. And then the shadow was a man, like none he had seen before. Hair wild in the wind, shouting in a foreign language, banging with his fists on the side windows, even as Vitaly's foot slammed onto the brake.

And then he heard the single word that the envoy had made him memorize, repeated again and again, screamed into the night. He wound down the window, suddenly aware that his passenger was also speaking. A few seconds went by before he realized the language was English.

"You'd better drive." Russert's voice was cracking, his breath coming in irregular jerks.

"My uncle," he yelled back. "He should be here."

Russert touched his arm. "He won't be coming." The voice had lowered, back again under control. "I'm very sorry."

Vitaly was about to get out and shake him, for he had to be lying. There was a mistake. However hopeless the situation, you can always save the man, this man—you can always get him back.

And yet when he looked into Russert's eyes he could see that he'd told the truth—and that out there in the wasteland of the eastern suburbs, nothing more could be done.

43

Jim Tuckerman had been damn clever—or damn stupid. They'd work out which later. But the flash cable had been marked for his attention—"eyes only"—and Fox could only give thanks to whichever gods were responsible.

He was airborne within forty minutes because the Agency can still move when it has to and—even with an image battered and sullied by leaks, findings, and failures—it has greater resources to draw on than any other intelligence organization in the world. If Fox wanted a plane to Norway, Fox got it.

The climb out of Dulles took him through the humid pall along the eastern seaboard, joining the jetstream off Newfoundland. By then he had called London, and had listened to the studied indifference of Foreign Office and been assured that "well, if he really had to . . ." the man would be there to meet him.

And then, he reflected, it's just me and the Atlantic and Tuckerman's shattering cable, for the next five and three quarter hours.

Fox shut his eyes and tried to piece together the scene in Moscow. Tuckerman calling Russert's apartment, getting no answer, calling again at midnight, starting to worry, waking himself at three, and calling again. Finally at five the man had gone there, jimmied open the door, and found the letter. Letter. The word didn't even begin to describe it.

Tuckerman would have thought first, sitting there in the apartment, wondering which of the signals clerks he could trust most, then waking and moving, fast but careful.

He could imagine the man's methodical mind. Send it, explain it, but cover each track along the way. Send it in a code that the Agency computers couldn't crack, that would go right to Fox's door, that wouldn't raise too many eyebrows and queries along the way. Although even now he knew there'd be plenty of unlisted phones ringing around the Washington area—and the moment he surfaced the monkey would fall on his back.

But he couldn't have stayed in the U.S. with this cable. If it got to the White House they wouldn't have a clue what to do with it. On a good day they'd leak it. On a bad day there'd be ranting and raving all over the building—and then the cowboys in the basement would have a say.

Fox knew how the final decision would go. When it came down to the line—it was all about the photo ops. No President could pass up the one that would kick off every election campaign from now till doomsday, the one the world would never forget: the shot of the Chief welcoming a Soviet leader into voluntary exile in the United States. The awful, unthinkable prospect that David Russert was now threatening to deliver.

She had to shake him hard before he came around. Marcus the idealist, she thought, Marcus the fool. All that Western education and experience, and he was still the child and she the adult. She had lived life. He'd been cushioned against it.

But there wasn't time for this.

"You have to move." Anastasiya rolled him over onto his back and slapped him hard. And he was stirring and cursing, fighting the dead weight that had forced him to the ground.

Hurry. Keep going.

She pulled him into a sitting position. And now they'd be looking for both of them. How long before they added up her contacts and balanced the equation?

Somehow she got Marcus to his feet, swiveling in surprise as the door opened and the photographer hurried in.

He didn't speak, not immediately, didn't need to, simply laid a black leather case on the sofa and snapped it open. In his hands suddenly, a pile of photographs and personal letters that answered Anastasiya's questions even as her mind began to formulate them.

"This was all in the apartment, packed and ready to go." He looked up at her. She could see he'd been running. His cool and his composure had left him. "It's pretty conclusive. He must have been going to take it with him."

She held the letters to the light. There was no doubt of their origin. She knew the General Secretary's handwriting—and you couldn't get more personal than this. Private notes on meetings, letters from his mother. A few reminders about the boy. "You did well to bring all this," she told him.

Marcus took the papers from her hand, trying not to look at the photographer, trying not to imagine what he'd done . . .

"He's left the Kremlin." Anastasiya sat down on the sofa. "We know that much. Maybe he went to this apartment. Maybe he didn't. The fact is he won't go there now—will he?"

She looked hard at the young Russian. His eyes told her what had happened. There was no need to ask. No need to talk—when your life and your plans are suddenly derailed in front of you, do you shout or moan, she wondered. Do you throw rocks at the sky?

"I don't know what to say." She glanced at the two of them. "You better lose yourself." This to the photographer. "As for us. What can I tell you, my dear. You can go to your embassy. I . . ." She pushed the hair away from her eyes. "It's over. All of it. Forget we ever began."

She gazed around the apartment as if to record the place and the time of failure—in this shabby little room, way out in the Kuntsevo suburbs, in a block that had begun to crumble and crack the moment it was finished. Far away she heard music, and the crying of a baby several stories below. I'm so tired, she thought.

Anastasiya felt pressure on her arm, half expecting Marcus to embrace her a final time and walk away. But he wouldn't let go, she looked up into his face and saw to her utter surprise that he was smiling.

"I know where he's gone," he told her, the old confidence returning, the strength that she had so admired. "It's all right. I know."

Vitaly headed the huge lumbering car out toward the military airfield. Late now, way past midnight. They're quiet and sleepy and they know me. And this is the way my uncle wanted it.

Behind him the two figures, still, barely talking, as if in shock. No sound penetrated the glass partition.

A wide boulevard, with the trees in full bloom, and through them he could see the perimeter fence, the runway lights still on. A hundred yards away—the control point. And you have to let the guard see him, otherwise you'll never make it.

Vitaly took a hand away from the wheel, moving it as he hadn't done since childhood, tracing the sign of the cross over his chest, bowing his head for an instant.

Wind down the window, show the pass, and it's the boy from Leningrad, the chatterer—and then you beckon him forward, like you're imparting a trust, and he must never, ever tell a soul, "swear it on the grave of your ancestors."

One furtive glance into the back, and the guard's face seems to lose all color and you drive through, choosing the service ramp, because that leads straight onto the stand and the runway.

Vitaly pulled up, sliding the partition just an inch. "I have to get the paperwork. Ten minutes: no more."

In the duty office sits Boris—lousy flyer, seconded to administration duties, hates them, hates everyone.

"I need a plane, Boris."

"Your plane is always in the same place." Boris doesn't even look up.

"I need a bigger plane."

Boris smiles. "Got a woman, have you? Dirty bastard. Just don't fuck about while you're flying. Okay?"

"Is there a Yak 40?" Easy now, keep the patter going.

"We have three. Only one has an engine. But it's your choice."

"Hmm, tough decision, Boris. I'll take that one."

"Okay. Keys are in the ignition. Sign here and get out before someone else wants it." He slides the log across the table. "Usual route, I assume."

"I can only do it one way."

Boris laughs.

Outside Vitaly feels the nausea climbing up his throat, the effort of snowing Boris. Sorry, old man, sorry about your career, and your family, and the rest of your life—but there was nothing I could do.

Out across the runway under a full moon, and for the first time you can see his face and watch him walk. *He looks so old.* Gone is the jaunty step, the little smile that played around the edges of his mouth. He looks at the ground, hands in his raincoat pockets, no one to wave at. When you're out, you're really out.

The plane stands there, white and blue in the moonlight. And you have all the coordinates in your head, the routing, the ident—and so does the tower.

"Vitaly," they crackle jokingly across the radio, "don't you ever sleep?"

"Of course not," he replies. "I'm not like you. Some of us work for a living."

They give him the weather and confirm the route—and now you're halfway down the checklist and the twin engines are starting to tell you they aren't that bad.

And now you know why you went through a hundred and one practice missions, flying straight lines to the north and back again, week after week, because no one is asking you questions and you're flying out of Moscow with the General Secretary in the back of the plane—and there's a clear sky ahead for a thousand miles.

Vitaly leveled off at 29,000 feet, where the stars shone bright and cold and the moon reflected off the cockpit windshield. Up here, he thought, I can pretend I'm dreaming. Just for an hour or two. Just till we land.

44

The guests had long since left the party—offended, as only drunks can be—by the sudden disappearance of their host. Yelena and the two nieces had been shunted, tearful and exhausted, into a dining room, where they slouched on gilded reproduction chairs, waiting for something unpleasant to happen.

Krichenkov was in charge, now considerably less composed. His little footsteps seemed to run in all directions. On his orders they broke down the door to the anteroom, and found Eduard half conscious on the floor, a bottle of whiskey at his feet, and nothing intelligible coming from his lips.

Again on orders they took pictures of him, where he lay. It seemed they were gathering evidence of the degeneration of the Soviet Union's first family—now that its head had gone. There were pictures too of Yelena and the girls, astride their fancy chairs, albeit wearing expressions of dejection: as if the people had finally found them out, and the lavish lifestyle (that they'd never had) was ending.

It was Yelena who realized what was being done. She who noted the indifference to her son's departure, the way they sought to exorcise him like a troublesome spirit. How quickly they had returned to old practices! Soon the lying would begin again in earnest—and if you lied long enough, that too would become the truth, the new truth, the most dangerous of all.

In the thirties Yelena herself had joined the party—well, it didn't mean much in those days, but at least you felt involved. It was like church, she thought, only without God. You just sat there, repeated the lines someone else had recited, bowed your head a few times, and paid homage to the man with the bald head and the goatee beard on the wall. What was so wrong with that?

Only later did they learn that lesson.

The door slammed back on its hinges and Krichenkov returned, shoes squeaking on the polished wood floors. They were going home, he said, by train, he said, staccato and officious, and she knew the type so well.

Somewhere, she felt sure, a stooge candidate was even now learning *his* lines, preparing to keep the seat warm. And by morning the radio and television services would be instructed to break the news of the General Secretary's departure. They wouldn't want the Americans to do it first.

As for herself, she had no worries. What mattered were Eduard and the nieces: who would forever be regarded as a traitor's relatives. Russians were like that, she realized—love or hate, black or white. A wasteland in between. The family would have to suffer because they'd see to it.

Northern Norway. A NATO air force base. A line of all-weather interceptors along the tarmac, and more sky than he ever remembered seeing. What do I know about this place? Foreign Office wondered. And then . . . what do I want to know about it?

He watched Fox checking in at the guest quarters. They might as well have met in Barbados for all the good they would do here. Maybe it felt better being close to Russia, but it wouldn't feel better for long.

Fox had given him the cable on landing. No pleasantries. No note swapping about flights.

"I wish you hadn't shown me this," he told the American.

Fox had put on a pale smile. "I wasn't going to be able to keep it to myself. That much was sure."

"How many people know of this outside your embassy?"

"Now there are two." Fox turned off the smile. "I needed to bounce this off someone who hadn't grown up in the States, didn't serve the U.S. government, and knew nothing about the role of a superpower. That seems to fit you people these days."

The two men surveyed each other unkindly.

"You also wanted to verify your instincts." Foreign Office paused. "By the way what exactly were your instincts?"

"I wanted to throw up."

"Is this the first time?" Foreign Office raised unsympathetic eyebrows.

"No, of course it isn't. I work for the government, remember? I was part of the Reagan revolution." Fox looked over his shoulder. "Shouldn't we go outside a moment?"

They walked out into the darkness. Just a forecourt, a lake, a wide road. Neither of them saw any of it.

"I believed in the doctrine." Fox was looking at the ground. "Less intrusive government at home, more intrusive abroad. We had to pick our targets and make them count. I mean look at Grenada, and Libya—forget the crap about rolling back the frontiers of communism—but we had to send signals to the other side. Show them that we were prepared to push buttons—not big ones. But if we had to we'd roll the planes out of the hangars and go for a drive in them. And they could draw their own conclusions." He glanced at Foreign Office as if expecting disagreement. "And it worked, to a point. We got an arms control agreement. For Chrissake, we got summits, where the world wasn't holding its breath, waiting for war." He shrugged. "It was something."

"And now."

"Now . . ." he sighed. "Now all this goes too far. You know that, don't you?"

Foreign Office looked away.

"Oh c'mon. It has to. If the General Secretary goes to America, there'll be civil war back in the Soviet Union. Open season for every political faction, military unit, factory brigade—you name it. This is the most dangerous time of all. They've just had their first taste of freedom and democracy in seventy years. That's a powerful drug. They're not used to it. If they overdose, it could kill them. You can't have power vacuums in a place like that. There's too much unrestricted power around. It's why they've always had to die in office or be stabbed in the back. Quick, brutal transitions with nothing left to chance or imagination. Why? Because Russia couldn't handle it any other way." He stopped, suddenly out of breath. "You know that. What's more, we couldn't handle it either. Oh the cowboys would—the White House would wet itself just at the thought. Your guys too. You don't get gifts like that in politics. Doesn't happen."

"So what are you saying?"

The American's face was just inches away from Foreign Office. "If he makes it out of Russia, he never reaches the West."

"You mean you'd want to send him back?"

"Right."

"And if he won't agree?"

"He goes in a crate." Fox turned away and walked back toward the guest house.

45

As they flew north, Russert felt the desperation rising. He wiped the sweat away from his forehead.

Across the aisle the General Secretary sat with eyes closed, but he wasn't sleeping.

Russert had tried talking to him, recalling the times they had shared, but he couldn't get through. There was barely a greeting, barely a sign of recognition. Instead a coolness, an air of affected detachment had settled over the man, as if personalities and relationships no longer counted, as if he were judging the world and finding it poor.

Russert rubbed his eyes. The man's face had been no surprise. He'd seen him on television a thousand times, exulting silently and privately on each occasion. He'd watched the smile light up the covers of magazines around the world, for here at last was a laughing Russian, a thinking Russian. The bear had shed its skin and revealed a human beneath it. Oh there was force and determination but his charm softened the edges. Such charm.

So many years ago and he recalled the two of them in Moscow, dating the same girl. Blonde, slim, with a smile that could wrap you up in bed and make you forget the world outside. And I had everything going for *me*, Russert thought. I was better looking, I think, and I was foreign. The girls in the student dorm used to look at us Americans as if we were passports with legs. Marry a foreigner—that's all they wanted to do. See New York and pick up all the gold that was lying around doing nothing on the sidewalks.

But I didn't stand a chance with him there. Fat, awkward-looking fellow, but he would smile that smile—and they'd feel his eyes bore into them. And this one girl we were after—the blonde—she just kissed me on the cheek and said I wasn't in the same class. And it was true: I wasn't . . .

Look at him, sitting, staring at his hands. This is the man I'm taking into exile. This old friend. This stranger.

He got up to stretch his legs. They were flying in thick cloud, at least 700 gray kilometers an hour. By now, he realized, Tuckerman would have got the letter and Washington would be hopping up and down on one foot—and they wouldn't have imagined, in their wildest moments . . .

He returned to his seat, taking comfort in the passage of time and distance. If you're not flying the plane, he thought, there's nothing you can do. We'll just refuel in Novaya Zemlya, see how the land lies, and then get the hell out West, before anyone knows it. Before it gets light. Before this day smacks the entire world in the face.

46

Belayeva knew. The moment she found out the flight was on course, she knew. Different plane, different time. Vitaly would be flying more slowly. But there could be only one reason for that.

An hour into her shift, she left the control room, saying she was going to the lavatory, went instead to her room and retrieved the automatic. "Why am I doing this?" she asked herself.

Back in the slot, she let one of the other controllers talk him in. But she turned on the loudspeaker and tried to glean something from the voice. Difficult. Conditions were poor that night. Storms forecast. He was calm though, damn him.

Someone had alerted the commander, she wasn't sure who. He came in still tucking his shirt into his trousers, hair uncombed, the major behind him.

"Right," he said, as if he knew what he was doing. Belayeva was certain he didn't.

She handed him the printouts, and he busied himself with them, checking figures and numbers that didn't need checking, peering at the radar screen. The major stood behind her and said nothing. Maybe it was always like that with the military. They didn't have to think. A bit like the Russian people. Only you couldn't go on like that forever . . .

Vitaly was requesting final approach. They all turned to look at the major. He nodded imperceptibly.

In that moment Belayeva made her decision.

Fox stood over the sleeping figure and shook hard. It wasn't easy to wake him. Foreign Office didn't do mornings.

In the light from the small bedside lamp he reached for his glasses, wiping the hair from his face.

"It's three o'clock."

"It's ten past three," Fox told him. He handed over a sheet of paper. "This is what Radio Moscow broadcast at three."

Foreign Office read it through twice. "It doesn't say much."

"No, I suppose it doesn't." Fox took back the transcript. "Only enough to set off a political earthquake right around the globe. Give it another two or three minutes and our people will be ordering us back. Who knows, we might be the first Westerners to share a labor camp."

Foreign Office sat up. "It said, 'resigned his position and has left the country . . .' "

"I'm afraid there's more."

"Ah!"

Fox sat down at the end of the bed. "We just monitored a Yak 40 out of Moscow, coming into Novaya Zemlya. It's our old scheduled route: the one we've been watching since Murmansk. But the plane's bigger and my guess is, there are passengers."

"Then he's on his way."

"Seems like it." Fox got up. "Take a look out of the window."

Foreign Office shifted around. At the side of the runway, where the interceptors were lined up, he could make out one or two tiny lights, some motion, a figure with a helmet crossed the skyline.

"Two of the fighter pilots here belong to us. Agency . . ."

"I don't believe this . . ."

"Believe it." Fox had his hand on the doorknob. "Whatever we decide to do—they'll go and do it."

47

With the landing lights on, the runway was a brightly patterned carpet, stretching out into the dark northern sky. The wind had picked up. And they stood outside the main dome, just a handful of them, their faces drawn and anxious.

"I'll be polite, but firm." The commander turned to the major.

"Don't be stupid," the officer replied. "Have you forgotten who he is?"

Out of the clouds they could make out the wing lights of the Yak, already fighting the surface gusts, its landing gear down, nose up, a white speck in the middle of the night.

And then for the first time the commander caught the movement at the end of the runway. He didn't need to ask what it was—the armored cars, the troops, the professionals were moving into position. Once the plane was down they'd surround it, block the runway, and the deed would be done.

The Yak's rear wheels hit the tarmac, and the commander could feel his excitement building. The moment of his career, his life. History in front of him. My God. To think . . .

The jets had gone into reverse and he turned away, shielding his ears from the din, aware suddenly that the major was no longer beside him, that he didn't know what to do next, and that the whole matter was now completely out of his control. And yet he couldn't take his eyes off the plane, the little white pin, roaring toward the far end of the runway, because in the end, that was all that would matter to any of them.

He was aware that the plane had halted. But it was too hard to see anything else. Across the flattened grass he ran to the Niva, paying no attention to anyone else, driving out onto the runway, against all the standing orders in the world, punching the gears, the engine rattling and screaming at him as his foot hit the floor.

It looked all right. The troops were in position around the plane. Maybe fifty of them, rifles pointed. But the door of the Yak remained closed.

The commander flung himself out of the driver's seat and ran over to the major. But even as he got there he heard the door open, the steps came down, and suddenly his breath was taken away by the figure who stood there, in overcoat and hat, his face expressionless, hands at his side. Calm, unemotional—the man fitted his image, exactly the way it had always been projected.

For a moment, nothing happened, and then without warning, without orders, the troops lifted their rifles into the air and snapped to attention.

Belayeva had run back into the control room, seeing the plane, knowing she had to retrieve her bag and get out there. In her mind she could picture Vitaly, strapped into the cockpit, alarmed, and what was worse, alone.

But as she entered, she knew something was badly wrong. The controllers had turned their chairs away from the radar screens and were looking at her in silence. As she swung around, a soldier held up his hands as if to bar her way.

"You must remain here. A temporary measure."

He wasn't more than twenty, the young face dotted with

acne, his combat uniform bulky from weapons and equipment.

Belayeva stepped down toward the radar screens, aware that she had to take control.

"What are you doing?" The soldier moved forward, disconcerted.

She ignored him. "Carry on with your work," she told the traffic controllers, and as they turned back to their desks, she surveyed the soldier.

"You may not be aware, young man, that this is the northernmost operations base of the Soviet Union, and I would warn you not to interfere with our work. Is that understood?"

He looked at her uncomprehendingly and returned to the doorway. You didn't argue with women in the military. These days you didn't argue with anyone.

At least a minute must have passed before they got the call. The senior controller spoke briefly into his headset. She couldn't hear what was said. The man unplugged himself and came across to her.

"Strange thing. Unscheduled Aeroflot flight out of Archangel. Headed our way. Pilot says he's on course for Vorkuta —in difficulties. What d'you want me to do?"

"Bring him in." From the corner of her eye Belayeva could see the young soldier approaching.

"Nothing is allowed to land," he said quickly, as if they were lines he had learned. "Nothing till further orders. Tell the pilot he can't come in."

And in that moment, Belayeva did something that surprised her for a long time afterward. She pointed to the screen and beckoned the soldier forward to examine it. Boy that you are, she thought, look at it, go on, can't you see the little plane out there? And even as he leaned forward, she brought the automatic out of her handbag and placed the steel muzzle against his neck.

"Young man," she whispered. "This plane *will* land here,

because I say so. Now sit on the floor, on your hands, and do as you're told."

For Marcus it was an overwhelming collection of images. Dreams, most of them nightmares, becoming real life.

Of course, when he had thought about it, there'd been no doubt where they had gone: it all came full circle. The training flights to Novaya Zemlya, the mounting chaos in the Kremlin. The way out.

But he'd been surprised at Anastasiya, surprised at the power that the privileged and influential could still wield in this land of confusion. Surprised at *her* power.

It wasn't so much the way she ordered them all to Sheremyetyevo, haranguing the airport authorities and the militia, employing both charm and steel in quick succession. Nor the way she could flash her government identity card, and demand facilities and access denied to all others. But she believed in it. Her confidence seemed irrepressible.

Not till they were on the plane, a civilian pilot in the cockpit, the photographer at the rear, did she retreat into her own domain.

She shut her eyes, and locked their arms together, pushing her face close against his neck. Inside, he knew, she was wandering. But she needed to be anchored, needed to know that there was firm ground to stand on and count on.

The plane moved into the northeast corridor, and he couldn't think of where it would take him. Whatever the circumstances, she always made him light-headed, made him feel the world was just a ball you could catch in your hand.

They refueled again at Archangel and she was out there on the tarmac, berating them before they could wake up and think. No the clearances were not in order, no there was no permission, no flight plan, no precedent. But if she was sure, if she would take personal responsibility . . . if, if, if.

And they were onto the final segment. Were they flying faster or did it just seem like it?

Marcus wondered where Foreign Office was. Had the man given him up? And wouldn't he have been right to do so?

They would know, all of them, that it wasn't the game for him. He was trouble, he was unreliable. Silly bugger, couldn't keep it in his trousers. Thinks he invented the hard-on. That's what they'd say, never knowing how deeply he felt.

The pilot wasn't interested in art. He was throwing the aircraft around the skies, without thought for his passengers. No gradual descent. The nose simply fell forward and dived.

Only when they hit the tarmac did Marcus realize there'd been no time to work it out, any of it. They were landing naked on a freezing runway, without backup or shelter. He could only remember what one of Foreign Office's men had confided in him: "When it's really big," he had said, "when it has a life of its own, it drives itself."

Apart from the landing lights, not a single sign of life came from the complex. They slid down the emergency chute and stood for a moment, lost in the Arctic silence, dwarfed by the dark expanse around them.

The pilot stayed in the cockpit, so it was just the three shadows that edged their way toward the domes.

Maybe it was wrong, he thought. There's nothing here after all. Anastasiya . . . But she had strode on ahead.

They stopped outside the main entrance and looked around them. The radar scanner spun crazily in the wind and without warning sheets of rain blew across the runway, as the eye of the storm closed over them.

You don't knock, thought Marcus, you just go in, hoping against hope that whatever they throw at you can be handled or thrown back. The guidelines for a life of peace and simplicity.

But it didn't prepare him for the sharp seizure of fear as they struggled into the warm cocoon, turned in confusion, and saw the lights of the hallway blaze on around them.

There must have been a dozen armed soldiers along the

walls, but it wasn't to them that Marcus's attention was drawn. In the doorway of what seemed to be a briefing room, a man with glasses and gray overcoat stood motionless, his hands by his side, watching them with nothing more than professional curiosity.

48

The four A.M. news bulletin from Moscow radio was fed onto the loudspeakers, and they sat under neon lights, listening to the tinny, self-righteous voice, as if they had flown into the Arctic Circle for that purpose and none other.

Marcus glanced over to Russert. How did I know you'd be here? he asked himself. Maybe because all roads lead eventually to a traitor, and you had to be one. You of the firm, dry, outstretched hand—that mark of an honest man, full of character.

The soldiers had taken up positions at the front and back of the room, their rifles in hand, but pointing toward the ground. They seemed to fill the place, with their bulky clothes and equipment, their blackened faces, blackened tunics. Silent, unthinking machines, now ready to act.

Somehow, thought Marcus, it always came down to a man holding a gun. Whatever the plan, whatever distant office you'd started in, whatever friendly little chat had set the ball in motion—at the end of the road there would one day be waiting a figure in black, with a weapon in his hand. And that would settle it.

At the far end of the room was a lecture platform. Russert stood on it, awkward and superfluous, the troop commander with him—a kind of high table. And there, presiding, was the General Secretary, taking in the broadcast, the diatribe about his self-confessed inability to govern, the apologies for mistakes (that he had never made), the pledge of continuity and further reforms (that would never be fulfilled), the lies that came tumbling out with all the practiced sincerity that true liars can give them.

He, it was, who rose to turn off the loudspeaker, who removed his overcoat, and balanced his elbows on the trestle table, as if to chair a meeting of the Politburo.

And now Marcus's impressions become disjointed as the room and the occupants rearrange to their final positions.

Russert whispers at the General Secretary's side, gesturing to the clock. But he doesn't like that, ignores him, brushes him aside.

"But we ought to get going," Russert says, loud enough for everyone to hear.

And Russert hasn't seen it, thought Marcus—but I have, watching the General Secretary assembling his own pieces on his own chessboard. We're all part of the game. We're all here because he brought us.

This isn't a man who's leaving his country.

He smoothes the hair on each side of his head and starts the speech. It's like a pep talk to a workers' cooperative. Same old jargon about critical problems and deepening crisis at home. They can't get away from it, Marcus realized. If only he sat and said: Look, I fucked up, it was an elaborate game, but I needed to play it. But he's still prattling on about economic revitalization, and Marcus was pinching himself that this was the middle of the night, just a couple of hundred miles from the North Pole.

And it's the pilot who's moving. Vitaly. He can see what's happening. The blood was rising on his neck all the time the General Secretary was speaking. His eyes have glazed over as if he's locked into a decision and is waiting for the moment . . . but he couldn't get away with it . . .

To Marcus it seemed like an act in slow motion as Vitaly

rose up from the second line of chairs and launched himself across them toward the General Secretary.

Even as his hands fastened on the man's neck, the troop commander leaned forward, pistol in hand, the muzzle pointing straight at the soft spot below Vitaly's ear.

Maybe Marcus got it wrong, maybe the speed of events was too great, maybe he only thought he saw it . . . the woman in uniform slamming open the door at the back of the room, her automatic rising to shoulder height and the round hole forming in the commander's forehead.

The soldiers were raising their rifles, but suddenly there was no one to give them an order.

And then he—the General Secretary is pulling himself up in the midst of it all, standing to attention, demanding the arms be shouldered, a voice of certain and unflinching authority, now, at long last, as the smoke from the automatic begins to fill the room and a man lies dead on the floor.

Vitaly is on his knees, the woman who saved him kneels at his side. He's weeping uncontrollably. Marcus could catch only a word or two about his uncle, about the price of a life, about the deceit and betrayal.

Russert's head is in his hands as if he's gone elsewhere and the General Secretary is looking straight at Marcus.

They both want to talk, that's clear enough, but neither feels able to begin. Only as he's heading for the double doors does Marcus catch at his arm.

"You know the West would never have taken you."

He stops and turns full face.

"You're too hot, you couldn't have made it," Marcus insists. "You were born here and you have to die here."

And then he was gone and a hand was cupping Marcus's face. Anastasiya.

"Marcus, I'm leaving with him."

He held her tightly.

"I can't agree with what he's done," she whispers. "He played with us all. Played with Russert and Vitaly's uncle, made us all think he'd leave. He's brought his enemies into the open and now he'll take his troops back into Moscow and be greeted like a conquering hero." She sighed. "I don't know the details, but that looks like it. He made himself look weaker and weaker. But all the time his own men were in place, just noting down the names of all his opponents, getting ready to move against them." She shrugged. "There was nothing else he could do."

"That line again."

"There's only one line in this country."

His turn to take her face in his hands.

"You don't have to go with him."

"For now I do."

"And later?"

"We'll see."

And there's a time, thought Marcus, when everything's been said, when the road has been traveled, when you can go no farther in any direction. This time.

"You know what I want to tell you, don't you?"

"Yes, Marcus." She put her arms around him. "Yes, I do."

49

The fighters were at the end of the runway. You couldn't see them, but you knew they were there.

The tie lines with London and Washington were on open microphones.

Their eyes were fixed on the radar operator and Foreign Office wondered how many fingers were on how many buttons.

Suddenly the man snapped his fingers, tore off his headphones, and got up.

"Southwest," he told them. "Moscow flight path. Seems to be going home."

The two of them made their way onto the terrace outside the control room. In the dawn light the planes were nosing their way back to the hangar, long, slow, and lethal, with the first of the sun's rays reflecting off the swept-back wings.

Fox stared straight ahead. "How many more of these d'you think we'll get?"

"A few. The Soviets have just bought themselves the biggest dose of instability since the Revolution. Some of us are going to wish Brezhnev was back in power."

"Makes a bit of a mockery of us trying to lend support . . ."

"It's not an argument for doing nothing . . ." Foreign Office turned to look at him. "Russia isn't just any old slab of earth. It's a sixth of the landmass of this planet, and if it goes to hell, it has the power to take us with it." He made a face. "That's why we're in this. Not for the good of the Russians, for their living standards, or democracy, or any of that nonsense—it's so they don't blow themselves to pieces. We can't take a civil war in that country—not another one."

The three planes had lined up again in formation, and the pilots in red flying suits were leaving their cockpits.

Foreign Office rubbed his chin. "As a matter of interest would you really have used them?" He gestured toward the aircraft.

Fox didn't look at him. "Would you?" he asked softly, and turned away.

The train reached Shelepin in the early afternoon as the summer heat wore down on the little town.

They looked a strange group, still in dresses and evening finery, now creased and dirty. Some of the passengers had sniggered at them. One had even asked if they belonged to a comic troupe, or the circus.

Eduard had slept long and badly, and he hung his head in fatigue as they stumbled their way, without luggage, along the pavement.

Yelena, as ever, took refuge in the present. What was past, was past, she told herself. And the future would go its own way.

She got them home, boiled water, and made tea. But by the time it was ready, the nieces and Eduard had fallen asleep where they sat and she had only herself for comfort. As the shadows lengthened, the night came to the town, and the noisy nagging wind blew in as it always did from the steppes around them.

Krichenkov had expected the chiefs of staff. From his office next to the General Secretary's apartment he instructed security to admit them.

One by one they had been coming to pay their respects: the head of the Moscow party region, a few trade union leaders, two or three "experts" from the KGB's second directorate—internal security. The hard core—with enough clout among them to bring the rest of the sheep into line.

As for the General Secretary—he had proved far easier to dislodge than anyone had imagined. Krichenkov sat back in his leather armchair and admired his manicured fingernails. Such were the surprises in politics. Truly, these were fascinating times.

He could hear the military men arriving in the outer office, so he rose to meet them, fixing on a bland, businesslike smile of welcome. Of course he wasn't looking for office himself. That was out of the question. But it had been agreed that he would help supervise the transition. If not king—then at least a king-maker—a chance to shape the glorious future.

As it turned out the three service chiefs entered Krichenkov's office before he could open the door to them. He noted in passing that they failed to knock, or indeed announce themselves in any way at all. At first he was reassured by the equally bland smiles of welcome that they themselves were wearing. It was only when he lowered his eyes and took in the revolvers each held in his right hand—that his confidence evaporated.

He tried, quickly, to press a button beside his desk, to summon the security guard. But the system seemed to have been switched off.

In fact, as they led him through the offices, he was surprised at how deserted the building had suddenly become.

50 _____

Autumn wasn't so far away anymore. The grass under the cedar tree was softer and damper, and you couldn't stay out so late. The sun was a memory, so too was the way they had sat together on the tartan blanket—Cressida playing and eating her tea—and he flat on his back, recalling the girl with the red hair.

There were not many moments, not many thoughts from which she was absent. He saw her before he went to sleep. He awoke with the vision of her beside him. Some days, though, her absence seemed to mock his dreams . . . as if to say: think on, Marcus, but I'm far away. Don't count on me, Marcus. We'll see what happens.

And yet it wasn't a dream that bound her to him. It was a certainty.

He remembered her many faces and sayings, recalled the constant desire to reach for her. Just a look or a word or a smile could trigger the impulse. Sometimes it was the silence they seemed to share, not vacant or awkward, but filled with the thoughts that passed soundlessly between them.

He would picture her back in Russia. Suited, maybe, in the inner offices of the Kremlin, laughing with friends, all of whom would believe they knew her. And yet there was the quiet place, deep inside her, that only he could touch.

She always insisted she needed nothing. And what she did need, she hid from view and never spoke of. You either found Anastasiya by yourself or you would miss her. She gave no clues.

"You're my friend," she had told him once.

"I can't be," he had answered.

"But you are . . ."

"I can't be just a friend."

She would incline her head to the right, look at him sideways and sigh so deeply. He recalled her saying, "It's as if I'm on one island and you're on another. I can see you. But I don't know how to reach you."

His mother was calling to him from an upstairs window.

"Just coming, Ma," he called back, "just coming."

He went inside and said good night to Cressida. And she lay on her stomach and pulled up the blankets till they covered the back of her neck, and smiled at the pillow as if the good of the world was locked in beside her.

Downstairs the two of them had dinner in silence, in the dark-paneled dining room where he had eaten himself all the way from child to adult.

As he sat there, it seemed like a sudden idea, and yet, when he thought back, he realized he had been carrying it all the weeks since his return to Britain.

Of course so many things were the same as before. There was the child and the job, the house and the mother, but now it all started from a different point.

Home, he realized, was a state of mind, even another person, and now his was somewhere else.

Marcus put his fork down and pushed the plate away.

"Ma, I'm going back to Russia for a while. I have to."

The old lady didn't look surprised, but then she had learned, as the English of a certain age so often do, to disguise her feelings.

"That's nice," she said.

She got up, went over to where he was sitting and ran her hands through his hair.

"We'll wait for you," she told him. "We'll still be here when you come back."

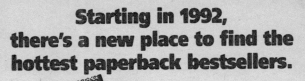